Rob Payne  *to* and *Live by Request* and is a former editor of *Quarry* magazine. He has edited two anthologies of Canadian short fiction, *Carrying the Fire* and *Pop Goes the Story*. His writing has appeared in numerous publications, including *The Globe and Mail*, *Canadian Fiction* magazine, *Write Magazine* and *Front & Centre*. Rob Payne lives in Toronto.

Visit the author's website at: www.robpayne.ca

Also by Rob Payne

Live by Request
Working Class Zero

Sushi Daze

Rob Payne

HarperCollins*Publishers*Ltd

To Lizzie, who took me to karaoke and later became my wife

Thank you: Cate Paterson, Julie Crisp, Anyez Lindop and everyone at Pan Macmillan for being the kind of publishing company every writer wants. Thanks to Nick Earls for his continuing support. Thanks to Otto, Peta, the Oz clan and Jolimont Westside Massiv. Ai!

Disclaimer: This is a work of fiction. Any likeness to individuals living or dead is purely coincidental. To the best of the author's knowledge, no language school can force an employee to climb a mountain. Yet.

Sushi Daze
© 2005 by Rob Payne. All rights reserved.

Published by HarperCollins Publishers Ltd

No part of this book may be used or reproduced in any manner whatsoever without the prior written permission of the publisher, except in the case of brief quotations embodied in reviews.

First edition

HarperCollins books may be purchased for educational, business, or sales promotional use through our Special Markets Department.

HarperCollins Publishers Ltd
2 Bloor Street East, 20th Floor
Toronto, Ontario, Canada
M4W 1A8

www.harpercollins.ca

Library and Archives Canada Cataloguing in Publication

Payne, Rob, 1973–
Sushi daze / Rob Payne. – 1st ed.

ISBN 0-00-639247-4

I. Title.

PS8581.A867S98 2005   C813'.6
C2004-905835-5

RRD 9 8 7 6 5 4 3 2 1

Printed and bound in the United States
Set in Bembo

1

Three years, and no sign that I'll ever be allowed on air.

As I leave Triple C Radio after yet another eight-hour shift, I wonder why I'm still slugging away doing panel work (glorified button-pressing, basically) for an ungrateful DJ and his emaciated, chain-smoking producer. I've been working at Toronto's Home of the Mellow Classics for a sizeable chunk of my adult life now, including a lengthy unpaid internship that I subsidised through a job at a coffee chain, replete with stupid mascot, silly uniform and logo-covered travel mugs. And now I ask, *for what?* I only got into panel work as a stab at fame, having been fool enough to believe older, wiser people when they told me, 'Do what you love and the money will come.' Looking back, I neglected to register the notes of resignation and regret in their voices, and didn't realise that I stood to be a lab rat of vicarious accomplishment in their unfulfilled lives.

Of course, three years on, if I were honest, I'd admit I'm not doing what I love. No doubt, radio is better than financial services or laying bricks at a construction site, but it doesn't provoke an all-consuming passion, and that's what I want my life to be about. I'm thirty years of age now. I can't die knowing that all I've done with this human existence is adjust levels and switch to commercials for carpet cleaners and roll-on deodorant.

Lately, I've been thinking the future is in movies, the last bastion of true artistic expression. I could become an auteur. After all, I've got attitude and ideas, and look great in a beret. But the creative arts world is all about contacts, which these days are made through overpriced training courses — several of which I'm eying seriously. I'm dreaming of a better tomorrow, just like in those smug election ads where problems cease to exist and everyone is wearing colourful polo-knit sweaters. Problem is, I need a great leap forward without reverting to cafe work or social assistance. I simply don't know where to begin.

I'm on my way downtown to meet Maggie, my best friend in the world. We've made plans to dine at The Market, an enormous culinary Disneyland that she loves for reasons I've never been able to comprehend. The place works on the same principles as a high school cafeteria, but with a food of the world theme. You pick up a tray and move around from station to station, getting a steak from the Mexican Grill House or a salad from the California Slim Zone. There are faux Bordeaux cellars selling mediocre French wines, and men in lederhosen pouring pints of domestic and international beers at Every Bit Alps.

Maggie is waiting in the foyer when I arrive. She's got long red hair, the naturally curly type that looks like tumbleweed from a Wild West film on a breezy day. Her skin is pale and dotted with freckles. We've known each other since elementary school, so there's no chance of romantic shenanigans, even in weak moments or on lonely Friday nights. I motion towards the door, but she stands waving her hands with an air of excitement.

'Guess what,' she says.

'The place is full and we have to go somewhere decent?'

'No, I got trapped in a door today.'

I pause and wonder how someone gets trapped *in* a door. I suppose she could have been the victim of a sci-fi style molecular dispersal and reconstitution, like on *Star Trek* when people get beamed onto the surface of planets inhabited by bodacious aliens in short Teflon miniskirts. Maggie would be the perfect abductee. She's sassy enough to make extraterrestrials curious and yet resourceful enough to escape and go on *Oprah*.

'I thought you'd like to know,' she says. 'It was the most unique part of my day, and I'm aware of your love for *authentic moments*. I was delivering roses and went through one of those glass-revolving numbers, but the box was too long. I got jammed in the opening and couldn't go forward or back out. I think the security guard thought I was flirting until he realised there was an impatient crowd forming behind me.'

'Was he nice about it?'

'Yeah, surprisingly. He had a chuckle at my expense.'

'It was probably the highlight of his day as well. You're not limping, so I'll assume you're alright.'

'I'm fine. The box took all the impact. I'm just glad I

didn't destroy eighty dollars worth of roses. My boss would have killed me.'

We stand in line until we get to the 'customs' booth, where a girl in a blue uniform asks us if we have anything to declare *besides good taste* and then hands us our passports for the night. For every menu item, the station gives you a stamp, like a visa, all of which get added up when you clear customs at the register. We take a couple of plastic trays from a large stack and begin to wander aimlessly into the crowd. There are lampposts and road signs, 'gipsy' bus-boys, and even movie posters in Italian and German on the walls.

'Where are you travelling to tonight?' Maggie asks.

'Don't make this any more humiliating than it already is.'

'I can't help it. But let's not dally, 'cause I'm starving. We were too busy to take a lunch.'

'That's terrible. It's the third most important meal of the day.'

We split up and compile wild mishmashes of meals. I feel like I'm walking through a museum of cultural stereotypes, moving from sitar music to 'That's Amore' in seconds, smelling lemon grass then wondering who might find mini bruscetta shaped like tiny gondolas an attractive proposition. I'm tempted to get matzo-ball soup and Middle East felafel just to force a spirit of international camaraderie in my stomach, but the joke isn't worth having to eat deep-fried chickpeas and whatever goes into tabouleh. We make our way to the far corner of the main dining area and sit side by side at a long, Munich-style wooden table that is perfect for people-watching and our usual game of Guess the Menu.

'You know what struck me today?' Maggie says.

'You're better at negotiating conventional doors?'

'No. All my deliveries go to banks, insurance companies or law firms. I'm always walking up marble corridors into rooms with leather couches and all the latest magazines in the waiting area. No one ever sends flowers to a girl in a cafe or a flower shop.'

'And this surprises you?'

'It would be a nice gesture.'

'I suppose, but it's a bit impractical. Of course, some might say yanking flowering plants from the ground and giving their slowly decomposing corpses to loved ones is a bit odd.'

'Don't pretend you're not romantic. As for lawyers, I bet they only appreciate our arrangements as symbols of power and money. It's so sad. It goes against the spirit of flowers.'

She cuts into her meatloaf, procured from Budapest Kitchen, slapped unceremoniously onto the plate by a university student in a white wig and apron pretending to be a Hungarian grandmother.

I'm feeling even more disenfranchised than usual tonight. Maggie knows me well enough to let my weary cynicism wash over her like so much car exhaust.

A family of four sits down at the table opposite us. The father is wearing new jeans and a grey New York Giants sweatshirt. The mother has got on a frilly ruffled white blouse with belled cuffs, the kind of shirt Beethoven might have worn. Of course, he was blind. The kids are between three and five years old, and appear utterly amazed by the concept of communal life. The girl is dragging her feet along the ground, one arm wrapped around a gender-specific doll and the other curled up to her lips. She watches the strangers around her eating and laughing, and I'd like to think she's mesmerised by the sheer energy and abundance of our first world privilege. (At least someone doesn't take it for granted.) The mother unfurls the kids' napkins and gently places them onto their laps, then they all take hands, close their eyes and begin to pray.

'Scary,' Maggie says.

Indeed it is scary, but that doesn't make this family any less worthy a subject for today's round of Guess the Menu. 'I'll wager the kids are having nuggets, pizza or hotdogs,' I begin.

'Naturally – what else do kids eat? Dad definitely looks like a steak and potatoes man, so I'm saying he went to the Mexican Grill House. She's probably got a plate of linguini from Roma Spectacular, because it sounds *exotic*.'

'Mags, you're neglecting to note the obvious: she's got two kids under five. That means she'll be caught up in the eternal young mother attempt to diet. I agree that she's probably gone to Roma Spectacular, but for a caesar salad with grilled chicken, because she doesn't think dressing is fattening. As for him, he does like steak, but tonight is an *international experience*, so I'm wagering he's gone to Munich Inn for sausages and sauerkraut. Tomorrow morning he's going to brag about it to his colleagues at the insurance company over instant coffee.'

Maggie puts down her fork and looks at me earnestly.

'Are we cynical and evil?' she asks.

'No, we're just bored. And don't think of this as mocking people. We're simply wondering about their lives – what makes society tick. This is scientific pontificating, pure and simple. You've got to get over this guilt complex of yours.'

'I can't help it, I went to a Catholic girls' school.'

'No you didn't. We both went to Robert Borden.'

'Well, I *know* people who went to Catholic schools. I've been emotionally affected by osmosis.'

We watch as the prayer finishes and our target family open their eyes, looking around fresh and revived like baptised puppies. Dad begins to lift the steel heat covers off the plates, piling them and the brown plastic trays on the edge of the table for one of the passing bus-boys to pick up.

Maggie digs into our breadbasket, shaking her head as every one of my predictions miraculously appear – nuggets, pizza, sausages and a caesar. For a few seconds we don't speak and I'm fully aware that I'm only one miracle away from qualifying for canonisation. I imagine anointing the kitchen staff with dishwater and Sprite, being carried aloft by spotty teens on minimum wage, my beatific portrait done in glued-together macaroni on a plastic serving tray as I'm presented with my lifetime two-for-one meal card . . . Ah, but who am I kidding? I don't have the energy to front a major religion; a small yet loyal cult in the hills would be enough.

'You really do have a gift,' Maggie tells me.

'Someone should give me a talk show,' I say. 'Or a radio show. I spoke to the morning producer about filling in during DJ Mikael's holidays, but she laughed and said I had *no DJ credibility.* They're giving his airtime to some dork who had a top forty hit in 1981.'

Maggie covers her bun in thick swaths of butter and devours it in two great bites, washing the mess down with several mouthfuls of water. If I didn't know her better, I'd be frightened; but this is the great thing about being a close friend, the total lack of having to appear couth. I love knowing I can show up at her place without having showered, put my feet up on her coffee table and watch reruns of *Starsky and Hutch* without feeling that I need to help with the dishes or feign polite excitement at her new curtains. And she is allotted the same freedom of sloth. Of course, the big difference is I never show up at her house looking like a hobo, whereas she makes full and regular use of her privileges.

'Any other news?' I ask. 'Entertain me.'

'Balloon Guy was in again today,' she says.

'Needed more wire?'

'Yeah. It has to be sixteen-gauge, and apparently ours is the best.'

Balloon Guy is a friendly stalker who comes into Maggie's flower shop at least once a week to flirt, show off his talent for making balloon animals, and buy forty-nine cents worth of wire. He's never plucked up the courage to actually ask her on a date, but there's been innuendo – not to mention borderline phallic creations, like horny vipers and dogs with very long tails. Personally, I think she should tell him she's married and save him the obvious pain of false hope borne of obsession, but she has a thing about honesty, something instinctive as a result of having two devious parental units and a brother who works on the Bay Street stock market.

'He seems to go through a lot of wire,' I say. 'I can't imagine business would be so good, but who knows. I suppose there must be a lot of prepubescent birthday parties in the suburbs.'

'What else is there to do out there? You can only cut your lawn once a week, maybe twice in spring. After you've washed the car on Saturday morning there's a great gaping mouth of existential darkness until it's time to light up the barbecue on Sunday night. You have to fill that somehow, usually through televised sports, kids or collecting antique Coke bottles, all the time your soul withering up like a blackened orange peel in the sun.'

'Geezus, Mags. I was wrong, you *are* cynical and evil.'

'Well, think about the word. *Sub*-urban: below urban life.'

'A couple of minutes ago you felt guilty about guessing a family's dinner choices, now you've condemned a large swath of society based on planned communities and identical housing. Do these two views not strike you as contradictory?'

'I'm a complex, multidimensional individual who has been raised in a world that embraces emotional capitalism – you know, that need to shape self-image in competition with others. Advertising and media manipulation have left me ethically confused. Haven't you read *No Logo*?'

'What did Balloon Guy make today?' I ask, changing the subject.

'A giraffe.'

'Good?'

'About a seven. Not as fine as his dachshund, but at least he comes in with new material. Hey, that reminds me: I got the strangest call this afternoon. Some guy was trying to sell me tickets to a charity basketball game involving midgets. Isn't that the cruellest thing you've ever heard?'

'You're not serious . . .'

'Yes, I am. Apparently this organisation decided that little people being forced to play basketball for other people's amusement was a good idea. Those poor tykes probably don't have enough strength in their tiny, puggy arms to get a ball high enough to go through the hoop. What are the baskets, nine feet up?'

Maggie lifts the next bun from the basket and tears it open more slowly. The frenetic tension of extreme hunger has left her and I can see her sugar levels topping out. I drop my napkin on the floor and, before I have a chance to grab it, watch not one, but two people tread across its bleached white surface. The second guy clearly saw me reaching for it.

'First of all,' I say, looking at the tread marks, 'they're not *tykes*. That pertains to age, not size or birth phenomenon.'

'Okay. *Dwarfs* then.'

'Secondly, you don't seriously think "midget basketball" refers to little people, do you? You *have* heard of the sport age group – atom, peewee, bantam, then midget? I think they're the eleven- and twelve-year-olds.'

She drums her fingers on the table. 'Why would anyone pay ten dollars to watch sweaty twelve-year-olds play basketball?'

'I don't know, *for charity*?'

She looks pained. 'No, I think you're wrong. I bet the game will involve dwarfs playing against some Harlem Globetrotters knock-off. It's like the circus: really big giants against freakish twerps.'

'Intellectually, that's what I'm up against every day.'

'We haven't evolved much since the Christians versus the lions in the Colosseum. The human race still needs to watch humiliating spectacle . . . You not enjoying your moussaka?' she asks as I push the mushie potato-hamburger mixture around the plate with my fork.

'*This* is a humiliating spectacle,' I reply. 'I'm never getting anything from Gods of the Parthenon again. I didn't take a good look at the cook until after I'd ordered – he was pretty sweaty. But they slap the dishes together so quickly in this place I couldn't cancel and go elsewhere.'

'But that's why I like The Market. I have the attention span of a gnat, absolutely no patience. I'm addicted to speed and efficiency. I can't wait until the day I can inject food directly into my veins.'

I move the conversation back to Triple C and my latest rejection. Maggie listens respectfully, even though I know she's heard all of my comments and complaints before. A tall guy with a spotty handkerchief tied around his head takes our tray away as the family across from us prepares to leave. This place is an industrial slaughterhouse of consumption, well set up and radically efficient.

'I bet your producer would enjoy seeing dwarfs suffer,' Maggie says.

Between Maggie and the porn industry, I don't know who's more obsessed about midgets right now. According to political correctness, I think, they're 'little people', even though that's a bit vague. I mean, my cousin is a little person, but she's eleven. I don't feel like arguing. I look around at the fake snowdrifts, and the Parisian street signs and cobblestone lane leading to the toilets, and decide I'm tired of the modern world. I'm worn out by pop culture, political correctness and fighting for recognition.

'Do you ever get the feeling that you've jumped the shark?' I say.

'Sorry?'

'You know, you've reached that point where you're as interesting as you'll ever be in your current persona and need a major overhaul. On *Happy Days*, the show went progressively downhill after the Fonz went water-skiing in his leather jacket and had to jump over a shark in a netted cage.'

She's staring at me, her neck craned forward, as if she's not seeing or hearing something correctly. There's a small smudge of tomato sauce in the corner of her mouth. I have the weirdest urge to spit on my finger and rub it off like a mother taking her kids into church.

'I didn't make the term up,' I say. 'When a TV show starts using implausible scenarios to mask a loss of originality, they've "jumped the shark". That's how I feel. My current sitcom life, *Radio with Jamie Schmidt*, has grown stale. I see it in people's eyes, like a few minutes ago when I was telling you about my latest episode with the Triple C malcontents. You were visibly drifting.'

'I told you, I didn't eat lunch. The sudden rush of carbohydrates has made me drowsy. I need to lie down.'

'Regardless, you weren't tuned in. My ratings are turning to shit. I need to reinvent myself, and I'm pretty sure the fates are with me. George Harrison came to me in a dream the other night and told me to listen to the first song on his last CD. The song's chorus goes: "If you're not sure where you have to go . . ." No, that's not it. "If you think there's a road to be on, any path will lead you . . ." I'm paraphrasing –'

'George Harrison makes the effort to visit from beyond the grave and you can't even remember one line from his song?'

'Basically it's about fate and faith, and how sometimes you have to take a leap and go blindly in a new direction.'

'Tell me you're not quitting your job.'

'I'm too young to be stuck doing panel work.'

'I knew you were getting snaky when you feng-shuied your room and started quoting horoscopes. My advice is to wait a couple of weeks before making your usual rash decision. Your mood might change.'

'Yeah, I suppose, but I've been mulling this over for a while, at least two weeks now. I'm not cut out to be normal – that kind of aspiration always gets me into trouble. University was a flop; this job is a total letdown. I've got to stop listening to sensible advice and practical people, because every time I try to fit in with expectations I end up oddly discontented, which feels like a constant mild stomach virus.'

'Well, don't give it to me.'

'I'm speaking metaphorically, Mags. But don't worry, at

the moment I'm not committed to doing anything, except perhaps getting out of this restaurant. The clatter of cutlery on cheap dinnerware is making me pre-migraine.'

We pick up our passports and head for customs.

2

If you look hard enough, you can find signs everywhere. And if you don't see big flashing billboards of fate, you can make them up – just wait for a coincidence to occur and call the whole deal 'destiny'. Maggie goes limp on me after dinner. She has to work in the morning and doesn't give in to my adolescent pressure to be social on a Friday night. I can't go home yet. My bones feel stale. There are a dozen people I can call – get-togethers to crash, card games, and crammed pubs – but they're all repeats.

As I walk past Rib Eye's Sports Bar, both the stench of deep-fried chicken wings and an odd feeling of enlightenment strike me. The flashing neon 'Welcome' sign calls to my soul, that nebulous space between the mind and its demons. Six beers later, I'm really beginning to dig the country music as I sit on a bar stool next to Jeff, a part-time construction worker who insists on buying my drinks, pulling hundred-dollar bills off of a thick roll of lucre. He's forty, with a puffy, bloated face that suggests prolonged alcohol and drug intake. I have to try hard not to stare at its sheer surface space, but his buzz cut doesn't help; there's nothing to distract the onlooker from all that pink flesh. He's been telling me about how he takes his boat up the Saint Lawrence River every summer to bring shipments of hashish to the metropolitan area.

'There's not much risk,' he says. 'Everyone takes to the water in July and August, so we're just another small boat out for a day trip. We got boarded once, but that was just an inspector looking for zebra mussels on the hull. You heard about them? Those little fuckers breed like shit in a sewer and eat all the plants in the water, so fish starve.'

'Yeah,' I say. 'I knew a person who had a cousin who worked for the Fisheries Ministry a few years ago. He was on TV when the problem broke. Mother Nature has a nasty streak.'

'She's a bitch.'

For close to a minute Jeff has been stabbing his thick hands into an old leather wallet, his cracked yellow fingernails striving to grasp the bent edge of a business card. Finally, he manages to pincer the paper. It's plain white and surprisingly tasteful.

Wrecking Ball
Metal Art of the New Millennium
Jeff Nelson

'You're an artist?' I say.

'I weld. That's how I clean my money for the government. Clients come in for drugs but pay for girders and corrugated iron pieces that I've stuck together, so the tax agents can't touch me. I'm even applying for grants. I know most people think guys like me are dumb, cause I didn't go to school, but if this is dumb . . .'

He pulls out the thick roll of bills again, winks, and downs the foamy dregs of yet another Export. There's a line of at least fifteen bottles in front of us – the staff don't seem eager to take them away, despite the large tips. I wonder if I'm a sucker for accepting society's illusionary order and mores of propriety when people like Jeff circumvent the rules and get rich. I have a moment of clarity in the midst of my warm drunken haze and again recognise my tunnel vision. I've been standing still for too long, surrounded by comfortable perceptions, not fully challenged or aware. There are worlds out there to be discovered. I look around at the wooden floorboards, pool tables, plaid shirts, fake leather jackets, tough man stances, sneers, laughs, thumbs in pockets, bottle blondes, baskets of chicken wings, and the advertisements for Wednesday night karaoke, pool competitions, and bands coming soon, with names like Steel Wheels, Nashville Louts and Tuesday's Lucky.

'You want to try the best goddamn hash you'll ever get in this city?' Jeff asks.

'Sure, why not?'

I could add *Couldn't hurt* or *What's the worst that could happen*? but for some reason, I don't. I finish my beer and we weave our way into the parking lot.

Signs. They're there to remind us that life is mutable. I've become so punch drunk with distractions that I've forgotten the potential for drama in my life. Shock can be good for the soul.

One minute I'm thinking vaguely about change and the future, the next my head is being slammed into the hood of a shiny new police cruiser. Surprisingly, considering the resounding thud on the metal, it doesn't hurt as much as you'd expect – the steel is thin and buoyant enough to take most of the impact. As my forehead rests on the cool surface, I realise that the cop has done this manoeuvre purely for effect. Cops love drama. They understand the need to keep life visceral.

'Put your hands on the car,' he tells us.

'This isn't what you think,' Jeff says.

'Are you telling me, if I go into that alley, I'm not going to find a joint? Do I look that stupid?'

I want to say something in our defence, but quite honestly I can't. My tongue won't make the enormous leap to my soft palate. My legs are cold concrete pillars and I'm not sure if it has begun to rain. I can hear drops landing, but don't feel anything on my skin.

The police officer digs his hands into my pockets, flips my wallet onto the hood and pulls out my ID. I was the one holding the hash pipe when he pulled across the alleyway, so obviously he thinks I'm the ringleader. Luckily, the pipe is now lying on top of a fish and chip shop, thanks to my spinning hook shot. Jeff wanders towards the cop, a faint smile on his face.

'We were taking a leak,' he says. 'I told you.'

'Stay where you are. Put your hands on the car.'

Jeff is amazingly calm considering he has a kilo of hash shoved down the front of his jeans. The cop is writing our names, dates of birth and driver's licence details onto a small white pad. I decide to explain. I'm not sure what my mind *thinks* it's saying, but the words come out as 'Wwru smelled wwz cccssigar smo . . .' Which is probably why the cop pulls my arm behind my back and jams me face-first into the hood again. He thrusts his hands into my every pocket, pulling out tissues and change, my car keys and a souvenir lighter from Boca Rotan, Florida. The scene feels sado-masochistic, like I'm being violated for kicks. Having eviscerated my pockets, he turns back to Jeff and, within seconds, finds and yanks the plastic Ziploc bag of drugs from his jeans. He directs my new friend into the back seat of the cruiser, gets in the front and runs our details through a small computer mounted on the dash. Jeff smiles, shrugs and waves from the back seat. After a minute or two, the cop tosses my licence on the hood. He seems disappointed.

'You can go,' he says.

I scoop up the fragments of tissue, the change and my wallet, and nod stupidly to the cop, who is lingering, looking young and almost skeletal under the dim streetlights. He waves sarcastically with a have-a-good-night sentiment. I'm confused as to what has just happened – in a matter of minutes – and feel the slow burn of blood in my cheeks. I walk for two blocks, reeling maniacally like an hysteric who needs to be slapped or Newton after the apple ricocheted off his skull. I wonder what this scene means in the grand scheme of life. It feels important and consequential. I turn onto Queen Street and stumble awkwardly into a large illuminated advertisement for an airline.

And suddenly, with desperate intent, the message is glowing ethereally before me. I stare at the rapturous, fulfilled faces of vacationing men and women, those who have successfully run away. The sign claims I won't regret the journey; it implores me to take the chance of a lifetime. I'm told to do it now, while there's still time, to book my tickets at the local travel agent.

'I'm going to do it, George,' I whisper to the former-Beatle from my recent dream. 'I'm going to find my own slippery destiny. And I promise to stop downloading your back catalogue.'

3

A few days later, Maggie and I are walking through Kensington Market. This area is supposed to be hip and bohemian, but it's really just a grungy assortment of stores selling army surplus clothing, mass-produced plastic junk from Taiwan, and mediocre tinned exports. If you need

Lebanese dill pickles or abalone-flavoured wheat gluten from China, this is your ideal destination. Personally, I think the whole area should be doused with gasoline and razed to the ground. It's the kind of place where white middle class artistes come to shop and pat themselves on the back for being 'multicultural', as if culture is a location.

I've been spreading word of my spiritual need for exodus via phone and email, and in person, as an attempt to brainstorm ideas from friends and associates. I'm vaguely hoping that someone has a cousin in the entertainment business overseas who will sponsor me and help me reach a pure and unwavering plane of contentment, those plateaus of nirvana that celebrities in tabloid interviews are always claiming to have reached. *It can happen to you too!*

Maggie is telling me about her illustrious co-worker, Hedgehog Girl, a twenty-something woman so named for her '80s retro spiky coiffure. Maggie is pumping her arms in stride and gesturing like a Tourette's patient.

'You know how Hedgehog Girl has been complaining about having no money for food?' she says. 'Well, she called in sick today.'

'Malnutrition finally get her down?'

'No, her pet rat started having seizures and she was up all night. Her husband eventually got their vet to make a house call at two in the morning. It cost them three hundred dollars.'

'Vets make house calls, but doctors don't. This strikes me as a mix-up in our social priorities. Did the rodent live?'

'No, it died this morning. Apparently it's been suffering from epilepsy for years.'

'They finally decided to take it off life support?'

'This isn't funny, Jamie. They spent two weeks worth of grocery money on a rat. And you should have heard her bawling on the phone – pure grief and agony. I'm torn as to what to do. Part of me wants to help this girl, but I also feel a great urge to strangle her. For years I've felt sorry for Hedgehog, but my patience is at an end. Take, for example, a couple of weeks ago. I saw her pocketing money from the cash register, but I didn't tell my boss, because at the time I still had some social conscience and figured it was only a ten-dollar bouquet of discount tulips that we would have thrown out at the end of day. No harm done. But apparently the till has been ripped off a lot lately and it's been noticed. When asked, the Hedgehog said she'd seen *me* putting twenties into *my* purse.'

'God, the irony is too great. I hope karma exists.'

We pass smelly fishmongers run by fourth-generation Italians and a cheese shop where I will never go again. Years ago I bought a quarter round of sharp Cheddar for a campus wine and cheese party; the girl behind the counter dropped the block on the floor, picked it up, gave it a quick wipe with her bare hand, then wrapped my purchase to go as if nothing had happened. I was too stunned to say anything – and granted, the cheese looked fine – but I stuck to brie and pepperjack that night. Today the place is doing a booming business, so I'm left to conclude that neither karma nor routine health inspections are up to much at the moment.

'Did they get to keep the body?' I ask.

'What would anyone do with a rat carcass?' Maggie says.

'I don't know, make soup? You said they spent their grocery money.'

She stops on the corner, with her mouth hanging open. The hotdog vendor nearby takes the momentary pause to pitch for his product in a deep, gravely voice. He is the clamour of throat cancer. He should be the centrepiece of an anti-smoking campaign. I look at the smouldering butt in my hand and stamp it out before hurrying across the intersection on a yellow light.

'I hope they're not paying to have the thing buried in one of those pet cemeteries,' Maggie says.

'Knowing the Hedgehog, I'd be more concerned about her burying it on the apartment property, like on the front lawn. But I'm sure there are regulations.'

'The vet probably cremated the body.'

'Or threw it down the garbage shoot on his way out.'

Personally, I've never had much sympathy for the Hedgehog, pegging her early on as a deranged misfit with a manipulative streak. Less than a year ago, she and her husband contracted a skin condition not seen since the Black Plague. At first, the hospital thought it might have been caused by a serious glitch in her apartment's plumbing or a mutated SARS flu strand, but the health unit did an investigation and found that the disease was a result of poor hygiene. Hedgehog and her husband hadn't washed their dishes properly for weeks and had been reusing filthy cutlery and crockery. That, coupled with living in close quarters with two large Dobermans, was a recipe for bacterial stew. Mags, being a walking guilt complex, covered the Hedgehog's shifts and kept in contact to make sure the penicillin was working.

We walk into the strangest food court on Earth. The Japanese sushi bar is run by Koreans; the pasta and pizza place is staffed by Chinese; the Chinese takeaway counter is run by an Eritrean woman; and the felafel is made by a Thai man with a thin moustache. I swear this city is becoming more varied every minute, all customs and traditions blending into a bizarre hybrid. The United Nations should move its headquarters to Toronto, if for no other reason than economics. Delegates from all the world's nations probably have at least one relative living in the metropolitan area, so they could bunk down in the spare room or on the lounge floor. In a single day you can run into Vietnamese boat people, Ethiopian computer programmers, and Chinese men who would rather talk about Bill Gates than Chairman Mao. I love it, and I have to admit, this convoluted mix has made me curious to see what's beyond my Canadian shores.

A familiar face looks at his watch as we arrive, exactly four minutes late. His sallow cheeks form a convex scowl.

'Ah, Samir,' I say. 'How's my token Indian friend today?'

'Impatient and hungry. How is my token jackass friend?'

'Yeah, good. If you had a dead pet rat, where would you bury it?'

'I wouldn't,' he replies.

'You'd leave it out to rot? No wonder there's still leprosy in Calcutta.'

'I would not have a rat for a pet. They are filthy vermin. Did I mention I am hungry and irritable? I am thinking about a slice of pizza.'

'You're no fun.'

Despite offering to help, Samir makes it perfectly clear that running away from home is not the answer to my problems. I thought he would have a greater regard for travel, since he is technically from another country, but he's too education-oriented to see the merits of wanderlust. Still, I know the only way to truly recharge my life is to leave the country, forsaking the built-in safety valves of my current existence. Only through disorder can I re-emerge anew like the prodigal son or, better yet, a male version of Eliza Doolittle.

'You should go back to school if you wish to change,' Samir tells me.

'Please, anyone can study. I need to *live*. And besides, you know I have a small mountain of debt thanks to two false starts at university and my radio course. There's a great film program I want to take, but the government won't give me any more money.'

'I thought you were dying to do graphic design?'

'That's so six months ago,' Maggie says. 'You have to keep up.'

'You must create a solid plan,' Samir continues. 'There can be no success gained by going willy-nilly all over the globe.'

'I am organising a plan. And don't say "willy-nilly". It sounds gay – not homosexual gay, but stupid gay, the old-style gay, like what my grandmother might say is gay.'

'I get it. I know "gay".'

'Yeah, but I want to make myself perfectly clear. I don't want there to be any ESL mix-ups, like that time when I said Andy Gerbin was queer and you tried to set him up with that guy in your dorm.'

'He looked lonely.'

'Poor Gay Andy, he's never lived the incident or the nickname down.'

I've known Samir since orientation in our university business program. I lasted a year with the hardcore commerce set, then lowered my MLII (Money Lust Intensity Index) and switched to media studies. I just couldn't take economics seriously. People call it a science, but that implies consistent and exact outcomes. The rules of economics are based on the assumption that human behaviour is a constant, knowable entity, when in reality people rarely act in predictable ways.

'I've been thinking,' Samir says. 'Maybe you should start a correspondence course on the Internet. I saw a segment on the news about how people will buy anything on-line. You could offer instructions on how to operate a radio station.'

'I don't know how to operate a radio station. My job isn't nearly as complex as you might think.'

We pause to watch Maggie slurp on her thick chocolate milkshake, the suction causing her cheeks to turn crimson. Samir looks at the burger and large fries on her plate and then back at her freckled face. She has the same build as she did in high school.

'Why are you not enormous?' Samir asks her.

'High metabolism.'

'I thought metabolic rates were a myth perpetrated by fat people unwilling to admit that they eat a lot and exercise too little,' Samir says.

'Sounds like the prejudice of a very thin man,' I say.

Samir makes the sound of a decompressing hydraulic lift. It's good to know precisely where to find a person's Achilles heel. He's always been defensive about his size, hiding his weedy arms in long sleeves and refusing to wear shorts in the summer. I wonder if he still drinks those disgusting carb-loaded protein shakes every morning to put on weight.

'Most obesity cases are genetic,' Maggie says.

Samir snorts. 'Please . . .'

'I can show you studies.'

'As if I have time for more reading with this MBA business. You're so full of wind.'

Maggie slurps the yellow straw again. This time she takes a deep breath and really sucks. Her face flushes and I think she's a few seconds away from an aneurism when she finally releases. Samir turns to me.

'Internet courses are the wave of the future.'

'I thought they were the wave of the present.'

'The key is to aim for people with either too much or too little money. You've got to peddle gluttony or exploit desperation. Make people feel that they're never enough.'

'That's beautiful. I never would have guessed you're in business.'

'He does have a point,' Maggie says. 'In the '50s, people were told to work hard, be honest and strive to buy a bungalow and their very own car. Today that's called a personality void – hey, I've got it! Why don't you write a self-help book for people who buy too many self-help books?'

I'm glad my friends are taking my cry for existential aid seriously. I look towards the exit, the sky outside turning Confederate grey. A doomed army of citizens is marching along the sidewalk, loaded with bags and briefcases, going nowhere. Samir crumples up his greasy burger bag, lemming-like crumbs tumbling off his sweater onto the tiled floor. He drops a scrap of paper down in front of me.

'It's my cousin's number. He might be in LA right now, but he might be back. I don't know. You must be nice to him.'

'I've told you before, Sam, I don't want to work for a Hindu radio station.'

'He has connections,' Samir insists. 'It's all about *networking*.'

'I thought it was all about the Internet,' Maggie says.

Samir holds up a finger. 'An excellent medium for getting in touch with contacts. I'll give you his email address.'

When he's done writing, he gives a faint wave, somewhere between the Queen's anaemic salute and an uninterested dismissal, and joins the sidewalk crowd. Maggie sits quietly. She looks like she's on the verge of a long and sensitive spiel. I've seen it before, the way she fidgets with her hands and looks at the table, forming her thoughts in her head before she begins to speak. I know she's got some profound advice, some insight that will help me formulate a plan to get to the next stage in my life.

'Okay,' she says, getting up. 'I've gotta get back to the shop.'

I buy a newspaper as I drift aimlessly towards home, where I pick up my mail and make some coffee. The first thing I turn to in the paper is my horoscope, which says I'll use my wit and charm to diffuse tension in the workplace. This, of course, is a total bust and rocks my faith in Grand Dame Lorene, Seer of Things Unseen. For years now, my wit and charm have gone unrecognised by my frosty co-workers. I scan the classified section, compare and contrast the newly engaged couples, and peg who's going to have a string quartet and whose best man will be wearing white tube socks with the tux. I give the whole disappointing mess a fold.

And then I stop.

There's a large ad on the back page:

BIGSUN English School
Bigsun Intercultural Company has been teaching for twenty-one big years. Since the time, we go large to be number one in size for all Japan. But we do not stop this motion, with also do textbooks, Internet to learn and vending machines to offer beverages throughout the nation.

Despite the suspect vending-machine side venture and a slightly crazed grinning teddy bear mascot (connection and relevance to teaching English unknown), the ad is promising. In fact, this is exactly what I've been looking for. Everything comes together in my under-stimulated brain, excitement clanging around with the first endorphins to meander through my bloodstream in weeks.

- 280,000 yen ($3200)/month
- Subsidised rent
- 5% income tax
- 35 hours/week
- Paid vacation and training

Who would've thought that having a working knowledge of my mother tongue could be so lucrative? I pick up the phone and am surprised when a woman with a perfect Canadian accent answers the call. I tell her how keen I am about the company and ask when I can leave for Tokyo.

'What's your file number?' she asks.

'I don't have one. I just saw the ad.'

Apparently, as with every other good thing in life, there is an elaborate, time-consuming process to endure. I've got to download an application form from the website and fill it out, write an essay on why I want to teach in Japan, and then wait for an interview/orientation session.

'Between you, me and the paper walls of the Kabuki Theatre,' I say, 'the sooner I can leave the better. I've been experiencing a great feeling of destiny lately. There have been signs. I won't get into those right now, but when I saw your ad, I felt a surge of karma not unlike a severe ice-cream headache. Can I speak to a recruiter?'

'That's not the way we work. Would you have a problem with the application?'

'Umm, no. I'm a bit slow typing, but my basic communication skills are fine.'

'I mean, do you have access to a *computer*?'

Obviously, the Japanese need for order is unwavering, because the girl on the line isn't budging. I spend the next couple of hours on my housemate Peter's computer composing an essay about my lifelong ambition to live in Tokyo. I strain my brain thinking of all things Japanese, most of which involve the Ho-Su restaurant on Dundas (which I think is mainly Korean). Given the history of hostility between the two countries, I have two options: do some research; or take a non-culturally-specific middle ground. I decide to play the challenge card, saying I'm a born adventurer who needs to get away from CNN. I make a few casual references to my love of teaching – having tutored several young cousins – and my fascination with Japanese technology. I simply have to know where all those DVD players come from.

With every word I type, I feel it, a sensation of freedom and possibility. I find my George Harrison CD and put on song one. As I listen to the chorus I realise two things: eventually, fate finds you; and I am really crap at remembering song lyrics.

4

I'm ashamed to admit that my family homestead is a twenty-fourth-floor condominium in Toronto's East End. Quite simply, there's nothing rustic or poignant about going home to a building filled with two and a half thousand residents. As usual when I make these visits every month or so, I shave, comb my unruly hair and wear casual pants instead of jeans. I need my father to think I'm leading a perfectly normal, contented life.

I clench a smile onto my lips as my dad answers the door looking groggy, like he's spent the night in his recliner after falling asleep watching television again. Except, of course, it's four in the afternoon.

'Did I come at a bad time?' I ask.

'No, no, just . . . hanging out.'

He smiles at his brilliant use of '80s vernacular. Thankfully, he's recently given up calling me 'dude'. The place is as clean and beige as usual, with magazines and pictures in their designated spots, and coasters strategically placed for hot and cold beverages. We crash in the living room and I tell him about my mid-afternoon epiphany.

'Why Japan?' he asks.

'Because they need teachers and pay outrageously well. And our dollar is so utterly low that I stand to make a small fortune on the conversion. Also, it's a great international experience, a good opportunity to learn self-reliance and consistency. What do you think?'

He shrugs. 'What do I know?'

He turns on the television and sits back in his recliner, flipping through channels with the remote control as his nostrils slowly flare in and out. In adolescent terms, he's sulking. I look at my mother's pictures on the mantle: her as a teenager, at their wedding, and kneeling with me in a panorama of autumn leaves. She had a brilliant smile, the kind that transformed her face. I sometimes used to watch her when she was concentrating on the newspaper or cooking. She would look like a stranger, so serious and placid. Now, of course, she looks like a fading picture.

'What's with the eye?' my father asks.

I reach up to the minor cop-car-hood-induced swelling. 'It's more of a forehead bruise. There is some puffiness around the eye, but my temple took the main brunt of impact.'

'You didn't get in a fight, did you?'

'No, I turned around in the DJ booth too quickly and got the mike square in the head. The room is pretty small and I had to get back to the panel to put on a commercial.'

His shoulders relax. 'You should speak to the station manager, maybe get the place reorganised.'

'That's a great idea. I think I'll do that.'

I take a deep breath, but my lungs still only feel two-thirds full. My mother died nearly seven years ago and we've never regained our balance. I don't think I fully appreciated her role in our family unit until she was gone. Like so many men, my father and I communicated our feelings through her. Testosterone is good for hunting and gathering, talking about sports and fishing, but not for emotional honesty. Of course my father's generation has the disease worse, an army of men raised on the '60s seam of social change, when nurturing a feminine side was just a vague theory spouted by shaggy-haired hippies and not an option for personal growth and self-awareness. My mother's death left a void, not just within us, but between us. For the first year or two, Dad was barely in his own head, constantly losing track of conversations, time, friends and family. Investments languished and bills went unpaid until my uncle finally talked him into getting counselling. In the last few years, he's been better and has taken to sporadically dating ageing secretaries, dental hygienists and social workers – the types who thrive on taking care of others – but they always drift away as quickly as they arrive. I look at the photos on the mantle and wonder why. Needless to say, we're still looking for a conduit.

'How's the social life?' I ask.

'Went out with Frances last night.'

'Which one is she?'

'The divorced sales rep, brown hair.'

I wait for more, but he's watching the technology stocks. He reaches across to a side table, picks up a small notepad and jots down some numbers. In the past three years, I've met two of Dad's women. They were very pleasant, both with my mother's brown wavy hair, height and general, pre-illness figure. My father is good looking for an older guy, with short, greying hair, a decent build and an even temperament. He likes to drink socially, doesn't smoke, and used to be able to hold a conversation. He probably has women falling over themselves, not that he seems able to care.

I wander to the bathroom, taking my time as I check out the place. He's got a new cabinet in the bedroom, but it's cheap pine, obviously bought at a generic superstore. I can't believe I used to live in this tiny condo. There's no personal space. I can't breathe properly. When I come back, my father reaches behind his chair and tosses me a catalogue.

'Mind picking me out a new shirt? No more aqua.'

'That was a great sweater,' I say. 'Luminous colours can be very therapeutic.'

'Sorry?'

I skim through the selection and am left to conclude that my father wants to look like a dead banker. There's nothing but sombre greys and blues, khaki shorts, and black-and-white-striped golf shirts. I toss the catalogue onto the coffee table.

'Do you have anything else?'

'No. Pick a shirt from that catalogue.'

'I'm leaving Canada as soon as I can.'

'Oh, don't be that way. I just want a nice, normal shirt.'

'This isn't about the shirt. I'm simply letting you know. I need to make some changes in my life and the sooner I leave, the quicker I start raking in mountains of lucre. Then I'll be able to come back and go to school –'

'Again.'

'Take a course I really want to do –'

'Again.'

'Do you have a better idea? Do you not want me to go?'

He looks at the coffee table, reaches for the catalogue and shrugs. 'There must be something in here . . . Frances wants to go see Bob Dylan. I told her I'm not very interested in music, but she's keen.'

I look towards my mother, no longer here to mediate. The air is as still and parched as a museum gallery, the windows shut up and latched tight. Finally my father stirs.

'Do what you like,' he says.

5

Within an hour of leaving the family condo, I've faxed off my application form and essay. I decide to cement the idea of exodus into my cerebellum by throwing an impromptu party for my nearest and dearest. Better yet, when I make a few calls, I find there's a party elsewhere in need of a good crashing. I phone the BIGSUN office, hoping that the Japanese reputation for chronic overwork is true. Sure enough, a man answers.

'Hi, is your receptionist still around?' I say.

'Betsy not here.'

'Well, I'm a friend of her brother's and I was told to look her up when I came to town. Our ship just came to port and I don't seem to have her home address. Can you do me a major solid?'

After I explain that this means 'a favour' in English, my overworked colleague-to-be-grunts. I'm pretty sure there are laws against giving personal information to complete strangers, but, being Japanese, he's probably got diplomatic immunity and knows he can always go home if I turn out to be a homicidal stalker. Within minutes I'm on the phone to my best hope for a speedy departure abroad. Betsy's voice is groggy, as if she's been napping.

'Hi, it's Jamie Schmidt. Remember me? I phoned about getting an interview for that teaching job in Japan.'

'Umm, how did you get this number?'

'Research. Being driven is a character trait. If that doesn't show I'm BIGSUN material, nothing will. If your husband doesn't object, I'd like you to come to a party with me tonight. I'll make sure your glass is always full and you can give me the lowdown on Japan and the job.'

Personally, I wouldn't come within a subway stop of me. I'm even freaking myself out. But life is an adventure – which is what people always say when they've never had anything bad happen to them.

'Okay,' she says. 'Why not.'

Betsy turns out to have a neat bob cut and a nice figure. At least, I think she has a nice figure. It's difficult to tell, because she appears to be wearing some sort of floral muumuu, a long shapeless dress that flows around her like the liberty bell.

'You don't look like how I imagined you,' she says.

Touché.

We catch the subway and I use the time to work my charm and probe her for useful details. She worked in Japan for six years, mostly in Hokkaido, which is in the north. When she wasn't teaching, she studied Japanese and went hiking, as there wasn't much else to do. There were only four other teachers in her town and it was winter for half the year.

'That's wretched,' I say. 'How do you say, "This place is cold"?'

'*Samui desu ne.*'

'So how do you say, "This place is fucking cold"? *Fucking samui desu ne?*'

The first person we see as we walk into the party house is my red-faced and obviously intoxicated friend Davis. It's not his party, but he's the link to this crowd. He comes over, helps us with our paper bag full of alcohol and explains that there are margaritas pre-made in the fridge and that a new batch will be made every hour on the hour until no one can stand them any longer. Honestly, everyone should have at least a couple of friends who work in the IT industry – the disposable income and desire for bacchanalia are outstanding.

'Have you had your shots yet?' Davis says.

'No,' I say, 'but my rabies has completely cleared up.'

He points to a bottle and a couple of glasses by the door.

'Two-drink minimum to get in.'

We wander over, gulp back a shot of cinnamon liqueur each and forgo the second. There's no way I'm subjecting my palate to more than one sampling of alcohol that is only one step removed from being mouthwash. Girls in low-slung jeans pass by, talking loudly and obviously lapping up the attention of half the men in the room. The kitchen and dining areas are hardwood, while the long, beautiful living room is covered in a lush crème-coloured carpet. Looking around at the crowd, I'm hoping it's stain-guarded, because everyone appears sloshed to incontinence.

'This isn't exactly what I expected,' I assure Betsy. 'One of the guys must be dating a university student on placement. It happens from time to time.'

'I can't stay long anyway,' she says. 'I've got to work at eight tomorrow.'

'I try not to see the sun until at least eleven.'

'Yeah, well, I can't complain. BIGSUN pushes the Japanese nationals a hundred times worse. The company doesn't expect much from us *gaijin*.'

'Gai-what?'

'*Gaijin*. It means "alien", or "foreign people" – non-Japanese.'

Davis appears with a tray of crackers that have been topped with creamy orange goop. 'It's crab mousse,' he says. 'On Triskets.'

We each take one and I watch as Betsy bites into hers. The creamy topping looks warm and slimy, like a forlorn sea creature that washed up on shore one humid summer's afternoon and has been decomposing for weeks. I toss mine back on the plate.

'Allergic to seafood,' I say.

Betsy excuses herself and leaves me standing in a room filled with strangers. Some sort of god-awful techno music is pumping from the stereo and there's a guy dancing by himself in the centre of the room, clearly off his head. I'd hate to think I'm getting too old for these sorts of soirées, so I tell myself I'm simply not in the right mood and am in need of a change of scenery. A guy in a University of Sydney shirt appears next to me, attempting to look cool and aloof while drinking bourbon from a canning jar. He's doing the Bono thing, wearing a pair of those ridiculous yellow-tinted glasses.

'When were you in Australia?' I ask.

'Shirt's from the Gap.'

'Oh,' I say. 'How exciting. When were you at the Gap?'

My youth is definitely running out. I'm getting old. Time is draining like blood from my face, my extremities getting cold, my eyesight failing. I'll trip and wake up aged eighty. My attention gets sucked back through a vacuum to Betsy, who is standing beside me tapping my shoulder and holding a breaded shrimp on a skewer.

'Oh, thanks,' I say, ignoring the small bowl of red seafood sauce in her other hand and popping the little bastard into my mouth. From the look on her face, I can tell she wasn't offering.

'I thought you were allergic to seafood,' she says.

'Did I say "seafood"? I meant I was allergic to *Triskets*. Say, do you want to get out of here and go somewhere nice? I don't feel like I can make a great impression professionally in these soft-porn surroundings.'

'I'm not really dressed to go anywhere. My room-mate told me to wear my least flattering outfit in case you were psychotic. In fact, I just called to let her know I haven't been abducted.'

An hour later, a small group of us have forgone the Roman orgy in progress and ended up at the Four Seasons' rooftop bar, the best night-time aerial view of the city without the need for droning engines and a seatbelt. I phone Maggie and she turns up only minutes after we've been seated.

A waiter in tux shirt, bow tie and white gloves brings rice crackers, roasted almonds and assorted nuts on a silver tray and tries not to look with too much disdain at our T-shirts, tattered Doc Martens and assorted muu-muus. Miraculously, the bar stocks Japanese Kirin beer, so we order a round to celebrate my pending metamorphosis.

'You're serious about going to Japan?' Davis asks.

'Absolutely. I've always had a borderline unhealthy obsession with the Orient.' I wink at Betsy. 'And besides, I need the money.'

'There are other ways to save,' Davis says. 'You could go out less.'

'I've been trying to drink at home at least twice a week.'

'Shit, you're practically a martyr.'

'You know,' Maggie says, 'according to a study I read today in *Metro*, you'd be classified as an alcoholic.'

'Yeah,' I say. 'Peter told me about that study as we killed a bottle of wine over dinner. I think the Repressed Assholes of America Foundation organised it. Their slogan: "Making Sure You Don't Enjoy Life Either". All studies have an agenda. I couldn't care less about what some evangelical Southern virgin has to say.'

'Forget the studies,' Davis says. 'Have you heard of *priorities*?'

'Of course I have, it's the scheme to get street kids off drugs. You know, there's nothing more fun on a night out than a lecture. Stop playing the moral role of my poor deceased mother, god bless her departed soul.'

I look to the heavens, located directly above the stunning skyline, and bless myself.

'Sarcasm is the lowest form of humour,' Maggie says.

'No, Mags, miming is the lowest form of humour. Sarcasm is proof of a marginalised soul.'

I do my best Marcel Marceau, pulling an invisible rope, finding my way out of the box, and culminating in taking the elevator down from the table – at which point I lose gravity and nearly knock all our overpriced drinks onto the pristine tiles. Maggie claps slowly and holds her glass up to our waiter, who is hovering at the far end of the room, looking disturbed.

'Priorities are something adults develop when they're working towards an important goal,' Davis continues.

'Yeah, but I'm still not convinced about this need to be an adult. Sounds like a crutch for really boring people. If I scrimp, sure I'll save faster for the film course, but I'll be one of the thousands of miserable souls in this city who go around slamming doors on people and not saying thank you. Having me as a happy person helps the karma of us all, as a city, as a living organism.'

'I'm sure the mayor will organise a Bring Back Jamie Schmidt campaign once you're gone,' Maggie says.

'Dare to dream. If my life is a case of arrested development, lock me up. I'm not going to waste another second being normal.'

'You're perfect for Japan,' Betsy says. 'They love weird, energetic foreigners.'

'So a tip for the interview might be to wear an outrageous shirt and be nutty? Should I juggle?'

'No, for the interview, dress like an accountant, but be *genki* — that's Japanese for "happy". Act like you're on a healthy dose of Prozac, but be a professional. If you can juggle, mention it, because hobbies are taken into account; but don't demonstrate unless you're asked. Trust me, you're exactly what Japanese students want.'

'Obviously the country's got bigger problems than economic deflation,' Davis murmurs.

Maggie tugs at my sleeve and motions across the room, towards the CN Tower standing in the distance.

'Isn't that Ben Affleck?' she says.

'No, it's a major landmark.'

'At the table by the railing . . .'

'Too thin,' Davis says.

Welcome to the great Toronto pastime: looking for celebrities in high-end bars. The waiter appears at my elbow.

'House champagne,' I say.

Maggie makes a squawking sound, but I know she wants to drink long into the night with me, because we're all in pain in the big city. Discomfort on public transportation, terror at making the rent, pollution, congestion and homeless crack addicts swearing at you are all part of the mystique of the metropolis. She goes into damage control mode, telling the waiter that beer will be fine.

'Ignore the lady,' I say. 'She doth protest too much.'

Because waiters are entrepreneurial and pragmatic types, he spins on his heel and zips away, knowing that fifteen per cent of a bottle of Moet is better than a polite, responsible smile and an empty palm. French champagne – a glass each as some sort of bet on my future earning power. Besides, Davis can afford it. When he gets inebriated enough he inevitably drops his credit card on the bill.

When the champagne arrives, no one complains. We make toasts to prosperity, to one another, and to great things yet to come.

6

My way of coping with a hangover is to deny its very existence.

Forget hair of the dog, a cold swim, hot bath, not eating, eating greasy food, drinking litres of water, sports drinks, brisk walks, sleep, vigorous exercise, sex, or homeopathic remedies involving Chinese herbal roots. Those simply reinforce the very idea that you *have* a hangover.

Denial is the cornerstone of my belief system.

I slip on my last clean shirt, the skin-tight grey one with 'Not Gay, Just Incredibly Charismatic' written across the front in bold white lettering. Maggie got it for me for my birthday – for whatever reason, she finds it hysterical. On the kitchen table, propped aesthetically against the salt shaker, is my quarterly letter of harassment from the government. I take the Thoreau view of taxation and student loan repayment and put aside any thought of remuneration until I find success. I don't understand why the government abides CEOs taking thirty-million-dollar buyouts and thinks I'll happily hand over my laundry money to keep the tainted carcass of a system afloat. I miss the communists. At least they kept socialism alive. Now there's no counter-ideology to keep government and business from screwing poor people mercilessly into the floorboards.

I toss the envelope into the garbage, make dry toast and go outside. As I navigate through the broken chairs and boxes of empty wine bottles, I wonder about my future life in Japan. Although Peter likes the communal areas of our house to be kept clean, he's left the backyard to my destructive influences. No doubt I'll have to tame my propensity for personal sprawl in a tiny, expensive Tokyo apartment. As I'm carting a box of wine bottles to the road, my next-door neighbour, Habib, comes running out of his house.

'What do you do?' he says. 'Never throw away these! My

friends make homemade wine. I give them bottles, they slip Habib free alcohol.'

He takes the box into his house, shaking his head in disbelief, and then nods towards my backyard. After the winter thaw, we fertilised a ten-by-twelve patch of the lawn and rolled it flat with a machine borrowed from a friend at Parks and Rec. We cut the grass super short, sunk several holes in the sod and made miniature flagsticks out of cleaning rags and old fishing poles. The pitch isn't perfect, but it's good enough for our bimonthly Friday night barbecue and putting competition.

Habib reappears dressed in his Toronto Maple Leaf hockey jersey with his putter in hand. We've been locked in mortal combat for over a month now, the score 22–13 in my favour, playing mainly for pride but always for a few bucks to keep things interesting. Habib came to Canada fifteen years ago from the Middle East and works at the airport refuelling 747s. I tell him about the turn of events in my life.

'Good,' he says. 'Now you can be immigrant too. You won't be so cocky.'

'I'm only going for a year.'

'But maybe you stay. One can never tell these things. Make sure you learn some language before you go. Half of my daughter's classmates have terrible English. She comes home and I ask her what she has learned, and she tells me the teacher has spent hours on reading. On the application form before coming to Canada, I was asked if my family spoke English. I marked the box "Yes", of course. And then when we learned we were accepted, we studied like hell.'

He lips out a downhill double breaker and curses loudly. I miss mine, we double the bet and I pick a new spot on the green. Habib juggles his ball absent-mindedly from hand to hand.

'If she doesn't learn now, what will become of her?' he says. 'I did not come to this country to have my only daughter cleaning toilets.'

He positions his putter behind his ball, closes one eye, then stops and steps back. He plumb-bobs, holding his putter in front of his body like a pendulum.

'How much is this for?' he asks.

'Three dollars.'

'Ah, that's not so bad.'

He gets back in position.

'Concentrate,' I say. 'You should think of every putt as your only chance to win the Masters. That way, you get used to playing under pressure.'

'I have enough pressure in my life.'

He drills the ball hard. It hits the back of the cup, jumps straight up, then falls into the hole. He smiles like a Cheshire cat.

'That was lucky,' I say.

'There is no such thing, only preparation and opportunity. I am impressed that you are going to Japan. I have long held the view that you are a bit *not serious* about life. I became a man when I left Lebanon.'

'They wouldn't do that sort of operation over there?'

His face goes blank. My stomach lurches and I think I've

just insulted his culture and/or his machismo in some irreparable way, at least until he breaks into hearty laughter.

'You think I am serious!' he says.

'That's not fair.'

'But I am honest when I say you are a man who needs to grow through challenge. A touch of heat is good for the soul.'

I'm so unnerved that I four-putt twice and lose an additional eight bucks. Still, the moment is significant, because I realise I'm going to be the mildly odd foreigner living in an entirely new culture. I'm going to have to adapt to ways and methods, a new language, strange foods in the grocery stores, sports teams I've never heard of, and bands I can't understand. The prospect is both tantalising and terrifying. I've never been much of a traveller, out of sheer laziness more than anything. I'm a community-based guy who likes to be surrounded by familiar faces and household comforts. For a few seconds I stand on the green and think I'm crazy to want to take off; but then the moment passes and I go upstairs to change.

None of my shirts is ironed, so I end up running late for my appointment at BIGSUN (as arranged by my new pal, Betsy). Although I usually try to avoid the local hospital like doomsday, I take a short cut through its back alleyway, past the steel waste receptacles and stray medicinal smells coming out of the air exchange system.

There's a woman outside the sliding glass doors sitting

alone in a wheelchair, her hands and legs bandaged. I'm thinking burns, but put the thought out of my mind. God knows I've spent enough time at these places. I've sat on these steps and attempted to make small talk with a person whose life had shrunk to a sterile white room, days in a bed, and a drip in the arm. Seven years and it could have been yesterday. Habib has no idea the kind of challenges I've been through – the heat on my soul – and can't understand how that experience has shaped me. I know I'm not perfect, that I'm sarcastic and jaded and have issues with the world, but at least I recognise my faults and want to try to change. I don't want to carry around these grievances against life. And if a hospital doesn't motivate me to *carpe* the *diem* and make an existential shift, nothing on this earth ever will.

The BIGSUN office isn't as impressive as I'd hoped. For an international organisation boasting several subsidiaries and a booming vending-machine wing, the place is pretty small. Betsy sits at the front desk.

'And your name?' she asks.

'You don't look so good,' I say.

'I think I'm dying. How about you?'

'I don't get hangovers; at least, not consciously.'

I'm ushered into a meeting room with a long table, a television screen at the far end and a dozen sullen-looking candidates ranging from their early twenties to mid thirties. All the candidates are fidgeting silently. The room is damp with nerves and I think, if this is my competition, I'm a shoo-in, because ninety per cent of a job interview is pure enthusiasm. Act like there's nothing in your life you'd rather be doing, even if the job on offer involves cleaning up blood at crime scenes. Leave no room for doubt: you love the smell of bleach and the feel of latex rubber against the palm of your hand.

In the middle of the table is an assortment of company and travel brochures, and for a second I wonder if I've stumbled into a Contiki-does-Japan sales session. Every photo features either a landmark or white people joyfully eating noodles and pointing at pagodas.

Simon, our extremely energetic host, bounds into the room – literally, the man *bounces*. He's Canadian, mid thirties, and very positive about the company, having spent seven years in Osaka. He runs over the basic economics, assures us that our apartments will be 'top-rate, first-rate and outstanding', and outlines the great things about living in Japan, most of which apparently involve the cherry blossom season.

'Well, that does it for me,' I announce. 'I'm convinced. How soon can we go?'

'Well, we've got two spots available this month. They're our rush order and we'll really be pushing the paperwork, so I'd like to send a couple or a candidate who has already been to Japan and won't need much orientation. Everyone else will be going in three months. Unfortunately, no one here today has been to Japan –'

'I have,' I say.

He leafs through the applications in a file folder on the table and pulls out my 'Why I Want to Work in Japan' essay. His forehead creases as he skims.

'It was a holiday,' I explain. 'I didn't mention it because I thought it might hurt my chances. I was in Hokkaido with the Ainu.'

I remember Betsy saying something about the Ainu last night, around one, when my focus was beginning to waver in and out. I know they're important, but can't recall exactly who or what they are. I'm hoping they aren't a sports team.

'You spent time with Japan's indigenous people?' Simon asks.

'Sure.'

'That's amazing.'

'It was nothing, really. They're like other natives in the world, selling arts and crafts and shunning our modern ways . . .'

The key to lying, once again, is denial. I'm quite sure that the Ainu have trinkets and paintings to flog to tourists, so most of what I'm saying *is* true. No doubt they have a company set up to handle sales of painted stones and native fauna skin golf-ball pouches to gullible tourists. My back has begun to perspire and I concentrate on nice, deep breaths. Simon looks disturbingly impressed. He has sat back in his chair and now has the plastic tip of his pen against his lips.

'The Ainu are one of the most endangered indigenous peoples in the world,' he says. 'Their population has dropped dramatically in even the last twenty years. What did your experience involve exactly?'

I can tell that he's actually going to listen, that he's curious, and isn't just putting on a fake-interested interviewer expression. The others in the room have broken through their malaise and are looking at me with life in their eyes. Somehow I think they've caught on that I'm talking through my puckered bunghole and are no doubt curious to see whether I pull this stunt off or flunk out of Interview 101.

'Well,' I begin, 'there were the crafts, lots of art, and dancing. They have special dances to the Fish God. And, of course, the food is sensational.'

'Are their eating habits different from the typical Japanese diet?'

'There's more seaweed,' I say.

'What sense did you get of their feelings towards the government – you know, the ongoing struggle for recognition as an actual indigenous people? And what's happening with the land claim issue?'

'It's an ongoing struggle. It's going on right now and probably will be for quite some time. I'm glad I could do my part. But we're not here to talk about my life among the natives . . .'

I look around the room, hoping that one of these corpses will murmur and get Simon back on track. I'm the centre of attention, which is normally my favourite place to camp out, but not today. Obviously last night's festivities were a bad idea. They've left gaps in my concentration just big enough to keep my brain from functioning properly.

'So, are you looking to return to Hokkaido?'

'No.'

Simon waits for more – of course he does.

'I'm done with that part of my life. You can only experience the wonder of native culture once. I'm looking for the extreme opposite: urban Tokyo, as fast-paced as possible. I need to embrace the panorama of the country. And besides, Sapporo is too damn *samui desu ne*.'

Luckily, Simon moves on. We're shown a video and quizzed on our strengths and weaknesses. All in all, the interview feels like a formality. We're told we'll receive an offer in the next week, by mail. As we shuffle out, Simon stops me.

'Listen, Jamie. I was really impressed by your energy, as well as your fascinating experiences in Japan.'

Outside the meeting room, Betsy's head jerks sideways.

'The Japanese Appreciation Society holds a regular lecture series, aimed at us Nipponphiles and Canadians interested in the country. I'd like to forward your details to our chair, Mrs Katatanabe. I know she'd love to have someone speak on the Ainu.'

'Absolutely,' I say. 'I can even bring slides.'

There's no reason why I wouldn't want to share my idyllic memories of time spent in a culture I love. Simon shakes my hand likes he's jacking up his car. I wink at Betsy on my way out, making a hand signal for her to call me later. Given the human tendency not to follow up on initiatives, I'm hoping Mrs Katatanabe never dials my number.

Like I said before: *denial*. It's not just a big river in Egypt.

7

Sure enough, my offer of employment comes four days later. I've been given a priority spot and have three weeks to quit my job, say farewell and get rid of my room. Unfortunately, I've still got six months to go on my lease. A sublet would leave me picking up a portion of rent (no thank you), and there's no way that my housemate Peter would absorb a loss out of the goodness of his tight-valved heart. I dial Maggie's work number and the new girl answers, sounding nervous.

'Fleurs Etcetera,' she says.

'Hi, do you do landscaping?'

'Umm, I don't know. Like, do you mean lawns and stuff?'

'Yes. My wife and I are thinking of a tropical theme. Hawaiian palm trees, a sand garden, and some exotic flowers . . . that sort of thing.'

'I think they might die in the winter. Let me –'

'How much would a pineapple tree cost?'

There's a few seconds of silence. I can hear muffled talking. Then Maggie gets on the phone.

'Fleurs Etcetera.'

I put on my best French accent, which turns out to be more Inspector Clouseau than Jacques Cousteau. '*Oui, allo. Ah wuz just talkeeng to ze other gurl about ze bunch of dead vegetation poseeng as roses that yer leettle shop as sent to ma home –*'

'Schmidt, I'm busy. I've got orders to go out and drivers waiting. And I'm supposed to be teaching the new girl how to wire wedding bouquets.'

'You just wasted twenty seconds with the details, Mags. I need a favour.'

'*No*. We're doing inventory tomorrow and, besides, there's nothing that's almost dead.'

Here's a tip for frugal guys: make friends with a florist. They're a great source of free, wilting flowers that are destined for the garbage bin but still have a day or two of physical integrity left. Nothing impresses a first date like a dozen red roses. (So the petals come off in two days – not your fault.)

'Is Hedgehog Girl working today?' I ask.

'She's here,' Maggie says.

'So, the period of mourning for the rat is over.'

'Apparently.'

'Is she wearing black?'

'Schmidt, bouquets to wire . . .'

'Convince her to come around to my place at five tonight. I'll pay her thirty bucks. She can use the money towards her vet bill.'

There's a pause. When Maggie speaks again, her voice is low and slow. 'Given the seediness of your proposition, I really need more details. And don't say this is slumming sex.'

'Oh, please . . . Don't sound so distrusting. I need her to wander around the house for a few minutes.'

'Clothed, right?'

'Absolutely. No hedgehogs will get harmed or naked in

this scheme. And remember, she owes us for being deceitful. Nobody steps on my friend Mags.'

At five-fifteen, Hedgehog is standing on my doorstep; her shoulders are slumped in her baby blue tracksuit and a fresh cold sore is eating away her top lip. After five minutes of drinking orange juice in silence (I thought she needed the vitamin C – it really is the cornerstone of good health), I'm praying that Peter doesn't stay late at work. Not that he ever does. The point of working at the Ministry of Finance, as far as I can tell, is the ability to leave at five no matter what utterly vital piece of work needs doing.

'Just pretend you're very interested,' I tell her. 'And mention your dogs.'

'I already have an apartment.'

'That doesn't matter. I'm playing a practical joke on him.'

A look of rancour flashes across her face. I decide to pay her up-front, which elevates her mood immediately. She eyes my wallet.

'Make it forty,' she says. 'This seems pretty important to you.'

I barter to thirty-five and understand Maggie's urge to choke her. She tucks the money into her bra and explains that she can only stay until six because her husband is cooking and the jalapeno cheese sticks go into the deep fryer whether she's there or not. Thankfully, at five-thirty, the loose doorknob rattles and Peter strides in. He stops dead when he sees the Hedgehog looming in the kitchen.

'Peter,' I begin, 'meet . . .'

I've called her Hedgehog Girl for so long, I can't remember her real name.

'Willy,' she says.

'I'm going to Japan, and Willy and her husband are looking to sublet my room.'

To his credit, Peter takes several long, quiet seconds to process all of this information. No doubt, he was expecting to heat up his usual two mini frozen pizzas, sit in the living room and watch *The Dating Game* with only minimal distraction. Now he's face to face with a herpes-infected future roomie. Most men would crack, but not our little diplomat.

'Why are you going to Japan?' he says.

'To teach. I've found a new vocation-slash-cash-cow.'

'If this is about reducing your part of the rent because you got the noisier room –'

I brush aside his rationalisation-as-self-preservation and explain my scheme as Willy inspects the house. She turns knobs on the stoves, opens and closes the blinds, and generally looks like she's never seen a real human dwelling before. I pretend not to notice as she takes several coins out of our laundry money jar.

'Let me see if I'm understanding this correctly,' Peter says. 'You decided to move to a country where you don't speak the language *this morning*?'

'Sort of . . .'

I hadn't mentioned any of my recent life-altering experiences to Peter because there's no way he could relate or understand. His idea of enlightenment is seeing his bank balance after the latest pay period. Personally, I can live life in a state of controlled panic. When you think of the true nature of existence, it's the most rational state of being.

Peter whistles through his teeth and looks over to Willy rummaging through the dish cupboard. He stares, no doubt running scenarios through his head: the odds of accidental shower exposure; the division of cleaning duties; and her friends, family and/or associates arriving to nest for a few days. I myself went through two interviews and several reference checks before being allowed to move in. Peter takes me gently by the shoulder. He still hasn't taken off his coat.

'Err, James, about the situation . . . Maybe you could draw up a list of say five potential sublets; then I can sit down with them.'

'I'd love to, but I'm not sure there's time.'

Willy is looking out the window at the backyard.

'Is that big enough for the dogs?' I call to her.

She turns, a big smile plastered on her contaminated face. 'Oh yeah. They'd love that. And we wouldn't have to walk them every night. Vance hates that. He says he wishes they could be trained to flush.'

Peter coughs. 'Are you sure you're not rushing into this? I mean, you don't have the job yet, right? What if there's a problem with your visa?'

'The company I applied to made an offer this morning. As for visas, I've never been *convicted* of anything.'

'There's still time,' Peter murmurs. 'What kind of dogs do you have, Willy?'

'Dobermans.'

'Shouldn't that be "Dobermen"?' I say.

She looks at me blankly. Peter takes off his tie and shoves it into the pocket of his pinstriped pants. He pulls his palm pilot from his briefcase and taps the screen with the mini magnetic stick.

'Let me contact a few people, James. There's a girl in HR who's living with her sister . . .'

'I don't want you to be responsible for my sublet,' I say.

'Really, I don't mind. I said I'd help this girl.'

8

Over the course of the next few weeks, I try to get my affairs in order – like I'm terminally ill – and spend some quality unemployed-but-no-longer-worried time with various friends. I know I should drop in on my father, but every time he calls I end up making excuses. He can't even fake enthusiasm for my trip.

Peter walks into my bedroom and claps his hands together.

'Cork's out in five minutes,' he announces. 'Our search for the perfect room-mate has finally ended.'

'I haven't decided to stay,' I say. 'So this person can hardly be *perfect*.'

'Oh, how I will miss your whimsy.'

'Lucky you. I've decided not to take it with me to Japan, so you can borrow it for the year. Just make sure it's dry-cleaned before you give it back.'

By the time I drag myself kicking and screaming down the stairs to be subjected to free alcohol, he's already yanked the cork out of a bottle of sparkling wine and finished half a glass. In all fairness, I should be the one providing the gratis refreshments, as finding a suitable sublet was more arduous than expected. At regular intervals, I've returned home to find Peter leading all types of freaks through the house. There was the man with the homemade 'Lara' tattoo sloped crookedly down his arm; the guy who poked through closets eating Doritos, until he touched Peter's suede jacket and was shown the door; and even a sixty-year-old woman from Chicago who *hoped no one played the TV too loud*.

But I tell myself I'm not responsible. Being a cheapskate, Peter advertised on telephone poles and in the accommodation section of *NEXT*, the city's most popular free weekly entertainment magazine. Maggie and I used to regularly contribute to the magazine's 'Seen You' section.

> Me: tall with a red baseball cap on. You: in that BMW turning the corner of Bay and Dundas. Did I catch a look? 416-299-8990.

> You were reading Nietzsche at the Bookstore Café on King. I was browsing Proust, too afraid to say hello. Can we catch up now and talk about our philosophies? 416-299-8990.

Finally, after enough unemployed performance poets had come snooping around, Peter got wise and took out an ad in a mainstream paper. He also raised the rent substantially, to weed out the weak, and set out strict specifications for the ideal room-mate. Apparently the new girl is studying law at U of T, doesn't smoke and is paying a hundred and fifty dollars more rent than me.

'In many ways,' Peter says, 'you leaving is the best thing that could have happened.'

I wipe away a fake tear. 'Oh, the sentiment. I'd be offended if I wasn't completely certain that my absence would be a blight on the household. Within a month, you'll be pleading with me to come back: "Make my life more exciting, Jamie! Someone has to fertilise the putting green and organise fantastic parties!" You'll probably offer to pay for my airfare.'

Peter loosens the cork on another bottle, turns and fires towards the fridge. The cork ricochets off the wall and lands next to the open garbage can. No points this time.

'She does most of her studying at the library,' he says. 'So she'll hardly even be around.'

'You'll get lonely.'

'You've got my email address, right?'

Our emotional bonding ends after the second bottle, as Peter isn't generous enough to splash out for more booze. He goes to watch *Hollywood Squares* in a warm cocoon of alcoholic indifference while I pace restlessly wondering whom I can drag out tonight.

As if by fate, the phone rings, promising jocularity and

high jinx. Unfortunately, it's a woman named Mrs Katatanabe, gushing enthusiastically about some upcoming lecture. For a few seconds, I'm sure it's a wrong number, but then I remember what I've so easily blocked out.

I could have a freak out over the Ainu–Sapporo debacle, except that BIGSUN is in the middle of obtaining my visa and desperately needs me, complete bullshit artist or not. I decide not to let Mrs Katatanabe down, as she is extremely nice and polite, and turn my mind to the second principle of fibhood: weaving an intricate web of deception. As with keeping warm in a cold climate, *layering* is the key.

I search the BIGSUN website for staff names. Neville Oliver is the head recruiter in the UK and will do nicely. I phone the Japanese departments of several universities and manage to get in touch with a PhD student named Burt who has a vast knowledge of the Ainu. He runs on like a spigot about their identity, history and the issue of recognition (but says nothing about the Fish God, I notice) until I interrupt.

'Well, my name is Neville Oliver,' I say. I spell it for him just to make sure. 'I'm with BIGSUN language schools. We're organising a talk for the Japanese Appreciation Society on the twentieth and would love to have you as our main speaker. You'll be standing in for Jamie Schmidt, who has come down with an unfortunate case of diphtheria.'

'That doesn't give me much time to prepare,' Burt says.

'Don't worry, just wing it. You'll be fine. Start with a joke and you'll have the crowd eating out your hand. Do you have slides?'

'No, but I could get some made. Is there a stipend?'

Being a great supporter of the humanities, I offer him two hundred dollars and tell him if there's any confusion with payment to refer the matter to me, Neville Oliver: N-E-V –

Hanging up, I tell myself I've done a good thing, really. Burt gets to escape from his lonely, academic life for the evening; the Japanese Appreciation Society gets its speech; and BIGSUN gets good PR in the community for a few hundred bucks. The only person who might cop shit is Neville Oliver, but he lives in the UK and is probably used to snafus from the colonies.

Over the course of the week, my visa arrives, my ticket gets booked and I pack my new life into two mid-sized suitcases. There's a certain satisfaction in the monastic lifestyle, a puritan zeal that comes with knowing that there's little that binds you to the flesh's demands. I just wish I could take a few more CDs.

I decide the best place to say goodbye to Maggie is outdoors, somewhere peaceful and open. Corners and small rooms breed emotion – that's the whole design principle behind prison cells and bedrooms – and there's no need to make this complicated. No doubt, I'm supposed to feel a certain amount of sadness at leaving my friends, but honestly, I don't feel much. The idea of leaving is abstract and conceptual, because I'm still here no matter how many times we wistfully talk about my pending absence. Besides,

I'll be back in a year and nothing will have changed. We do live in Toronto, after all.

I sit on a bench in High Park with a bouquet of flowers, lunch and a bottle of wine. Giving flowers to a florist still doesn't strike me as a sensible practice given the mark-up on comely vegetation, but I want to make a last impression. The arrangement is a rocking mixture of black and red flowers, limes and asparagus. Apparently the whole produce section is now fair game for floral art. But I did stress to the girl at the flower shop that Maggie was a florist so the arrangement had to be cool, not some slapped-together job for a grandmother or person in a coma. A voice filters into my brain from the peripheries.

'Excuse me, sir?'

A bald Asian man is standing beside my bench. How he got there is beyond me. Either he's been trained in SAS-style covert manoeuvres or I've been completely spaced out.

'Do you mind if I pray for you?' he asks.

'Knock yourself out,' I say.

I'd rather he didn't, but he's caught me off guard and my first reaction is to be accommodating and polite. He closes his eyes and begins a whispered chant, his mouth moving incrementally, like he's chewing on a very small piece of gum. He has miniature cymbals on his right thumb and forefinger, which chime every few seconds when he hits a new arch in prayer intensity. This is the fast food, consumer society path to redemption. I sit doing nothing while scoring points towards redemption. I imagine drive-through salvation kiosks around the city dispensing burgers, coffee and blessings. What a brilliant concept.

Finally, just as I'm beginning to get bored, my bald friend finishes. He opens his eyes and smiles. I wait for him to ask for a donation.

'How do you feel?' he asks.

'Oh, good. My neck is a bit stiff, but that's because of the way I slept last night.'

He probably wants me to tell him I've been spiritually transformed, or felt the power course through my body, but I see no cause to feel so obliged. He's just another sign in a litany of signs, fate working through the masses.

'I am a Hare Krishna,' he says. 'We are all about channelling good karma. This is why we don't drink, smoke or eat any animal products. They get in the way of enlightenment and true joy.'

'You obviously haven't been to one of my parties. You guys still hang out in the airport?'

His beatific smile wavers but then he laughs. 'I only go to the airport when I'm off to see my cousins in Wisconsin. If you would like to discuss the spiritual advantages of Krishna, please come to our drop-in centre.'

He places a brochure in my hand and bows slightly. This strikes me as a strange way to drum up business, but I suppose with all the post–September 11 security changes, they've had to change strategy. He spies a couple sitting at a bench further down the path and beelines towards them to spread the love.

Maggie appears from behind a lilac bush.

'What was that about?' she asks.

'That was Dave. He's going around offering free hand jobs. I agreed to meet him in the public restroom in a half-hour, so we'll have to eat quickly. Tell me you weren't hiding from the Hare Krishna.'

'I didn't want to interrupt,' she says. 'But if free sex is on the menu, maybe he can slot me in. I haven't had a decent orgasm in months. Sorry I'm late, by the way. We had a bunch of deliveries that had to go out by ten and the couriers didn't show up until eleven-thirty. They don't seem to understand that flowers arriving an hour after a funeral aren't poignant.'

'So hire a new company.'

'They're all like that.'

'Well, it is hard to get good help at two dollars a delivery.'

She air-kisses me on the cheek as I present her with my bouquet. She inspects it carefully, looking at how the greenery is stuck into the foam base, and poking around petals. I'd been hoping for a slightly more emotional response.

'Very nice,' she says. 'Did you get this at Sal's Flower Emporium?'

'Amazingly, yes. Your clinical receipt of my gift is heart-warming.'

'I know their head designer. We did a couple of courses together.'

She places her canvas bag between us and pulls out Tupperware containers of various sizes and colours. Passers-by might think she's a rep enticing me to buy.

'I've made a spinach and asparagus salad,' she says. 'Because it's your favourite and that's the kind of friend I am. I've also got a pasta salad and some veggie sticks. What have you brought to this relationship?'

I pull out my bottle of wine and a container of my own. 'Cracked pepper risotto with pine nuts and real shaved Parmesan, not that grated sawdust sold in supermarkets.'

'Are you trying to belittle me and my salads?'

'It's no big deal, I had time to cook. This is our last afternoon together and I wanted to have something special. Besides, it's just rice, the staple food of the third world, and pepper, the most universal spice. If anything, I'm serving you peasant food. You should be upset.'

She grunts and slaps down two plates as I pour red wine into plastic cups. The topic of conversation meanders to Triple C. I dreaded quitting for a solid week, running scenarios, rationales and self-defence techniques through my mind, expecting the worst. But in the end, my good old stony producer didn't even flinch. Apparently she didn't see our rise to the top of soft pop in the city to be in any way a team effort. She mumbled something about having a cousin that would take over.

'So we're at the end,' Maggie says. 'You're really leaving me.'

'I'm not leaving *you* – but thanks for the added guilt.'

My Krishna friend scoots by on the sidewalk. For a

second, he looks about to stop and offer Maggie the midday park special, but notes the feast in progress and wisely moves on. It's the right decision on his part. I'm so hungry I couldn't be held responsible for lashing out and breaking his little cymbal-clad fingers.

'Have you been studying Japanese?' Maggie asks.

'*Atsui desu ne?*'

'Does that mean "Yes"?'

'No, it means "It's hot, isn't it?"'

A while back, I bragged about buying *The Busy Person's Guide to Japanese*, thinking that my last week of unemployed freedom would allow me enough time to learn a few basic phrases; but there's been too much packing and socialising. At the moment, '*Atsui desu ne*' and '*Samui desu ne*' are the only phrases embedded in my brain. Those and '*konichiwa*', but everyone knows that one, so I score no points for being diligent.

'There's no use trying to learn while I'm still here,' I say. 'I need to be immersed in the culture, and then I'll have no excuse but to learn the really vital phrases, like "I've just cut off my index finger with a de-boning knife and am rapidly losing blood." The motivation factor will go way up.'

'You might be bilingual in a matter of weeks.'

'Or dead.'

'Maybe you should buy de-boned fish fillets, just to be on the safe side.'

We have a nice enough lunch, but the day feels oddly stilted, because our futures are about to divide drastically. I wonder if this is how old people feel sitting on park benches, knowing that most of their memories are behind them. The scene was no better when I said goodbye to my father. He spent half the morning talking about how nice the cotton fabric of his new shirt feels, which I'd like to think is his way of telling me he cares. He said I did a great job ordering it off the Internet – which could loosely be interpreted as him saying he's proud of me as a son. I could read a lot into the nuances, but half of me fears he is only talking about a shirt.

At the subway station, Maggie surprises me with an octopus hug, which is not her style and is therefore doubly touching. She has said it all for us both. My solitary train ride home is spent gazing at a city I'm no longer a part of: ads for radio personalities hip only to dull people; graffiti on concrete overpasses; and people reading their various newspapers.

I'm ready for a perspective shift.

9

The Japanese bus driver has seen the movie *Speed* way too many times. He's wearing a blue polyester jacket and hat, and thin white driving gloves, giving the offhand appearance of a person certified to drive public transportation. I'm holding on to my seat as we careen around another corner towards Terminal 3. My luggage has already flipped off its rack, coming dangerously close to amputating the stiletto-clad feet of a Japanese girl wearing heavy make-up and a micro-miniskirt.

I check my watch. My flight was delayed an hour in Chicago and I'm hoping that the BIGSUN rep sent to meet the incoming group hasn't left without me. Nerves and high humidity have left the back of my shirt soaked, and my pants feel as if they've been welded on with marmalade after fourteen hours of flying.

But I'm here. I can tell by the ads inside the bus.

Brad Pitt, Julia Roberts and Meg Ryan are among those gleefully hawking canned iced coffees, flat screen TVs, blue jeans, palm pilots, cars and insurance. The Japanese writing looks like hieroglyphics, creeping down the edges of the posters in red and black. Even more confusing are the English translations, which appear to have been written by someone on the wrong end of a two-day methyl and lighter fluid binge. A beer ad reads: 'Asahi for much the big taste. When I am being of the sporting life, my one refreshment is going large to the big clear taste of Asahi Super Dry. Now is the time of the great excitement.'

As we skip over a speed bump, I'm forced to agree. The English couple behind me gasp, the impact no doubt worse on their cellulite-depleted old person bums. We met at the luggage carousel, all looking mildly bewildered. They're here to see their son, his Japanese wife and their first grandchild.

Another ad grabs my attention: 'Pizza-La sauce of the secret recipe emphasises the taste of specialty beef.' I take a closer look and see that the 'original pizza' is topped with beef and lettuce. But this isn't the only original idea for a pizza that the locals have come up with: there's curry potato; teriyaki chicken and mayonnaise; seafood, seaweed and mayonnaise ('new diet'); and a selection of mystery pizzas with names like Get's, TNT Dynamites, Bomber, Bingo and Busters.

We take the corner at Mach 3, my fingers straining painfully to maintain a grip on the steel pole. The pinky on my right hand slips, and for a second I envision myself being thrown through the window, over the immaculate roadway and into the bamboo grove. *I'm sorry, Mr Schmidt, but your son is much dead in the big Japan.*

A silky voice drifts out of the speaker above my head.

'We soon will be arriving Terminal 3. Please that all belongings get accounted for. Thank you for the use of Narita inter-terminal shuttle service.'

The female tone is smooth, like warm honey sliding towards the glass edge of the jar. She might as well have said: '*We will soon be giving you slow and deliberate fellatio. Please sit back and give in to every wave of pleasure. Thank you for using Narita inter-terminal shuttle service.*'

My seduction is interrupted by what I assume is the same message in Japanese, except recited in a helium-fuelled voice by Minnie Mouse. I'm not sure if this is the same woman or another speaker. The language slides together as one long word. I feel momentary panic and wonder if I should turn around, take the hairpin turns back to Terminal 1, get on the next flight home and be happy with my predictable life. There is no slow immersion into Japan. I am here and it is exploding all around me.

We slam to a stop and the driver jams on the parking brake. He frantically hauls suitcases down the steps as a milling crowd stands outside. Voices and machines rev as a homogenous block of faces shift en masse towards exits and ticket machines. I feel like scurrying to a corner to stand with my back against a concrete wall until I can judge the ebb and flow of the tides.

'This country is bloody *obsessed* with punctuality,' the British man behind me says. 'You better get used to it. They'd rather be killed in a road collision than fall behind schedule.'

He steps off, takes the handle of a suitcase and disappears with his wife into the crowd. I'd never fully appreciated the idea of a people being swallowed by a crowd before, but seconds later I can't see even a glimpse of my momentary allies. Terminal 3 is a heaving, solid block of torsos that might be easiest to navigate by body surfing. Sombre business suits and new stylish clothing – short skirts, thin cotton tops and high heels – collide and part, bump and merge, shuffle and accelerate. Hands, arms and flailing limbs surround me.

I drag my suitcases through the entrance, watching hundreds of cardboard signs being held up by corporate reps and personal assistants. Yes, I'm Mr Wakayama and I'd love to be taken by limousine to my hotel. I go to a service desk and have BIGSUN paged. A few minutes later a small Asian woman in her early twenties bounds up. This Tigger-like joy of movement must be a company-wide phenomenon, no doubt taught during our orientation and training. She's wearing jeans, a T-shirt and running shoes instead of the standard-issue high heels and skirt. I'm instantly confused. Do I bow or shake her hand?

'*Konichiwa*,' I say.

'Are you Jamie?' she asks.

'Yeah, that's me.'

'I'm Taya. God, this place is a zoo, isn't it? How was the flight?'

'Good. No complaints.'

I didn't manage to get upgraded, but I did convince the very lovely head flight attendant that my 'reconstructed knee' required as much space as possible. She moved a couple of people and managed to get me a seat next to the emergency exit.

'We have to wait for the LA flight,' Taya says. 'Then I'll buy you all tickets for the express train into Shibuya, central Tokyo. You'll have to find your way to the subway from there. I'm pretty sure you're on the Yamanote line. Someone from the company will meet you in Azamino and get you sorted with your new digs.'

'You've got an excellent grasp of the English language.'

'Thanks, I'm from New Jersey.'

I think about telling her I was making a comment on the American educational system, but decide to swallow my embarrassment. At this moment, I feel like someone has punched me in the stomach or I've ingested too much speed. My pulse is machine-gunning. Taya looks up at the arrival board. The LA flight is unloading passengers.

'I heard this place was busy, but this is insane,' I say.

'You should see it during peak hours. The subway is even worse – some stations have men in white gloves to push you through the doors like sardines. But don't worry, most days you'll be starting work at ten, so you'll miss the rush. And you get used to it.'

She hands me a cardboard sign embossed with 'BIGSUN' and the innocuous teddy bear mascot. We mill through the swarm, trying to gain position around the cordoned-off entry area, where dazed travellers are wandering around like stunned tunas, their mouths gaping slightly and their eyes bugged out. Together, Taya and I round up a collection of overwhelmed Caucasian faces. Their discomfort makes me feel better, almost giddy, because at least I'm not alone. I help a girl from Vancouver with her heavy suitcase. She's biting her nails as we walk and seems to be having trouble breathing.

'Don't hyperventilate,' I say. 'You're not covered by the company medical plan until you're out of the airport.'

'This is manic.'

'You get used to it.'

She yelps as a man in a blue suit drags the wheels of his travel suitcase over her toes. She takes several gulps of oxygen, her face crumpling up like a four-year-old deciding whether or not to cry. We descend to the bowels of the airport along a series of moving walkways – like it's 2066 – and circle our wagons of luggage as Taya buys tickets for the express to Shibuya. For a second, I wonder why I'm being asked so many questions, and then I realise that they think I'm with the company.

'So,' a short girl with pigtails asks, 'is tomorrow's orientation session all day? I really need some time to chill out. And will my hair drier work in the power plugs here?'

'I don't know,' I say.

'What do you mean you don't know?' she snaps.

'Well, tomorrow's not really an orientation session. You don't technically have a job, right?'

'What?'

'Yeah, see, you still have to be interviewed by the CEO, Mr Ko. If he doesn't think you can handle living in Japan, or if he doesn't like your *belligerent attitude*, you'll be on a plane home by tomorrow night.'

She points a finger in my face. 'No way. I've got a job. I signed a contract.'

I duck away from the protruding digit. 'That doesn't matter. You're in a different country now. The Japanese do things their own way. They're original thinkers – except of course when it comes to TVs and automobiles, which they copy and then sell to North Americans at a cut price.'

A tall American raises his hand tentatively.

'Umm, I wasn't told about not having a job either. I was recruited by Dave in Maryland.'

'Oh yes, Dave,' I say. 'He's been having trouble filling his quota for teachers lately, which is probably why he left out the disclaimer. You did read your contract thoroughly, right?'

The American blinks. His eyes move slowly to the floor. A couple of new recruits are smirking and whispering, and I get the sense the joke is coming to an end.

'I have a job,' the short girl says. 'I don't care what you say.'

'Yeah, probably, but don't underestimate Mr Ko. He was the only kamikaze pilot in the Second World War to crash his plane and survive. He's got two glass eyes, which is very unnerving when he's asking questions.'

Half the crowd laugh and I have the feeling that we're all beginning to relax. The line between tension and frenetic laughter is thin.

'And then there's the medical,' I say.

'Medical?' the American guy says.

'Drug tests, stamina, all that sort of thing. They don't take drugs lightly in this country, even if you're a former Beatle. Paul McCartney got locked up for having some pot residue on one of his ties.'

To my horror, the girl from Vancouver begins to freak out. As before, she looks like she's about to cry, and I realise I'm paving the road to hell with every well-meaning word. She must have misunderstood the sarcasm.

'Please don't cry,' I say. 'You have a job. You're great and you'll make a perfect teacher!'

'Do I have a job?' the American guy asks.

'How long can you hold your breath under water?' someone asks him.

'About a minute and a half,' he replies.

I'm waving my hands to kill the game when Taya appears with our tickets. She pauses to gauge the weird level of conflicting tensions, and looks directly at me. I shrug and decide to leave bad enough alone.

We're all going to Shibuya, except a guy in cowboy boots from Texas, who has to catch a connecting flight for Hokkaido. I tell him to say hello to the Ainu for me and wish him the best of luck. He and Taya go back upstairs to the main terminal and the rest of us step on board a long, sleek train from the future – clean, modern and with the rounded nose of a supersonic jet.

We make small talk for the next forty-five minutes. I regret taking my game as far as I did, because I end up answering stupid questions for most of the trip. Sure, I could tell everyone I'm a new teacher too, but the recrimination would be too great, and besides, we're all working in different areas around Tokyo, so we'll probably never see one another again.

Shibuya is a madhouse. Its frenetic pace makes the airport look like a seniors' home. I take the train alone to Azamino, a residential area halfway between Tokyo and Yokohama. Everyone else is living in the arteries of the big beast.

The urban landscape blazes against the night sky. For miles, there is nothing but dense city, no open spaces or parks, just concrete and neon, and an astonishing number of 7-Eleven stores. The symbolic alphabet – *kanji* – drives home the fact that I am far away, in a new life with no parameters. I can re-create myself here, because no one knows the first thing about me.

I get off at the station and am met by Roger, a Brit in his forties who is married to a Japanese girl and has been with the company for close to a decade. He's polite, but seems generally uninterested in my life. I get the feeling he's done this task hundreds of times as he explains a bit about my new neighbourhood.

'A decade ago, this was farmland,' he says.

'I thought there'd be more skyscrapers.'

'Not in Japan. They can't stand up to the earthquakes.'

I remember Betsy saying something about tremors, but she didn't mention architectural imperatives. I had the feeling they were faint rumblings that shook the place up every five hundred years or so.

'But earthquakes aren't common,' I say, hopefully.

'Oh, yeah, they are.'

This is as animated as UK Roger has been so far. He appears genuinely pleased that the earth moves several times a month, or at least by my discomfort. He details the devastation of the Osaka quake in 1991, in which several hundred people died, recalling the television shots of collapsed homes and security camera footage of supermarket shelves coming down. He describes how the walls bent before giving way.

'Tokyo is well overdue for a big one,' he says. 'We'll certainly be next. And this year has been particularly bad. There's a lot of seismic activity off Izu, which is a peninsula that juts out from the coast and ends in a small chain of islands. You might think about stocking up on dried food and bottled water.'

'You're joking . . .'

'The best place to hide is under your kitchen table,' he

continues. 'I suggest purchasing a safety helmet equipped with a light.'

I'd like to think he's playing Torment the Tourist, which I obviously deserve, but there's none of the signs of deceit in his expression. He doesn't avoid my glance, isn't twitching or faintly smiling, so I have to accept that he's telling the truth. This is not what I need to hear after travelling halfway around the world and being exposed to a fit-inducing over-abundance of neon.

UK Roger walks and pontificates as I struggle behind, dragging my two suitcases along the narrow sidewalk, up and down the undulated route. Patiently, he slows down when I begin to fade from exhaustion. We take the elevator to the second floor of my new home, Azamino Sunny Palace, a five-story nondescript white building, and make our way to apartment 207. He knocks, unlocks the door and makes a big deal of bringing my suitcases the final two feet through the doorway.

'Thanks for your help,' I say.

'My pleasure, and part of my job description.'

We take off our shoes and I follow him into the main room, which is small, unadorned and appears to have been severely trashed by feral monkeys. The carpet is stained with dark liquid, the table and chairs are covered in clothes, books, magazines, videos, spare change, assorted lint balls and festering takeaway containers. The kitchen is even worse. I might not be the most orderly person in the world, but I'm not completely undomesticated. After living with Peter, collector of detergents and cleaning supplies, this is a change.

'Well,' UK Roger says.

He stands in the middle of the room, surveying the landfill. No doubt he wants to ditch me and get home to his wife, put his feet up and watch *The Iron Chef*. He takes a stick of gum from his pocket, delicately unwraps a piece and begins to chew. He cranes his neck to look in the rooms, his feet glued to the floor, as if he's afraid to move. He attempts to look jolly and reassuring — which is probably easy for him, because he doesn't have to live here.

'Seems someone has already moved in,' he says. 'There wasn't supposed to be anyone until tomorrow.'

'Maybe they're squatters; though I don't smell urine. No, wait — I *do*.'

Roger busies himself clearing away some of the rubble, dumping armfuls of clothes inside a room full of luggage. A dozen CDs are strewn across a floor that appears to be covered in woven straw.

'That's *tatami*,' UK Roger says. 'It's traditional Japanese flooring, known to keep rooms warm in the winter and cool in summer. But you've got to keep it clean, otherwise it'll be teeming with mites.'

We both look around. Mites are nothing; I'm wondering how long before the sewer rats move in. I've got the pick of the two remaining rooms. The first is small with a balcony but no closet; the second is even smaller, but with a storage cupboard the size of a pantry. I take the balcony and open the sliding door. A blast of hot air filters in. Roger fumbles with a remote control, directing it towards what looks like a vacuum cleaner turned on its side, stuck high on the wall. A faint humming permeates the room.

'Air conditioner,' he says.

'That's a nice bonus.'

'A necessity, trust me. Once your adrenaline wears off, you'll start to notice the severity of the heat. Get used to it.'

He gives me instructions on how to get to orientation, then leaves. I sit at the kitchen table, feeling the apartment slowly filling with cool air. Somehow it feels wrong to be here and be inside, like I'm hiding from this country or giving in to my sense of intimidation. I'm terrified, but can't help laughing at what I've done – where I am. *What the hell am I doing?* Normal people don't pack up their lives at the age of thirty and fly to a completely foreign culture where they know no one and can't even speak the language. A few weeks ago I was jumping the shark, working in radio, and living in a city I know far too well; now I have my own spin-off series.

Various forms and envelopes are scattered on the table. I recognise the logo for the company's health plan and look over a claim form filled out in a looping hand.

Reason for being sick: *I ate seven hotdogs and felt severe stomach pain.*

'*Geezus*,' I say. 'What kind of animal have I been set up with?'

I decide to find nourishment, which is my first step into my new world. But as I stand on the sidewalk watching the cars, high school boys, beautiful women, businessmen and lights all zipping by, I think there's no need to rush towards total independence. I go into the Lawson's convenience store next door and spend ten minutes trying to figure out what exactly is in the frozen food containers. There are bowls of mystery dumplings, soups, corn-topped pizzas and TV-style dinners featuring happy smiling squid. I curse myself for not learning a few basic expressions, like 'Does this contain raw eel?' I play Russian roulette with two items, then load up on my essentials: coffee, milk, and cheese that comes pre-grated in child-size servings. The bread selection is nonexistent – there's only four-packs of giant white bread, each slice the size of a large hardback book. For a country where everyone is so small, the gargantuan bread is clearly an anomaly.

I take my selections to the counter, where a teenage guy with spiky hair runs each item over a scanner and double-bags everything. He's very polite, points to the monitor, and accepts my childlike naivety with good grace. I fumble with this new currency and smile weakly.

I have arrived.

10

As if I'm not disoriented enough, when I drag my weary butt out of my closet/room the next morning there's an enormous man with nipple rings in my bathroom. He's wearing a towel and is shaving his head in front of the sink, a thin coating of shaving cream covering his entire skull. He makes a long, deft pass with the razor, sees my reflection and stops. He turns and juts out a huge hand. His accent is English.

'Marcus Clayton,' he says. 'You must be the new prisoner.'

'Jamie Schmidt.'

He bustles out of the bathroom towards the table, his towel swinging wildly, and clears up papers and empty containers. He looks around for a new place to squirrel away his garbage and tucks them under the TV.

'Get in last night? Sorry about the mess, but I've been here by myself for two weeks and have become a real ratbag. How much do you think a maid might cost in this country? We could have her come in once every week or two?'

He stops and looks directly at me. I'm trying to follow the flow of conversation, but his accent mixed with my jet lag, and the distraction of the two gold hoops swinging on his chest, is too much.

'Yeah, probably too expensive,' he says.

We look at each other for a few moments, sizing one another up. He points to his skull – at the cream beginning to turn runny and move down his head – and goes back to the sink and the act of delicately lining up the razor in the mirror. He's thick and muscular, with sharp definition around his shoulders, and looks like he might be good in a fight. I go to the kitchen to put on the kettle. Sounds filter through the open window, cars and chimes and voices speaking gibberish from the streets. I peek through the slats to see Japan in the daylight. The place isn't as metallic and shiny as the neon had made me expect. I look at last night's dinner container of rubberised seafood dumplings, and groan.

'I think you'll like it here,' Marcus shouts.

'Based on what?'

'Based on the fact that I like it, I suppose,' he says with a laugh. 'And I've got brilliant fucking taste. Azamino is close enough to the hustle of Tokyo without getting completely bombarded. We're termed a "residential suburb", which in Japan means there's only two department stores within a three-block radius.'

I return to the lounge room and watch him tilt his head to look for residual stubble. He begins to shout again until he notices me.

'I notice you – oh . . . I notice you made it in time for dinner last night. Any good?'

'I wouldn't recommend it.'

'Most of the restaurants are near the station, but if you can't be bothered walking all the way, there's a bento box takeaway across the street. You know, a tray full of bits and bobs of rice and meat and veg. You'll see the plastic food in the window.'

'*Plastic* food?'

'Models of the various dishes. My students tell me the better quality the fake food is in the window, the better the restaurant. Did you do much research into the country before you came?'

'Some.'

I refuse to feel bad about neglecting to learn about Japan when there were abundant emotional goodbye drinks to consume. Marcus gives me a complete run-down of my nutritional options. Apparently, every convenience store has fresh, pre-made and easily identifiable meals in a refrigerated case near the cash register – how I missed this entire section gives a good indication of my fatigue and fragility. A lot of young workers eat convenience store food for their evening meal, because they work fourteen- or fifteen-hour days and don't have the energy or inclination to cook.

'Either that,' Marcus says, 'or they go to an *izakaya* and get completely legless. It's a beer hall where everyone shares small plates of snacks, like chicken cartilage and octopus balls. Do you drink?'

'Definitely.'

'Then you'll enjoy Japan.'

'But I don't eat chicken cartilage.'

'You will. I'm not saying you'll like it, but at some point a Japanese person will order a dish and you'll either be curious or feel obliged. Or, as in my case, you'll think the cartilage is grilled pieces of squid and whack a load in your mouth. It's certainly not the worst taste in the world. I suppose you'll be off to get your alien registration card today.'

Every non-native resident has to sign up with the government, which strikes me as positively Orwellian. The ID features a head shot and a thumbprint and has to be carried at all times. Marcus sweeps the last line of creamy froth from his skull and rinses the razor in the sink. He then drops his towel and steps through the shower door in mid-sentence, still speaking as the spray begins to drown out his voice. I go to the kitchen and make a giant piece of white toast in the oven. It tastes like soft white nothing.

The apartment didn't strike me as spacious last night, and now it seems much smaller with two bodies moving around. I'm not eager for our third to make an appearance, which is supposed to be soon. I do a brief inspection of the cupboards and closets: we've got a full set of dishes and accessories, a vacuum cleaner, TV, VCR and even a small washing machine. There are no pictures on the bare white walls, and we're not allowed to put any up, but overall I'm impressed with the set-up.

I flip through an English-language newspaper as Marcus bangs around the medicine cupboard. He steps into the lounge room dripping wet, with an electric toothbrush in his hand.

'I notice you're a hard bristles man,' he says.

'Am I?'

'None of my business, right, but if you get a chance, pick up one of these electric models. I had a bit of gingivitis a while back – there's a history of suspect gums on my mother's side – so I invested in one. My mouth stopped bleeding within days and I haven't had a problem since. If you want to give mine a try, go ahead.'

He turns to spit, thus missing my uncontrollable look of horror and revulsion. I'm not quite sure what to say. No one has ever offered me their toothbrush before, especially not a grown man who I've just met, who has bloody gums and two gleaming pieces of metal shot through his tits.

'The engine part, that is,' he adds. 'You'll have to buy your own head.'

'I don't pay for that sort of thing.'

'They're only a couple of hundred yen for a pack of three. It'll make a world of difference to your mouth. I'm not sure what the Japanese attitude is to fluoride in the toothpaste, but why take chances? And yes, I get your joke. Good to see Canadians aren't as deadly boring as I've heard.'

'Who said that?'

He winks, zips his lips and sashays into his room. A few minutes later, he emerges in a pinstripe suit looking remarkably professional; he's been transformed from a club bouncer into a figure of style. He apologises for having to go – his first class is at ten – and disappears within seconds, leaving the room feeling incredibly empty.

I'm not accustomed to being alone without knowing there are a dozen people within reach with a simple telephone call. I make myself very still and small and just listen to my new surroundings: the neighbours walking upstairs, engines, and a voice on a loudspeaker in the distance. I can smell the *tatami* matting, toast and lingering deodorant. Marcus has left his balcony door open a foot and the humidity is creeping in, wetting my lungs, walking across my skin with wet soles.

A smile overtakes me, nerves churning like new love.

11

Orientation is tedious. It takes place at BIGSUN's head office in Tokyo, in a large conference room, where a hundred or so foldout chairs are arranged in a semicircle around a podium. The newest batch of recruits is milling around anxiously in their new suits, skirts, old thrown-together pants and ties (likely only ever worn to job interviews, funerals and weddings), and expressions of expectation. Everyone is handling the sheer novelty of this venture according to his or her personality type. Several are overly chatty and enthusiastic, others completely quiet, wringing hands, and the rest are somewhere in between.

We're shown a couple of corporate videos, one about the company and the other about the nation, both packed with exuberant, smiling individuals teaching English to overjoyed students. Everyone is so intoxicatingly filled with BIGSUN love and contentment that I'm momentarily convinced we're a subsection of Aum Shinrikyo, that doomsday cult that made headlines briefly in the 1990s. After the films, we sign our contracts (sans drug tests) and receive our schedules.

With technicalities out of the way, we're cattle-prodded into groups of ten and forced to fold origami swans as an exercise in teamwork and grace. We're no longer individuals, but part of the loving and contented BIGSUN team. We will give ourselves to the company. We will worship at its altar. A head priest moves around the cells of origami martyrs, handing out sample medical claim forms. I immediately recognise the looping handwriting and words on the form.

> Reason for being sick: *I ate seven hotdogs and felt severe stomach pain.*

Well, that's a relief.

After lunch, we're given a brief and uninformative language lesson, from which I'm now able to say, '*Ringo ga suki desu*' (I like apples). That should come in very handy if I ever get lost in the countryside or am stuck for ideas at the greengrocer's.

During our afternoon break, my second room-mate makes his appearance. Eldon Jones is five foot nine, with square shoulders and a short fringe cut like a Roman emperor. He's a thirty-five-year-old public defender from Louisville, Kentucky, and speaks with an ultra-slow Southern drawl that makes me think his battery might be low.

'I must have just missed you this morning,' he says. 'I got in late last night and stayed at a hotel near the airport. Hey, I see y'all left me the small room.'

'Technically, they're all small.'

'S'pose that's finders keepers and I can't complain. This country is weird, ain't it? Two people have quit today alone. They couldn't cope with that paper bird, or something, and packed up. I guess a whole lot of people decide they can't cope when they get to this place. I was talking to one of the trainers —'

'You were talking to a *shoe?*'

'No, that's what the company calls its managers.'

'Oh right. Well, you went through the interview process — they weren't doing much beyond weeding out the wackos. Apparently BIGSUN will hire anyone with a tongue.'

'Yeah. At least we're normal enough. What's say we get a drink after this shindig is over?'

An hour later, we're wandering around Shibuya, the main artery of Tokyo. The place is wall-to-wall spectacle, with signs blasting on all sides and a giant TV screen looming over the main square advertising iced coffees and new cars. The sight of swimming mermaids on screen holding cold cans contrasts completely with the dense moist heat rippling off the asphalt. The humidity crawls like a living creature over my arms, legs, neck and back with clammy puckered hands. I can feel the slow pull of H_2O from my blood as cars and buses groan by in puffs of exhaust and acidic smoke. The sidewalks are jammed with heaving bodies, a solid mass. We're an ant colony following the scent on concrete and asphalt, bumping along blindly into oncoming arms, stopping, starting and realigning towards our ultimate destination — which in Eldon and my case is unknown. We simply have to move or risk being buried alive in swinging briefcases. I've taken off my jacket and tie, and can feel a waterfall of perspiration running down the back of my shirt.

'If I don't get into air conditioning soon,' I say, 'I'm going to have to take all my clothes off and douse myself in bottled water.'

'Ah, this ain't so bad. The heat's fine and I kinda expected the crowds. Check out this gal coming now.'

Eldon trails off to rubberneck a passing *kugaru* girl, the Tokyo valley girls who sport bleached blonde hair and panda white make-up, and walk around like circus performers in stilt-like platform shoes. They were a hot topic among the recruits at lunch.

'We're not in Kansas anymore,' Eldon says. 'There's nothing like this in Kentucky, that's for sure. You like Oriental chicks? I heard they're easy. They like foreign men, because the country's like ninety-nine per cent Japanese. I plan on finding out how easy as soon as possible.'

He walks with jerky steps, as if his spine is loose or bent, or both. His arms swing akimbo and he's doing a poor job of navigating the flood of bodies around us. We pass under a canopy of glistening silver lights, through winding side streets clogged with delivery vans and the smell of sour cabbage. Eldon is attempting to find a bar he's been told is good, but his sense of direction is abysmal.

'Guy told me to take the second left out of the station. Did you know there are no street names in Japan?' he says.

'No easier place to be young and lost,' I say.

'Shit, I need a drink. I thought that sports bar was down this street, but they all look the fucking same. What's say we take a gamble on this place?'

We're standing in front of some steps leading down to

Water Bar. Above the door is a heartfelt greeting: 'No one really goes to Water Bar for the drinks. But we make sure our drinks won't kill you. This is something you should remember.'

'More eloquent words were never spoken,' I say.

'I reckon that demands investigation. You'd think these Japanese companies would hire proofreaders. There are thousands of English teachers scattered around the city. They could pay a couple of westerners to fix that shit.'

The stairs are narrow and wind sharply to a cool lower corridor, like a tunnel. I feel like we're entering a secret lair, or tunnelling into a mythical world, through the wardrobe to find the Lion and Witch. The establishment is very small – an ornate oak bar fills two-thirds of the total area. There are no tables, only stools, four walls and a dozen people leaning over multicoloured cocktails. The air conditioning is cranked high and there are two empty seats, so there's no way I'm going back to the urban jungle any time soon. By the time we peruse the retro '70s drink menu (Boxcars, Fuzzy Navels and Singapore Slings), my skin is completely dry, wiped clean by frosty air. I order a 'Long Island of New York Tea' and watch the young bartenders flip bottles Tom Cruise–style as they swizzle and mix. Eldon orders beer.

The crowd is young and fashionable: boys with spiked hair gelled up high against gravity, and girls in silky shirts, skirts and the requisite high heels. There are no blue suits for a change, but then I consider that it's only five o'clock and most office workers – the reverently corporate 'salary-men' – won't leave for home until seven or eight, at the earliest. This is a university crowd, albeit a more up-scale version than at home. A young girl with a daisy clip in her long black hair slips off a stool and weaves towards the door on drunken toes. The spirit is good. I can't say I love the urban density, but there's certainly energy to the place.

'You know why scientists believe flies love to drink beer?' Eldon says. "'Cause they're always sitting on *stools* . . . So how'd you end up on this crazy island?'

'I had my face slammed into a police car; but that was more a symptom than a catalyst. I suppose I don't want to be old. I want to retain my freshness, like Wonderbread.'

I talk vaguely about my desire to make movies, realising that I can say whatever I want because there's no context, no frame of reference for my life. The more I pontificate on my ambition, the more possible the idea becomes, as if my greatest hindrance to success all along has been the admission of desire. And yet, if I were to be honest, the film industry is probably a lot like the radio industry – too much politics, not enough extended lunch breaks. Frankly, I don't know what I want out of a career. Luckily, with my new life, I can put off all real life decisions for at least twelve months, which appears to be Eldon's idea as well. He tells me about his life as a lawyer, about his fifteen-hour days and low salary.

'I had enough, you know,' he says.

'You burned out?'

A slight iciness not unlike the air conditioning creeps into his eyes. He takes a swallow of beer. We've been here for forty-five minutes and he's already halfway through his fourth Asahi Super Dry.

'I needed a change,' he says. 'Besides, money is to be spent, and life is to be lived. I was working so much I didn't have any time to go out and experience anything. I could buy stuff, but once you fill the rooms of your house, there's nothing much to do except look around and wonder what might need replacing. I'm like you: I'm here for a good time. That's why I cashed in my retirement fund, rented out the house and hopped on a flight.'

'You cashed in your retirement fund?'

'Absolutely! I plan on spending every dime I earn. Some people come to save, but I'm going out partying and only coming home when they drag me.'

I swear to god, he says 'Yee-haa!' at this point. The more Eldon consumes, the more his Southern drawl accelerates and becomes a one-way monologue. He fails to notice my ever-increasing monosyllabic responses of 'Ah . . .' He finishes his sixth beer, looks at the bottle quizzically and laughs.

'Shit, they do make things small here. Let's get one of them weird Japanese waiters over here.'

As he waves his fingers towards a wary bartender, I'm reminded of high school and the way that early friendships of convenience were formed. No fourteen-year-old wants to be seen wandering around the cafeteria alone – that's instant social death. I briefly latched onto a group of guys who were into cars, metalwork and smoking pot. What they weren't into were life's bigger issues, like moral philosophy, oral hygiene or talking about anything that didn't have a transmission. After a couple of months, I managed to make new connections and find my people, leaving behind for eternity all conversations about welding techniques and homemade engine blocks. I look at my new room-mate and wonder where I'll find my locker. I'm a priest hearing a tormented confession. Half the time he doesn't even look at me.

'As a lawyer, there's nothing better than getting someone off who you know is guilty,' he says. 'Some people might say that sounds bad, but I figure it balances out the people who get falsely convicted. Understand what I mean? And knowing you won despite the odds is a mindfuck, absolute pure joy.'

'Sounds like the black heart of the American Dream.'

'What's that?'

'I said this is going to be my last Singapore Sling. They're really sweet.'

'Yeah, my wife used to like those.'

Eldon excuses himself to go take 'a vicious slash' and I'm left to sip what's left of my drink. If I didn't have to live with this guy for the next year I'd bolt right now.

'Hello.'

I turn to see a Japanese girl in her early twenties, with dark hair and eyes, and the smoothest skin in the world. It looks as soft as rose petals. I bow slightly and she giggles.

'I buy you drink,' she says. 'You speak English to me.'

Her pronunciation has it come out as *Eng-rish*, which is about the cutest thing I've ever heard. I pull up Eldon's stool and pat the seat.

'Why don't I buy you a drink *and* speak to you in Engrish?' I say. 'I'm Jamie.'

'My name Megumi and I from Asakusa.'

She giggles girlishly again, looking very coy, with a hand in front of her mouth. She glances at the drinks menu and points to a 'Grasshopper Very Much Special'. The bartender takes the order, yelps '*Hai!*' and begins spinning bottles and pouring shots. From the look of her flushed cheeks, Megumi's either nervous or has already consumed a few 'very much special' insect cocktails.

'How long you Japan?' she asks.

'My contract is for a year.'

'You one year in Japan? Ah, long time.'

'Oh, no,' I say with a laugh. 'I arrived yesterday.'

She looks confused.

'I came yesterday,' I say. 'On a plane.'

I make the universal symbol for airplane, splaying my arms wide and making a deep, grumbling engine noise. Her eyes light up and she makes a surprised high-pitched sound.

'*Sagoy!*' she says. 'You come in Japan person house?'

'Err, no, not yet.'

She grabs my arm. 'We go. I show you. We no drink now so much.'

She says something to the bartender, cancelling her green frothy beverage, and pulls at my arm persistently. I think of Eldon, wondering vaguely if he's passed out in a toilet stall, and convince myself that drinking longer with him wouldn't be beneficial to either of us. He needs to sleep or detoxify or learn to meditate, and I need to polish my karma with positive kicks. And really, this is why I've come to the country: cultural exploration coupled with very pretty females. There's no reason for me to decline her offer.

I slide off my chair, throwing down a couple of bills on the counter. Megumi is excited and we giggle girlishly together. As we approach the door, Eldon comes out of the bathroom and stops dead, looking generally perplexed.

'Change of plan,' I tell him. 'I'll see you back at home later. We're going to Disneyland. Her brother works there and he's going to let me try on the Goofy costume!'

Eldon says nothing, just looks from me to the girl holding my hand, with his mouth open.

We re-emerge into the stagnant hell of humidity and wander along Hachico Square. Megumi points to a bronze statue of a dog and works very hard to explain how the dog used to meet his master here every day, and when the old man died, the dog would still come and wait. She does pretty well with her explanation, but when she gets stuck, I feed her the correct word or expression.

'Where did you learn English?' I ask.

'It very bad.'

'No, it's great. I'm amazed that so many people in Japan have some language skills. I thought doing the basic things here would be really difficult, but the subways have signs in English and the supermarket was fine.'

I'm pretty sure this goes over her head, but she smiles politely and pats my arm. I vow to make a better effort to keep my sentences short and simple as I wipe the oh-so-seductive fountain of sweat from my forehead.

'*Mushi atsui desu ne*,' Megumi says.

I point to my head. '*Atsui?*'

'Hot-*to.*'

'Yes! Hot! *Atsui!*'

We're both overjoyed at my first successful communication in a foreign language. I'll be Canada's ambassador to Japan in no time.

On the train Megumi tells me she's been to the United States twice on language exchanges, both times rooming with families. She doesn't have much to say about Utah, and doesn't understand my probing for dirt on the Mormons. It seems an unlikely place for cultural immersion, like some nefarious language-for-religious-conversion scam.

She teaches me the words for 'train', 'seat', 'shoe', 'sock' and 'hat', which leaves me overwhelmed by the sheer effort of communication. Learning a language is essentially extreme memorisation, and I'm a preschooler in this country. As we squeeze together on the train, I let my hand slip down to her hip and she makes no effort to move it away.

Megumi's apartment is in a complex tucked away down a winding back street. We race up the stairs. As we slip our shoes off at the door I'm convinced that she's thinking the same thing as me: we're young, lusty and open to cross-cultural experiences. The air conditioner must be on maximum, because once again the perspiration is shocked from my body instantly. I put on a pair of blue slippers embossed with a round blue cartoon figure, and follow

Megumi into the main room, where my exuberance gets a quick cold cure as well.

An older woman is sitting watching daytime soaps. She gets off the couch, beaming widely, and bows to me. She's so short and withered, she could be the spokesperson for osteoporosis. I hadn't even considered that Megumi might live with her parents. I'm having quite a lot of difficulty determining the age of some Japanese females.

'My mother,' Megumi says.

She says something in Japanese, the only part I understand being '*Hajimaemashite*', which is what you say when you meet a person for the first time. I say '*Konichiwa*' several times and bow, because any time I try to say '*Hajimaemashite*' the word comes out in a mangled heap. I could say 'Shoe' or 'I like apples', but that wouldn't make the best first impression. There is much smiling and more giggles before Megumi takes me by the arm.

'Come in room.'

She leads me into what appears to be a seven-year-old girl's shrine to life. Everything is pink and lacy. The bed sheet is covered with a smiling cartoon cat and there are pictures on the walls of characters from kids' movies. The Littlest Mermaid winks at me. The Lion King stands majestically. A ceramic Donald Duck, pantless as ever, holds court on a small dresser. Megumi slides the paper door closed, puts a Celine Dion CD on her stereo, and sits down on her futon, patting the space beside her. She points to the speaker.

'From Canada, yes?' she asks, referring to the music.

'Yeah, unfortunately,' I say. 'Every nation is cursed with some evil. I see you like cartoons.'

We sit and listen to Celine shriek, Megumi moving her head back and forth to the beat with a placid smile on her face. Despite my every instinct, I smile and pretend to enjoy the power screeching, not quite able to bob my head joyously. There's a knock at the door and mother comes in with a teapot and two small cups not much bigger than shot glasses. She pours me a drink and offers it with both hands.

'Greenu tea,' Megumi says. 'Very nice for body.'

Mother waits expectantly until I take a sip and say how amazed I am by the taste. She's overjoyed.

'*Atsui*,' I say.

She claps. What had begun at Water Bar as a fun jaunt into the delicate feminine world of the Orient is quickly descending into a shambles of pantomime and improvisation. I'm embarrassed by my interpretation of the situation. Megumi did say she'd buy me a drink to practise her English, and teaching is technically my job. I laugh to myself. Mother looks at me intently and seems to understand, laughing heartily with me. We stare at one another, really cracking each other up. Finally, my wacky ways too much, she leaves, and I sit back down on the futon, my legs outstretched onto the *tatami*, which doesn't feel cool, just scratchy.

'Futon is nice place for language exchange, yes?' Megumi says.

'Fine by me. When in Rome . . .'

'Ah! You like Italy!'

She gets up and brings back vacation photos, as well as a video of the movie *Roman Holiday*. Megumi loves Audrey Hepburn and views her as the ideal western woman: feminine, graceful and anorexic. Megumi went on a package tour of Europe and passes me pictures of herself and sixty other Japanese people with cameras and bum bags, standing in front of the Forum, the Colosseum, and a Giorgio Armani store. She points to a girl making the peace sign, her head tilted slightly to the left in what can only be described as a cute pose.

'Bestu friendo,' Megumi tells me. '*Tomodachi.*'

'I should be taking notes.'

She points to a gladiator impersonator (some swarthy Italian guy in a tin vest and helmet), the warmth of her breath cascading down my neck. Megumi is speaking only a few inches away from my ear now, and when I turn she stops speaking and looks me directly in the eye. With Singapore Sling courage, I lean forward. Her mouth is warm as we descend slowly onto the cartoon cat's left eyeball. I begin to say something about mom in the other room, who probably doesn't want to hear her daughter making out with a complete stranger, but Megumi shakes her head.

'Sleep time,' she says.

I thought Eldon had been blowing smoke when he said *gaijin* men were highly desirable to Japanese women, but suddenly I feel like a rock star, special simply for being different. Either that or she's a sucker for such sweet nothings as 'I like apples' and 'The weather is hot'.

When we come back out into the main room, mother is on the couch, still watching soap operas. I'm not sure that naptime ever occurred. Regardless, she looks up at me with the same wide smile and begins to laugh.

'Good?' she asks.

'Yeah. Very good English speaker,' I say, motioning towards Megumi. Mother gets up and quickly shuffles to the kitchen, returning with a backpack, a pair of running shoes with Velcro straps, and a polystyrene container. She holds them out to me.

'Please,' she says.

'These gifts,' Megumi explains.

They're acting like this is a normal thing to do: bring a complete stranger home, make out with him on a bed covered in pink cartoons, then load him up with dinner and ugly fashion accessories. I thank them both, slip on my shoes and merge back into the crowds heading for the train station.

12

I've got a day off before training begins in Yokohama, but there are lots of errands I have to do. For one thing, my alarm clock has begun to lose ten minutes for every hour. At first I wonder if time moves more slowly in this country, but then Marcus explains that the voltage in Japan is probably slightly different from that in North America.

I register for my *gaijin* card at the prefecture office, which is part of a community centre. I wander around, looking in on judo classes, badminton and a small gym that has one of those archaic fat-burning machines from the 1970s – the type with the belt you put around your waist, which shakes you violently while you do nothing. A small lithe man with thinning hair jiggles vigorously as he reads a magazine. I sign up for free Japanese lessons, hoping to surprise Megumi with a few key phrases next time we meet up. There are only so many soft pop ballads I can handle to fill in the silences.

When Marcus gets home from work, I tell him about the previous night's events and show him my loot. He can't stop laughing at the Velcro shoes.

'They're top trainers,' Marcus says. 'Did the old woman make them herself? There's barely a heel on them.'

'I guess she felt she had to offer me something. I've read that being hospitable is very important here.'

'What kind of grub did she make?'

'It appeared to be fish head, celery and tofu soup. I had a glance as it was winding its way down the toilet. I saw at least one eye.'

Marcus whistles through his teeth as he cuts vegetables and fries chicken pieces in hissing oil. He's cooking curry and drinking Pocari Sweat, a sports hydration drink. Eldon has been in his room for the past hour or two and finally emerges, yawning and squinting like a baby mouse. He extends a hand to Marcus.

'Hey, I've been dead to the world for ages. That jet lag is a killer. You must be the other guy.'

'That's my Christian name, yeah,' Marcus says. 'Get a good kip?'

Eldon smiles and looks into the pan. 'I'd love some, if you made enough. Smells real good and I can't seem to get full on the small portions here. I suppose cooking at home is a good idea – must be hard for you to get full on those bento boxes, being such a big boy and all.'

'*Big boy* . . . Yes. Well, I am toilet trained, if that's what you're worried about. Whereabouts are you from in the United States?'

'Kentucky.'

'Ah, fried chicken. That's brilliant. Can I ask you a serious question? Is it really true that no one knows what those eleven herbs and spices are? I mean, if scientists can map the human genome, you'd think they could figure out black pepper, cumin and the rest, right?'

'Err, yeah,' Eldon replies. 'I don't rightly know . . .'

Marcus tells us how he used to be a prep chef in Brighton, a seaside town in southern England, before he decided to travel. He guts and dices a red pepper like a propeller, then hands around a plate of poppadums. Eldon looks at the snack suspiciously, breaks off a piece and chews slowly.

'That's not bad,' Eldon says. 'Japanese?'

'No, it's Indian.'

'Geezus, we are multicultural,' Eldon says. 'A Brit, a Yank and a Canadian, in Japan, eating Indian food. We should get a medal from the United Nations. 'Course they'd have to form a subcommittee, vote seven ways till Tuesday, and would probably end up giving the medal to some tribal lord in Africa.'

Eldon runs to his room and returns with a bottle of booze. The neck is covered by red molten wax that streams down the sides. He unscrews the cap and pulls three small cups from the cupboard.

'Maker's Mark,' he announces. 'The finest whisky you can buy, but they sell it in the grocery stores here for next to nothing. Costs me way more back home. How about we have a drink to toast us being room-mates?'

'Sorry, mate, never touch the stuff,' Marcus says.

'You don't like bourbon?'

'I don't drink.'

Eldon whistles. 'I've heard of you people. Tell me, what's the point of life if you don't get smashed?'

'I come from a family of violent drunks. I made a decision a long time ago to give myself the best possible chance of staying out of prison. You wouldn't like me intoxicated. I'm what you might call a nasty prick.'

'What do you do for kicks?'

'Exercise.'

Marcus turns down the heat on his curry and wipes his hands slowly on a tea towel. He holds up his Pocari Sweat like a talisman. Eldon shakes his head like he's been slapped.

'Fuck me,' he says. 'Even the word "exercise" makes me sore. All right, Jamie, y'all drink up in Canada, don't you? Have to stay warm somehow, I suppose.'

Eldon pours us two shots, then slides on the hardback chair so that his spine, the seat back and cushion form an isosceles triangle. I look around my new home and think the place is screaming out for pictures, knick-knacks, or maybe even a house-plant.

'So you're from England, hey?' Eldon says.

'That's right,' Marcus says.

'My granddaddy was stationed over there near the end of the Second World War, when we came to bail y'all out. I don't remember exactly where. Canadians were around somewhere too, I'd imagine. Or did you stay out of that one, like Vietnam and Gulf II?'

'Canada was in the war,' I say. 'Of course, my father's family were in Germany.'

Eldon sits up. 'No shit, you're a Nazi?'

I look down, wondering if I've mistakenly slipped on my SS uniform and jackboots again.

'I'll have to sleep with a gun under my pillow,' Marcus says.

''Course, we're in the land of the kamikazes now,' Eldon continues. 'They were a bigger deal to the States than the Germans. I don't hold any grudges for Pearl Harbor. Bygones are bygones.'

'The company will be pleased to hear that,' Marcus says.

'You always make smart comments?' Eldon says. 'I don't appreciate people making jokes about me.'

There's a strange moment of tension. I can't gauge Eldon's seriousness, but he seems genuinely offended. To his credit, Marcus moves the conversation to our one area of commonality: Japan. He tells us that one of his regular students is a professional porn-movie reviewer. And we learn that the best band names he's heard so far are Doggy Bag, Sads, and Blanky Jet City, the last of which is a leather-clad rock band and all the rage.

By the end of dinner, Eldon is well on his way to getting stewed. I've drunk enough that my residual jet lag begs me to hit the futon for some solid coma time. I've forgotten to buy a new alarm clock. Actually, that's a lie – I remembered, but couldn't find the clock section of the department store and neglected to look up the word (*tokei*) in a dictionary before leaving the apartment.

I set my alarm for four in the morning, hoping it will go off at what is really six. This of course is a stupid plan, because I suffer through a night of extreme paranoia, waking up every hour to look at my watch. By six, I'm blurry-eyed and exhausted, ready to begin my new job. This should be interesting, as I've never taught anyone anything.

13

My four days of training are generally insufficient. There are six new teachers in my group, but we don't get much chance for talk, as most of our time is filled watching qualified teachers, making lesson plans and smoking outside the school entrance.

In class, we listen attentively like scared first graders to UK Roger, the man who met me at the station when I arrived in Azamino. If I thought my mild case of nerves was bad, I'm a diamond cutter next to almost everybody else. People are *terrified* of being sent into a classroom. One guy throws up during our lunch break and another walks out halfway through his first practice lesson. The students, as they should be, are generally perplexed and I can only hope they're getting a reduced rate for being guinea pigs in these lessons.

Roger tells us to entertain the students, because most aren't here to *learn* English. Our mandate is to give them a place to speak to foreigners. That's why BIGSUN promotes itself as a speaking academy, not a school. The thought that I'm being paid thousands of dollars to make small talk is both comforting and shocking. I've got no problem chitchatting, but it doesn't strike me as an ultimately fulfilling career.

My final practice lesson is about going to the beach and involves the use of 'tag' questions: 'I've got my sunglasses on my face, *don't I?*' 'He doesn't like sand, *does he?*' 'You didn't buy your swimsuit at the supermarket, *did you?*'

I think of the many times I've gone to the beach and had to confirm that my sunglasses were on my face. Roger gives me a supportive pat on the back, and I walk into the classroom to find my student, a Mr Takamuri, slumped in his chair with an expression of extreme indifference on his face. He's in his requisite blue suit and his hair is parted perfectly in the middle. I greet him with a hearty 'Hello' and bow politely. His response is barely audible and comes with absolutely no expression change. I feel a slight, clammy finger of panic on my spine and resist the temptation to look at my watch, knowing there's only a mere fifty-nine minutes to go before I can burst out of here.

'So,' I say. 'I thought we'd start with some beach vocabulary. Do you like the beach? Not the movie starring Leonardo DiCaprio, of course, but the place: water, splash splash...'

I'm utterly horrified that I've used the term 'water, splash splash' with a grown man in his late forties or early fifties. I speak to people from other cultures all the time and don't know why being trapped in this tiny glassed-in room makes the simple act so intense and agonising.

'You are new?' Mr Takamuri asks.

'Yeah, I'm training.'

He nods thoughtfully. I think for a second that perhaps he's tired of having inept vomiting recruits as instructors, but he doesn't seem particularly upset, just . . . well, inanimate. He has no interest in sand, surf or the location of his sunglasses, so I babble inanely about why I've come to Japan. I'm even boring myself. At least, I thought I was bored until he deems me worthy of an effort to speak and begins to share information. He's a paint salesman and spends the last thirty-five minutes of class telling me about his products. He sells three different types: latex, enamel and a magnetically charged paint that sticks to ionised surfaces. This has something to do with cars, but by the time he's detailing its benefits and drying time, I'm poking the sharp end of my pen into my leg, digging my nails into my palms and craving a cold beer. Every time I try to interrupt or steer the conversation to something remotely appealing, he waits two seconds and resumes his speech.

'So have you been overseas?' I ask.

'I want one day to go to conference in America.'

'A paint conference?'

He nods. 'In Las Vegas. I maybe get many showgirl.'

Of course, I want to say, *With your good looks, perfectly parted hair and paint knowledge, you can't lose. The women will be flocking to your table.* I look over to see Roger standing in the hallway monitoring lessons. He smiles and gives me a wave. When the bell finally goes, I thank Mr Takamuri for the irreparable brain damage and follow Roger into the teachers' room.

'Didn't want to ruin the surprise,' he says. 'Taka has demonstrated an important lesson for a new teacher: you have to suffer the bad students to appreciate the good ones. And think of it this way, you probably learned a lot about paint.'

He suggests beers to celebrate our triumphant graduation and promptly leaves, telling us to meet him downstairs. When I step off the elevator he's outside Yokohama station, smoking and drinking a tin of Sapporo beer.

'I thought we were going for drinks,' I say.

'Welcome to *eki* beers. "*Eki*" being "station", and beer being . . . well, you know. If you're in a good school, you'll end up drinking half the nights of the week. Japan is a very social place. *Kampai!*'

He toasts, swigs back a large mouthful and motions towards a small magazine kiosk. I wander over, see a cooler of beers set back near the skin mags, give the peace sign, smile and say, 'Beer'. The woman asks me a question, to which my only response is confused silence. I can't even order beer correctly in this country. I suddenly gain a new respect for every immigrant in Toronto, understanding for the first time what it *feels* like to be a complete outsider. In a way, I'm useless to this country. If I can't teach, I'll be deadweight.

I look around at the station teeming with people. I've been to big cities in my life, but nothing like the hive of Tokyo and Yokohama. There's so much energy and such a seductive vibe about both places, as they pulse with humidity, sweat and bare skin. Even the smells are sexy, the mix of diesel and perfume smouldering in my nostrils. I wonder where the girls in the short skirts are going tonight, taste salty sweat on my tongue and feel right. Forget the future, movie aspirations, houses, cars and career, because Japan in the moment matters more. With people surging and trampling all around, complacency doesn't strike me as an option.

The party doesn't last long. Roger has to get home and everyone else appears fit to collapse, the stress and heat pulling the energy out of us. We say our goodbyes and drift off. I begin to walk towards the station.

'Hey Jamie,' Roger says.

I turn around, expecting him to throw me his suit jacket like in the old Coke commercials and tell me I've done a great job. Instead, he points to the opposite end of the square.

'You live on the *subway* line. That's over there.'

When I emerge from my room the next day, Marcus is in his boxer shorts, humming and moving around the kitchen with those quick sprightly motions of a true morning person. He fills the room, being in all spots at once, and I concede that I'll have to wait my turn before getting into the kitchen.

'Hello, hello, hello,' he says. 'See you survived your training. Students didn't break your spirit and dash your hopes then?'

'Yeah, it was fine. I even learned the Japanese word for "acrylic".'

He goes to work opening a tin of meat. Seeing my expression of interest, he stops and flashes the label. 'Corned beef,' he says. 'I brought a few cans with me for special occasions, that and Yorkshire tea. I figure just because you're away from home doesn't mean you should go without.'

He goes on to explain the secret of making scrambled eggs (don't add cream, whip them well, lots of butter and keep stirring). I'm not very interested in perfecting my skills, don't really dig eggs and am generally unreceptive to taking instructions in the morning, so I excuse myself and drown for twenty minutes in the shower. When I come back, Marcus is sitting at the table watching the news. I put on the kettle and sit vegetable-like on a kitchen chair. I shake a cigarette from the pack and put it to my lips, then notice Marcus looking at me.

'Hate to be a bugger,' he says, 'but mind killing yourself outside?'

'I thought all English people smoked.'

'I thought all Canadians lived in snow houses.'

'Igloos?'

'That's the one.'

Point of cultural ignorance taken, I drop the cigarette back on the table and stretch my shoulders. BIGSUN isn't much into comfort. All the classroom chairs are cheap, poorly padded foldouts, and my muscles are aching. I might suggest investing in some ergonomically correct recliners for teachers.

'You need exercise,' Marcus says. 'You have to loosen up those muscles.'

'You're far too energetic in the morning. What are you doing up, anyway? I thought today was your day off.'

'I have aikido, the martial art. Three times a week I pay men half my size to throw me around a gymnasium.'

'I'd do it for free if I could.'

'See, that's the thing – you *could* do it with the proper training. These little blokes can drop me like a load of stones. It's all about maintaining your centre of gravity and using your opponent's energy and momentum. And there's a whole mental philosophy as well – you know, the mind–body–soul as one.'

'Yes, Grasshopper.'

He gets up and goes into a stance, simulating a throw, his mouth still full of egg. I've always thought of martial arts as a sport for men with small penises and aggression issues, but that's probably just a result of high school gym class. Somehow I don't think most of the Neanderthals in grade ten grasped the subtleties of holistic oneness.

'Is this a class for foreigners?' I ask.

'No, it's all in Japanese.'

'How do you understand anything?'

'I don't usually. There are a couple of blokes who translate the important parts; the rest of the time I smile and try to pick up on the room's vibrations.'

'Are you good?'

'No, I'm terrible. But everyone gets a kick out of having a *gaijin* in the class, and it keeps me in good shape.'

We hear shuffling in Eldon's room. For the past four nights, he's headed out to Roppongi, Tokyo's most chaotic nightclub district, and has not come home quietly. The walls of the apartment are literally paper-thin (several layers, but still), so there has been a 3 am wake-up call every night. Eldon's door slides back and he stands bristled and unkempt, his hair matted and his eyes raw as bloody steak. He's wearing a stained sleeveless undershirt, boxer shorts and slippers.

'Hey y'all,' he says. 'What a night. We met these girls in this bar in Shinjuku and they gabbed to us for hours. Fucking gorgeous legs. I think they were models or something. Man, we got hammered.'

'Why didn't you bring them to breakfast?' Marcus asks.

Eldon grins and runs a hand over his rough face. 'That would have been good. I don't think I could have done anything, you know, in that way, but I would have tried.'

'Problem with the package?' Marcus says. 'I'm sure you could have Viagra shipped from home.'

Eldon doesn't say anything, just nods absently and wanders to the bathroom. Marcus wolfs down his final slab of compressed gelatinous beef and slurps his tea. I make coffee and my usual giant slice of disgusting toast, and come back to the table as Eldon emerges from the bathroom, his towel around his waist. He's in surprisingly good shape – lean and stringy, but with some muscle around his arms and shoulders. There's something about his slow Southern speech that makes me think of laziness and mounds of flab.

'You know,' he says, 'I'm glad you're all here. I forgot to mention about the dishes. Could you all wash them *the right way*?'

'And what way is that, exactly?' Marcus asks. 'Is there an American way of scrubbing pots? Sounds like cultural imperialism to me. Remember, England was once an empire. If anyone is doing dishes the wrong way, it's bound to be the colonial.'

'They should go into the sink according to the order they go to your mouth,' Eldon continues. 'Cutlery first, then glasses, plates, pots and pans. You cut down on bacteria by sterilising the most important dishes with the freshest, hottest water. You know? Make sense?'

Marcus looks at Eldon for a long few seconds, then roars with laughter, shakes his head and goes into the kitchen, as if this is a comedy routine or some sort of practical joke. Eldon follows him.

'It only makes sense,' he says. 'From a hygiene point of view.'

'You're taking the piss.'

Eldon stares blankly. 'I already went.'

Marcus bellows again, harder, runs water over his plate, and scrubs it with the white brush. He holds his fork under the tap and cleans the tines with his fingers, then places both items in the dish rack.

'This is the way my mother taught me to do dishes,' he says, 'and I've never once contracted typhus or malaria or whatever disease a person gets from doing dishes in the wrong order.'

'I'm saying there's a better way,' Eldon says. 'You know, it's like science. If you clean the fork with your fingers like that you're probably making the situation worse. Here . . .'

He puts the stopper in the sink and turns the hot water tap on full. He squeezes several long ropes of detergent in and puts everything currently air-drying into the water.

'You wash your hands after going to the bathroom, right?' Eldon says.

'Mate, what are you saying?'

'The bacteria from faeces can go through eight layers of toilet paper.'

'You're serious?' Marcus says. 'Have you done some sort of study?'

'No, I just read stuff – you know, like in science journals.'

'What, the *Harvard Journal of Faecal Medicine*?'

If I'd been smart, I would have skulked back to bed after my shower and waited until everyone was gone before emerging. There's no place in my life for tension first thing after waking. Mornings are for nursing coffees, slow breakfasts, reading the paper, and long lie-ins, preferably with someone female and scantily clad. Marcus squeezes by Eldon and picks up his gym bag in the hall.

'I'm late for class.'

'Don't forget your Zen,' I mumble.

He gives a brief wave and disappears. Eldon stands with a hand on his hip, mid-demonstration, a wet knife in his hand. He lets out a sigh and goes back to the bathroom, closing the door behind him. I finally get to light up my cigarette and drink my coffee in peace.

14

Shin-Yokohama school is easy to find, its ridiculous mascot waving electronically from a large billboard directly across from the station of the same name. I take the elevator up to the third floor, grinding my teeth nervously, and walk into a generally unremarkable and mildly sterile office containing a large Formica-covered reception desk and two small leather couches for waiting. I present myself to a Japanese girl in a blue blazer who beams widely, makes an exclamation of sheer joy, and bows. I bow back, which she thinks is the most fabulous thing ever, then she takes me to the teachers' room, which, like everything else in this country, is small and cramped. I've arrived an hour early to prepare for my lessons – six of them, each lasting an hour. I can hear English conversation going on throughout the building.

'Here are your files and the schedule. I am Aka. Please to punch in time card.'

We've got time cards, like some sort of factory. I slide mine into the machine, the date is stamped next to '*Suiyobi*' (Wednesday) and I put it back in my slot. Aka runs out of the room on her high heels to greet an incoming student with a high-pitched call of enthusiasm, and I'm left to snoop around on my own. There are rows of 1970s-style textbooks, with lessons on the Soviet Union and disco, as well as stacks of supplementary materials, such as playing cards, board games and giant dice with vowels instead of numbers. I thought teaching English would be a high-minded pursuit, but I've landed back in elementary school.

A second staff member comes in, bows and introduces herself as Akiko, the manager.

'Aka and Akiko,' I say. 'Just close enough to be confusing.'

'Jamie-*san*,' she says. 'Thank goodness you are here. Sheila is very late on subway and you must take her lesson next period.'

In my most friendly manner, I explain that the class starts in twelve minutes, I haven't prepared my lessons for the day yet, and I'm not ready to walk in cold and wing it, as there's simply too great a risk of paint monologues. Akiko notes my reservations, making several affirmative humming noises, but looks horrified when I suggest we cancel Sheila's class. Oddly enough, the more I try to persuade her, the less Akiko appears able to understand English. The end of the session is announced by a series of chimes that sound like a cheap front door bell being rung. Men and women in suits and skirts come streaming into the room as I frantically look for Sheila's workbook. A blond guy with square glasses, aged in his early forties, juts out his hand.

'You must be the new meat,' he says. 'Eugene Plotz. Anything you hear about me is a lie. You look scared.'

'I'm fine.'

'No, I sense a definite glint of sheer terror in your eyes.'

The others mumble greetings and put their heads down to write in their files. Sally is an Australian girl with straight, thick brown hair. Paul is Scottish, with round wire glasses and a slinking walk – a sliding gait that sees his feet barely lift off the ground. He's got a soul-brother sway and wears his tie lose around his neck, the top button of his shirt undone.

'You're in kind of early, aren't you?' he says. 'Don't be too keen. You'll make the rest of us look bad. I'm going for a smoke, who's coming?'

'Right behind you,' Eugene says.

'I know, it tickles.'

'Wait,' I say. 'I could use some help. Someone named Sheila is running late and I've been given her next class, which should be interesting considering I don't know how to teach.'

'Mate, yeah,' Paul says. 'Sheila is never on time. Don't worry too much about having a good lesson. The BIGSUN staff are just happy to have one of us teachers in the room – any teacher, as long as he or she has a pulse.'

'You could be in a coma and no one would complain,' Sally says.

'God knows most of the students are,' Paul says. 'BIGSUN could prop a dead body in the corner and no one would notice. Hey, I'm surprised they haven't come up with that already. It'd save paying us.'

'About that help?' I ask again.

Paul tosses his files casually onto the table, digs out a crumpled pack of cigarettes and a silver flip-top lighter, and swaggers towards the door. 'I'd like to, mate, but if I don't smoke at least one cigarette for every two lessons I completely lose my focus. No use both of us having bad lessons.'

Eugene puts a hand on my shoulder and runs a finger over the schedule. He digs a book out from the cupboard and assures me that these sorts of glitches happen all the time, always at the last minute. I run through my student's file, keenly aware that I now have six minutes until the start of class. I look at the teacher notes to determine the student's area of weakness, but the comments are either superficial or an illegible mess of chicken scratching.

Atsuko, the lucky student, is a twenty-year-old hotel clerk who stares at me the entire lesson, parroting back what I say while smiling weakly. Our basic lesson point is the use of 'Do you' (do you like, do you have), and our vocabulary is fruits and vegetables.

'Do you like lettuce?' I ask.

'Lettuce?' she says.

'Do you like lettuce?'

'Lettuce?'

'Do you like?'

'Like?'

'Lettuce?'

'Lettuce?'

I know for a fact that in my brief job interview, Simon told me teaching was easy. I run my hand over the cartoon of two women with shopping carts at the grocery store.

'We're not practising repeating, Atsuko. You know, no repeat?'

She blinks several times. Her eyelids are decorated with sparkling eye shadow that catches the fluorescent lights. She smiles widely.

'Repeat,' she says.

I've met my linguistic doppelganger. I think of Megumi and know I'll have to call her once my life settles into a routine. I see productive lessons going on all around me involving rote repetition, comical role-plays, and discussions about current events with advanced students.

'So you work at a hotel?' I say.

Atsuko looks at me blankly. Suddenly a woman with long blonde hair appears at the window. She holds a clipboard, smiles and waves jubilantly. This must be my boss, popping in to see how much progress we're making.

'Do you like lettuce?' I ask my student again.

'Lettuce?'

When the bell goes, I bolt into the teachers' room and collapse into a chair. Cora, the clipboard-holding boss, introduces herself.

'Interesting lesson,' she says. 'I like Atsuko. She's a very enthusiastic and hard-working student.'

'Does every female name start with A in this country?' I say.

'No,' Paul says. 'Most are named Yoko.'

At lunch, I find a small takeaway shop at the train station and return to the teachers' room with *tonkatsu*, a breaded pork schnitzel coated in egg and laid on rice. Paul is chewing through a cheese and tomato sandwich, reading the newspaper. Akiko, the manager, comes into the room and claps happily as I pick up a piece of pork.

'Ohhh, you can use chopstick!' she says.

'Ohhh, you can use a spoon,' Paul says. 'Don't be so condescending. And when I attempt to speak Japanese, please stop clapping, because it doesn't help my confidence.'

Akiko giggles, pinches his cheek and places a file in Cora's box before sauntering back to the main desk on her slinky high heels. Paul is shaking his head.

'Get used to people marvelling at your abilities to do anything remotely Japanese. I'm convinced it's passive-aggressive. Mind you, if you want some tips with the chopsticks: don't point with them, make a stabbing motion at anyone, or stick them in your rice bowl – that means someone in your family will die.'

'Can I stick them up my nose and pretend to be a walrus?' I say.

'Of course, mate. As foreigners, we're expected to be zany and ridiculous.'

On my way home, I stop at a 7-Eleven and buy a long distance phone card, and then go to a public booth. BIGSUN in Toronto failed to mention that apartments don't come with telephones and that to install one costs several hundred dollars. You have to buy the phone, rent the line, and then even the basic fees are exorbitant, hence the reason everyone has a cell phone the size of a chewing gum packet. Maggie sounds groggy, but pleased to hear from me.

'It's five in the morning,' she says.

'I thought you were an early riser. Aren't you supposed to be at a dawn flower market?'

'It's not dawn. But let's not quibble over my impending day of extreme fatigue or the fact that I'll probably get a cold because of this. How's Japan? Bending the company to your will yet?'

'I wish. I hate to admit that I'm intimidated, so I won't, but this place will take some time to figure out. Today, I had a student spend an hour detailing his prostate examination, which apparently involves the doctor putting his finger up the man's rectum. God knows I'm hoping medical science makes great leaps and bounds before I reach check-up age. I have to say, teaching is a strange way to make a living.'

'What about life outside work?'

'Well, my local supermarket sells birds' nests for making soup. Apparently twigs, grass, bird spit and mucus are a continental delicacy. Everybody sleeps on the subway and I had an old woman chase me down the street to give me a Kleenex that had fallen out of my pocket. All in all, I'd have to say the place is weird and fantastic at the same time.'

Though Maggie is clearly entertained by my new life, I can already sense our distance, like I'm describing a movie that she should see. She can't understand what *wasabe*-covered peas taste like, the way the green radish stings your tongue and gets stuck in your teeth. Nor can she imagine being immersed in a homogenous culture. The smells of our streets aren't comparable. We are suddenly left on different tangents of life and I'm gob-smacked by how quickly this schism has occurred.

'Listen,' I say, 'I've got to go. These public phones are killer expensive and I'm starving. I have to go point at plastic food.'

'Sorry?'

'There's a great take-out restaurant across the street from my apartment, but the menu is all in *kanji* – the Chinese alphabet – so every night I have to drag the woman at the counter outside and point to the fake plastic food in the window. She's very good about it.'

There's a moment of contemplative silence. 'Is your new life everything you hoped for?' Maggie asks.

'Oddly enough, yeah.'

My week gradually improves. Saturday and Sunday turn out to be the killer days, every lesson booked to capacity with office workers who can't come at any other time. Personally, if I were a salaryman working eighty hours a week, I'd be passed out on my *tatami* floor in a pool of exhausted spittle, but our students are dedicated, industrious and nearly comatose from fatigue. For many, this is their chance to glimpse a life outside of Japan and speak to a foreigner. Others simply can't handle the prospect of free time.

I ask my first weekend class, if they had three wishes, what would they be. An older man in his fifties looks pensive and tells me his only wish is to live with his family. He works in Osaka during the week, and many weekends can't come home to Yokohama. He's been there for seven years and his company refuses to grant a transfer. Although I want to be sympathetic, and curse the wicked ways of the national conglomerates, my only real thought is: *Why are you at BIGSUN on a Saturday morning instead of with your wife and kids?*

Sunday night, I drag my weary arse home, the dense humidity leaving me to gyrate down the narrow sidewalk on a pool of sweat like some giant tie-wearing amoeba. I perk up considerably when I spy Megumi standing at the bottom of the stairs to my apartment, wearing a silk skirt, high heels, and a dark blue T-shirt that has 'Fuck Housework' written across her chest in white lettering.

'I am here,' she says.

'Yes, you are. How did you know where I lived?'

'I phone BIGSUN.'

Once again, the company proves that employee confidentiality is simply not a big issue. Maybe this is because Japan is a safe country, or a *safety country*, as several students told me today. Theft and assaults are rare; women walk alone at night; and some shops will leave their merchandise outside for the night unprotected, covered in tarps. Megumi moves towards the stairs, pausing only to make sure I'm following. Thankfully she's not toting any of mother's cooking.

'You good day?' Megumi asks.

'Yes, very informative. Eight people suggested I visit Kyoto.'

'Ah, Kyoto is temple city.'

'So I understand.'

'Kyoto girls very pretty.'

She pauses and then begins to pout. After a few seconds, my tired brain deciphers this little game as fishing for a compliment and I tell her I'm sure she's much more beautiful than any Kyoto girl. This makes her instantly and joyously happy. She wraps her arms around me and we go upstairs. I get changed and she puts on one of her CDs, a wistful boy band named SMAP, which quite logically stands for Sport Music Assemble People. Her other CD is GLAY. Both prove that shitty manufactured pop music isn't a strictly western domain.

'What does "GLAY" stand for?' I ask.

'You know, colour *glay*.'

Despite my best intentions to be a culturally sensitive teacher type, I begin to laugh uncontrollably. She seems surprised and embarrassed, and apologises several times for not knowing; but then after watching my face redden and contort, she joins in and giggles. I tell her it's no big deal, which is a confusing phrase for a non-English speaker, and end up explaining the idiom.

I make dinner, take the used dishes to the kitchen, and wash them to keep Eldon content. When I come back, Megumi is standing in the middle of my room looking at the pictures tacked to the wall of Maggie and assorted friends. I'm divided as to where to take this relationship. I like Megumi, but the language issue is a stressful one and I don't want to rush into anything.

'I bring you gift,' she says.

I sniff the air for soup, but she pulls out a small paper envelope. Inside is a five-yen coin tied to a clasp and ornamented with ribbon.

'*Go-en*,' she tells me. 'This is good luck in Japan. When you get the good luck or see this coin, you will know me. Okay?'

I'm so touched as to be speechless.

15

My nearest place to email is a subterranean arcade/gambling den called The Deep, which has a giant glittering neon whale over its door. The place is located down two flights of stairs, and as you descend, the atmosphere becomes shady, electronic and dense with ozone. Deep metallic pings of slot machines and the cardio-effecting deep bass of synthetic gunfire replace the sounds of cars, trains, human voices and footfalls.

Today, a kid of about seven is playing Ronan Kill, a Samurai game involving gross mutilation with a large sword. He's kicking and yelling as his character swipes, and I wish that a parent or member of staff might swoop in to restore my sanity and enforce the game's probable NC-17 rating. But there's no one hovering in sight. Cartoon violence isn't seen as harmful in Japan. In the corner, two girls in school uniforms are playing Dance Dance 2000, their pigtails bouncing wildly as they imitate dance moves being flashed across a large computer screen. Several of the older gamblers leer as short skirts move upward to reveal white cotton underwear.

Schoolgirl porn is another perfectly acceptable form of entertainment in Japan. In fact, it's a national industry. There are smiling teen girls on magazines, an entire wall of videos at our local shop, and tons of *manga* cartoon books devoted to their sexual exploitation. Up until a few years ago, one of the hottest commodities in vending machines was pre-worn schoolgirl underwear – the choice masturbation aids for businessmen. After years of pressure, the government gave in and banned them *indirectly*, passing a law stating that *used goods* couldn't be sold in vending machines. Of course, there are still plenty of mail order companies willing to help a man get his fix of pubescent panties.

My workday is slow, which is nice after the insanely busy weekend. Cora comes into the room in the afternoon and holds up her hands for attention.

'I'm glad you're all here,' she says. 'I've got some bad news.'

'You're staying on as head teacher at Shin-Yokohama?' Paul says. 'BIGSUN renewed your contract so you can continue to torment us?'

'Very funny. No. Sheila has left the company. She's gone back to South Africa without giving her one-month notice for either her job or her apartment. I can't impress upon any of you how irresponsible and unfair that is to the company and to you all as professionals. We'll be getting a replacement in two months and until then we'll have supply teachers coming in from other schools.'

'How does this effect my life?' Eugene asks.

'Aren't you sad to see Sheila go?'

'She was an idiot.'

'That's not the right attitude. Remember, we're all part of the BIGSUN family.'

'Makes you realise why some animals eat their young.'

Eugene goes back to his files and Cora leaves us to our apathy and rapid-fire planning. I've noticed some tension between these two and wonder if Eugene resents working for someone younger than him. He's always friendly and helpful with the rest of us, acting more like a mentor than a colleague, but with Cora he's terse. Paul takes a black marker and draws a Salvador Dali moustache on a photo of Sheila, before dumping the contents of her teacher drawer into the garbage bin. He hands the tray to me.

'Welcome to the team. You're official now.'

'What am I supposed to put in here?'

'Teaching aids, special lesson plans, and sandwiches. Mine's mostly used for the latter, because BIGSUN is too cheap to buy us a fridge.'

Eugene digs into his compartment and hands me a special lesson he wrote. It's about exploration to Mars, outlining the probability of life, space stations, myths and facts. He points to his highlighted vocabulary list.

'My student asked what a light year is. I said it's like a regular year, but with half the calories, and spent the next forty minutes explaining the joke. My advice is to keep humour simple, like nothing more complex than a knock-knock joke.'

'Tip noted,' I murmur.

'Mate,' Paul says. 'I don't feel that we've had a chance to bond properly yet. Quite frankly, I've been waiting to see if you'd stay the week. We have a lot of meltdowns within the company. But I've deemed you worthy enough to have a drink with me. How are your next few days shaping up?'

'You've asked at a good time; my social calendar is barren. Can I say I'm flattered?'

'You should be. I'm the most interesting person in this school. Just promise you won't bore me with too many personal stories or get maudlin when we've had a couple of beers. I hate that sort of thing.'

The chime goes and the next round of serious language education begins. I have a pregnant student, Sumi, who tells me she 'feels fake'. I get excited, thinking we're going to have an existential/intellectual discussion about the emotional impact of creating a new human life. Then I discover she means she feels *faint* and isn't interested in having a difficult lesson.

The following class includes a thirty-five-year-old guy named Kozo, who insists I call him Mike, for reasons never fully explained. He's lived in Chicago and San Francisco, has a very unique accent and keeps saying 'Hey man, you know,' 'Let's go for beers' and 'We should hang out.'

By the time the bell sounds, I'm dying for a cigarette, but when I walk into the teachers' room I'm stopped dead in my tracks. Cora is talking to a woman in a tight skirt slit up the side to mid-thigh and a silk shirt that clings to her body like wet leaves. Her neck is long and beautifully pale, and her blonde hair sprawls like drunken seaweed. She purses her bold red lips and looks at me over tortoiseshell glasses.

'Are you with us, Jamie?' Cora asks.

Apparently we've been introduced.

'Sorry,' I say. 'I zoned out.'

'That's a quality we like in our teachers. This is Cassandra. She does evaluations for the district and used to work here until you took her place.'

Her hand is cool, almost cold. She stares at me with blue eyes that are like ocean currents, and wiggles her pixie nose like a curious rabbit.

'I'm Jamie,' I say.

'I know,' Cassandra says, laughing. 'We were introduced ten seconds ago. I do the evaluations for the district.'

I feel my cheeks flush. My mind searches for a witty remark but comes up empty, knowing instinctively that anything trite will bounce off this girl, ricochet and kill me. Rather than be hackneyed, I stand paralysed and mute until she can resist my incredible charisma no more and turns her attention back to a folder containing the seven-day advance schedule.

Her accent is Australian, but not strong. Wherever she's been for the past few years, it hasn't been home. Or maybe the feral hair makes her seem more nomadic that most. I can tell she's comfortable in her skin by the way she tilts her neck and shakes the watch on her thin wrist.

'Jamie, are you with us?'

Cora and Cassandra are staring at me. I'm told that Cass is going to observe one of my afternoon lessons, then give me feedback and a written evaluation. *She's going to judge me like a side of beef, watch me fumble, and shake that beautiful curly hair until I ache.* I nod as I'm informed and the chime goes for class. I'm not sure I have the right files, but I squeeze by Cassandra's chair and stumble to my room.

'Don't feel any pressure,' Cassandra says. 'I'll be in the classroom next to you with my head down. Just do your normal lesson.'

'What if my lesson isn't *normal*?' I say. 'What if my students want to tell me about the Japanese tea ceremony in excruciating detail for the entire hour?'

'Try to stay as close to the lesson plan as possible. But

relax. You'll be fine. After a few minutes, you won't notice me or remember you're being observed.'

As she leaves the room, I find it difficult to believe I won't notice her. She's very noticeable, the kind of person you could pick out in a crowded train station. Her sweet-smelling perfume doesn't help. The first girl I ever kissed was wearing strawberry lip balm and I've been a sucker for even the faintest whiff of berries ever since.

My blissful state of attraction drops substantially when I see my students – Yumiko, Mrs Yamaguchi and Yoko – three sexagenarians decidedly low on sex appeal.

'I miss my class yesterday,' Mrs Yamaguchi says. 'My husband is in hospital all day. He has problem with his brain. He is dizzy and cannot drive well.'

'I hope he's alright.'

'Maybe no. We get picture of his brain.'

'A CAT scan?'

All three students write this down in their notebooks. Apparently Mr Yamaguchi has been suffering from frequent blackouts, headaches and bouts of disorientation. I had planned to do a jovial lesson on shopping, but feel the joie de vivre of buying kitchen appliances slowly ebb from the room.

'I have to be waking him for two hours, the doctor tell me, or he go into the big sleep and die. What you say, coma?'

'Who's looking after him now?' I ask.

'No one.'

'You left him alone to come to BIGSUN?'

'I have lesson booked. I call after class finish.'

Yumiko, one of the other students, is waving her arms, trying to get my attention. 'The father and mother belonging to my husband are in hospital. I make bet with him who will be die first. I say mother and think I will win because mother have big cancer in stomach and not eat very much.'

'Are you sad?' Mrs Yamaguchi says.

'No, this okay. She old and when die, we have lots of money for vacation and shopping. What say this?'

'Inheritance,' I mumble.

They write this down too. My third student is enjoying an amused giggle. Cassandra's head is down and I wonder what she's writing on my evaluation form. *Jamie Schmidt managed to introduce the lesson point while promoting an atmosphere of macabre ghoulishness.*

Except I haven't actually introduced the lesson, even ten minutes in. I can barely inhale. They ask me the word for 'killing someone with a pillow'. I feel a desperate, almost superhuman need to drink a bottle of scotch.

'Our lesson today is on shopping,' I say.

'We buy coffin!'

'New dress for funeral!'

This is met with peals of laughter. After several more bleak comments, I lose my nerve completely and restrict all conversation to drills, listen-and-repeat and student reading. The mound of tangled blonde hair nods from time to time. At the end of class, I fall into the teachers' room and pour myself into a steel chair, my spine as slick as Jell-o on a hot day. Cassandra motions for me to follow and we sit in one of the language lab rooms for privacy.

'Interesting class,' she says.

'They seemed to enjoy themselves. We're supposed to keep the students entertained, you said so yourself. I'm really learning a lot in this job — like I didn't know that Japanese people wear white to funerals.'

She smiles. 'Believe it or not, your lesson was better than most new recruits, even with the talk about cremation.'

'The big fire oven.'

'I liked the way you segued from that into shopping at the bakery.'

'I did my best.'

She looks over her notes, sucking on her teeth. Her eyelashes are painted blue, but you can only tell when you're close and her head is bowed slightly. There are no rings on her fingers, and no tan lines, like she might have removed a wedding band for work.

'Beyond the unusual warm-up, your lesson was solid,' she says. 'You kept them moving, followed the task progression, and did all the drills. You might want to leave more time for role-playing, seeing as we are a conversation school more than anything.'

'I was afraid we'd have a mock funeral or a doctor being told to pull the plug on a coma victim. But yeah, I admit I need to work on my role-plays — most of the time students sit silently and stare at me.'

'You can play a part in the scene.'

'I do, but they still stare. How do you get your hair so curly?'

She tucks a strand behind her ear self-consciously. 'It's the humidity. I don't have any control.'

'Why would you want any?'

She looks at her notes with a faint smile on her lips and puts a finger to her chin. The nail is painted bright red – *sexy red, that sunset blazing red, fire engine red, half-eaten cherries dripping cognac red*. Hair is falling onto her shoulders and the curls look mysterious, deep and wild.

'Listen, Jamie, I'm not big on these evaluations. The company wants me to enlighten you on how to best keep students engaged, but quite honestly, I don't know that secret. If the students are having a bad day or are corpses – pardon the expression in light of your last lesson – there's not much you can do. But you're smart and obviously have some social skills, so you'll be fine. If you want to minimise your pain, and this is not to be repeated, draw out your warm-up discussion for as long as possible, shoot through the reading and drills, and then let them role-play. Most of our students aren't here to learn. They want to have a laugh and think you're their mate.'

'I'm a surrogate friend for lonely Japanese people?'

'Well, yeah, quite often. We're the cheapest English school in the country, so we tend to get some eccentric students. That applies to teachers as well, as you might have noticed. My last room-mate wouldn't spend money on anything but records and DJ equipment. All I ever saw him eat was white bread, Vegemite and bananas. He used to lock himself in his room every night and mix with a set of headphones on.'

She's beautiful, those large blue eyes staring right into me. That's the only thought that comes to mind – nothing about teaching or students or supplementary materials. I want her to keep talking, to say anything, to make that mouth move. I want her to be my surrogate friend, too.

16

When I get home, Marcus tentatively pokes his head from behind his door, exhales in relief and steps into the living room.

'Oh good, it's only you. Say, did you feel the earthquake last night? I thought it was my alarm clock going off, so I got up, brushed my teeth and was putting the kettle on when I realised it was two in the morning. Hope I didn't wake you.'

'I think I'm in love with my boss,' I say.

He cocks an eyebrow and frowns. 'You just had to trump my witty earthquake story, didn't you?'

The front door rattles and Eldon flies in, dripping with sweat. His eyes are red, his shoulders are slouched with fatigue and his clothes are so saturated that they look heavy, weighted down and unwilling to remain properly tucked.

'Geezus, mate,' Marcus says, his nose twitching. 'Looks like you swam home . . . across an ocean of vodka.'

'Air conditioning on the train wasn't working right,' Eldon replies. He's been keeping up his dual life of central Tokyo drinking champion and daytime teacher, and his reaction time is slower than usual, on pace with his lethargic speech. It has occurred to me over the past few weeks that I'm sharing living space with an unknown quantity. Eldon has told us a bit about his life in the States: he quit law more than two years ago; his house has five bedrooms and the pool room has a bar with two kegs; there's an ex-wife, but at what point the marriage collapsed, he hasn't said. I have a feeling it was in or around the same time his love of the law dissipated. How he spent the interim to now is a mystery.

Eldon looks down at the landing and frowns.

'Can y'all put your shoes in the cupboard?' he says. 'This place is a pig's sty.'

He stumbles off to his room.

Every morning I wake up to the sound of Eldon's breakfast routine: two flat eggs, a slice of ham, one giant piece of bread, and orange juice prepared precisely at eight-fifteen. He sets the table with a knife, fork and empty glass, and brings ketchup, the container of juice and butter to the table. Above his plate he lines up seven vitamins and supplements in a row, to be consumed immediately before his meal, one after the other with a small sip for each. He refills his glass, chops up his eggs into equal-sized pieces, and butters his toast in long swaths beginning at the top crust then coming down. None of this should bother me – logically it has no bearing on my life – but it's driving me absolutely mad.

Marcus motions for me to follow him out the door and we walk down the road to a ramen noodle restaurant, determined to stay out of the apartment long enough for Eldon to get changed, showered and bolt out the door for yet another night in Roppongi. Except tonight, for unknown reasons, he's still around when we return, watching a video and drinking bourbon.

'Hey y'all, can I have a word?' he says.

He hooks his finger so we follow him into the bathroom. I'm afraid for a second that Eldon wants to show us some rash he's picked up in a hostess bar, but he points to the sink, runs his index finger along the bowl and holds it up.

'See this?'

'My god, it's a finger,' Marcus says.

'There's these whiskers,' Eldon says. 'They're all over the place. I was just wondering if after you shave, maybe you could wipe down the basin, 'cause otherwise it gets filthy. And we should start a cleaning schedule so this place gets a good scrub once a week.'

He gets some toilet paper and demonstrates the best way to clean up the almost invisible shaving fragments, slowly dragging the tissue in descending strokes. Marcus is expressionless, the muscle at the base of his jaw bulging slightly.

'Do you think you might be a touch sensitive?' Marcus says.

'Yeah,' I say. 'We're all pretty busy with work. I don't have a problem if someone can't clean every day. We've all got to make concessions.'

'I see what you're saying,' Eldon relies. 'But a clean sink

is the minimum I can put up with. I'm not asking you to vacuum. I'm a reasonable man.'

'Though perhaps slightly mental,' Marcus says.

Eldon has a silent conversation with himself; his lower lip jangles, then silently he pushes past us to his room and closes the sliding door. Marcus picks up Eldon's toothbrush and casually scrubs the basin, pressing so hard that the bristles bend almost flat. He runs it under water and drops it back into the holder.

'We all take some time to settle in,' I say.

'Mmm,' Marcus says. 'Unfortunately, we've been here weeks. I realise he's been living alone in a big house in Kentucky, but that doesn't ease my annoyance. There's adjustment time and there's being an absolute wanker.'

Marcus examines the damage he's done to the toothbrush, a satisfied smile on his lips.

17

Everyone is gathered in the teachers' room waiting impatiently for Cora to arrive for our weekly staff meeting. I leaf through an English-language magazine and learn that Morioka in Tohoku Prefecture is famous for *wanko soba*, no doubt a very salty broth. Under entertainment, there's an interview with Tsuyoshi Kusanagi, one of the members of the boy band SMAP, who is currently in ten different TV shows, including *Food Fight*, in which competitors attempt to out-eat one another. Last week he ate fourteen plates of squid, but lost to an Osaka baseball player. Paul slides a piece of paper towards me.

Role-Play One: YOU ARE THE FATHER I NEVER KNEW.

Student 1 is an angry salaryman who left his family without cause or provocation.

Student 2 is the child, abandoned since birth.

Start by telling Student 2: 'No one loves you, and you're living in a cardboard box next to Yubisu station. You meet your birth father while scrounging for discarded rice.'

Role-Play Two: HAVE YOU BEEN SAVED BY JESUS?

Student 1 is a wandering missionary trying to convert pagan Japanese to Christianity.

Student 2 is a housewife/student/salaryman.

Start with Student 1 saying: 'Excuse me, do you fear the eternal hellfire of Satan?'

'You don't honestly do these?' I say.
'Four years of teaching puts strange thoughts into a man's head.'
'He's right,' Eugene says. 'I do a great hostage-taking lesson that always goes over a treat. You'd be surprised how

lightly students hold human life. They're always keen to shoot after about two minutes of negotiations.'

With a great dramatic flourish to let us all know how busy and important she is, Cora arrives with her hands full of photocopied papers. The first item on the agenda is earthquake preparative training. We get led around the school and shown the stairwells, are told not to use the elevators, and are taken into a small storage closet containing bottled water and several rope ladders that we can use to get out of the windows if the need arises. When we're back in the teachers' room, Cora unfolds a large sheet of paper and pins it to the wall. She gives us her disappointed face.

'Well, folks, these are the quarterly BIGSUN school rankings, and as you can see, we're near the bottom yet again. I had a phone call from our AGM.'

'Area general manager,' Eugene translates.

'And he's very concerned. This doesn't reflect very well on any of us, and the staff are absolutely ashamed. They've lost face and don't feel they deserve to be among their peers. But I told them not to despair, because we're going to win the Summer Challenge Day!'

A ripple of groans moves around the table. Apparently, in an attempt to promote goodwill and teamwork (and generate publicity), BIGSUN organises four seasonal events in which teachers from all the company's schools compete in a *physical challenge*. They've done rock climbing, sailing, cross-country runs and scavenger hunts. Cora is beside herself with glee.

'This season we're having a relay race to the top of Fuji-*san*!'

'The electronics company?' Sally says.

'That's Fujitsu,' Paul says. 'And they don't just make electronics, they make everything: tyres, furniture, mopeds . . .'

'Five companies own everything in this country,' Eugene says.

'So what are we climbing?' Sally asks.

Cora slaps her hand gently. 'Oh, come on Sally, you know Fuji-*san*. You've been in the country long enough.'

'Mount Fuji, for those of us not pretending we're Japanese,' Eugene says.

'Is this mandatory?' Sally asks.

'Of course not,' I say. 'You can call the mountain whatever you want. I'm sure Eugene means we shouldn't neglect our own language.'

'Exactly,' Eugene says.

Cora holds up her hands for silence. She takes a deep breath and explains that under the Other Duties section of our contracts we're bound to promote the company when required. The terms 'promote' and 'mountaineer' are marginally different in my world, but I let others do the bitching. This is the first year that the clause will be enforced, due to teacher apathy in previous events. The mood is dark, bordering on openly hostile.

'This event is good for company prestige,' Cora insists. 'And thousands of people climb Fuji-*san* every year, including grandmothers, so there's nothing to worry about.'

'Well,' Paul says, 'my gran can take my place, because

there's no way I'm hiking up a poxy mountain. I'm not Sir Edmund bloody Hillary. I'm an English teacher.'

'I guess you don't want the bonus,' Cora says. 'And you can kiss a raise on your next contract goodbye.'

'I don't care,' Paul says.

'What bonus?' Eugene says.

Turns out BIGSUN in all its generosity (and feverish desire to get on the front page of *The Japan Times* newspaper) is offering one month's extra wages to every member of the winning school. This adds up to several thousand dollars for a day's work. Eugene slaps the table.

'I'm sold,' he says. 'Looks like I better call my Sherpa.'

That night, we sit around a bench outside Shin-Yokohama station with 'tallboys' of Kirin beer, watching the scene. I swear, this place never stops – it doesn't even slow down. People finish work and stay out, go to karaoke, a pub or to the game centre to play Pachinco and the slots. In some ways the minuscule size of apartments is a blessing, because people are forced to get out and interact, not squirrel away for extended periods of time in front of a television or video game.

'So, Jamie,' Eugene says. 'How are you finding life in our idyllic small town?'

'Mildly crazy, but generally good. I wish I could speak more and point less, but I suppose that'll take time. How long did it take you to master the language?'

'My youngest kid is six and he speaks better Japanese

than me. I get by, but my wife usually does the talking when we're out. This country has a way of keeping you humble.'

'Try shopping for women's clothes,' Sally says. 'I always assumed "big-boned" was a polite way of saying someone was fat, but I really do have bigger limbs than Japanese people. Do you know how humiliating it is to go into a shop, ask for the largest-size pants they have and still not be able to squeeze into them?'

'Have you thought of having your clothes custom made?' Eugene asks.

'How much is BIGSUN paying you?' she says. 'And besides, I can't speak the language either, and I don't have a six-year-old to help me out.'

'You can borrow mine. Just make sure to feed him before dropping him home – which will cost you twice as much as pants, because he's got my American appetite. But seriously, if you need help with the language, let me know. Fitting into this place isn't easy.'

We linger in near silence soaking up the swell of humidity. After hours in frosty air conditioning it's nice to be breathing marginally fresh air, letting the heat pull open our pores and ease every muscle.

Things I've found out about my co-workers: Eugene's been in Japan for nine years, having met his wife while stationed at the naval base in Yokohama. Fifteen years at sea had left him satiated and lonely and ready for love. Sally is here for a year, nothing more or less, having put off the universally accepted Australian need to backpack until she finished her university degree. Paul, meanwhile, is a mystery, always ready with a comment but not much personal information. So far, he has told me he came to Japan on a bet; by mistake; because he's wanted for tax evasion; and because George Harrison came to him in a dream (I let that one slip while drinking in an *izakaya*).

Eugene finishes his solitary beer, makes his apologies and goes home, followed shortly thereafter by a tired Sally. Paul and I continue to work our way through a plastic bag filled with cans of beer. He pulls out a container of roasted nuts covered in crust and offers me some, which I decline. I still haven't gotten used to the snack food in this country. Even the potato chips are a danger, as likely to be squid or seafood flavoured as barbecue or salt and vinegar.

'So, Paul, why did you really come to Japan?'

'Does it matter?'

'Four years is a long time to be away from home. You must have an interesting reason. Don't you ever want to go home, get on with *real life*?'

'Real what? Never heard of it.'

'How about a career?'

'Appears that I've got one, mate. Think about it: I live like a king in Japan, with loads of money, an easy job, women who want me, a furnished apartment and ready-made friends who arrive through a turnstile every six to twelve months. I never want to go home. Someone else can work at Marks and Sparks for three pounds an hour.'

'You don't miss Scotland at all?'

'No.'

'When was the last time you were home?'

'A long time ago. I spend my vacation time in Thailand – fantastic place. The sponge baths are so cheap that you can have one every day, sometimes with two or three women. I'm thinking of taking six months off next year and living on the beach, shooting smack and seeing the temples. They're an untouched culture, very profound. You should come.'

'I'm not sure that's my thing.'

He finishes his last beer and tosses the empty into his small plastic bag. 'Suit yourself.'

He hauls himself unsteadily to his feet, wavers and picks up the knapsack he always carries. Standing before me with his crooked tie, wire glasses and red cheeks, he strikes me as a British schoolboy ready for the ride home. He thinks for a few seconds, then motions for me to follow and we head in the direction of the school, the lights still blazing as the staff work out lesson schedules and do their paperwork.

'I want to take you somewhere special,' he says.

'I'm not going to a massage parlour, if that's where you're headed.'

He scoffs and keeps walking. We stumble through the revolving doors of the five-star Prince Pepe Hotel and enter a lobby filled with marble and silk, and staff in blue blazers with gold buckles. There's no hint of perceived impropriety in Paul's manner as he leads me to the magnificent elevator and presses the button for the top floor. Framed behind glass is an ad for the underground shopping complex proclaiming this to be 'Climax Summer'.

'I can't help but be excited by the prospect,' he says.

There's also a poster advertising the upcoming baseball series between the Giants and the Lions. Two players are smiling beneath the slogan 'Hit! Foot! Get! More Runs!' We emerge with a gentle swish and stand on a thick spongy burgundy carpet, my feet sinking down. Paul leads me into an up-scale bar, orders us more beers and we sit on a black leather couch in front of a floor-to-ceiling panoramic view of Yokohama. Because every building here is low, I've forgotten about vistas and views. The city spans for miles, a mash of bridges and highways and railway lines. The harbour lies in the distance, seemingly within reach.

'This is the best view in the city,' Paul says. 'Drinks are dear, but it's worthwhile. I come here at least once a week just to look. If you squint hard you can see the world's largest ferris wheel, in Sakuragicho.'

He tells me that the last time he was home, he spent two weeks in his parents' house smoking pot, unable to feel any connection to his home town, culture, or friends. He wanted to be in isolation, cocooned with no obligations. He asks if I know Bobby Sands, an Irish IRA suspect who was falsely imprisoned and went on a hunger strike in protest during the 1980s.

'There was a picture in the newspaper of a protest in support of Sands,' Paul tells me. 'My father was at the front wearing a "Free Bobby Sands" T-shirt. The next week he was let go from his job at the mining company. Those were the Thatcher years, so everyone was getting the shaft, if you get my pun, but there was also the point being made that you don't want to protest too loudly or stand up for anything as trivial as human rights and democracy in the British Empire. Except it's not an empire, it's a shitty little collection of damp countries full of cruel tossers.'

'What happened to your dad?'

'We're not on *Oprah*, mate. Don't get feminine on me. You asked why I came to Japan, and I'm telling you. I learned not to believe in the world, full stop: we're all powerless, democracy doesn't exist, and the planet is on its way to complete oblivion. Sorry if that makes you sad – I can get you a tissue. Did you know there are more people living in China today than populated *the entire planet* a hundred and fifty years ago? And do you see people getting any smarter?'

'Sure they are. Look at technology.'

'Yes. Okay. Five per cent of the population is getting smarter, but they're not the ones having babies. By logic, stupid people having the majority of children makes for a progressively more inept population. Things can only get worse.'

'You paint a gorgeous picture. Why not give up now?'

'Because I've won the lottery, being western and English-speaking at this point in history. I'm riding the crest of the tainted system. We're in Asia being paid exorbitant sums to *speak to people*. Does this not strike you as ridiculous?'

Admittedly, I'd never thought of my new career in these terms. I've long suspected that I'm being overpaid for what I'm doing, but that's the market value. And I'd like to think I'm making some sort of positive contribution, helping

Japanese people work towards increased job prospects or travel opportunities. I can't feel guilty about speaking the most common language on the planet.

Paul orders two more beers from a passing waitress and disappears to the toilet. When he comes back, his mood has transformed and he turns the conversation back to neutral ground, until midnight when I catch the last train and stumble towards a distant futon.

When I get home, I'm surprised to find Eldon sitting at the kitchen table with another stack of movie rentals on one side and a half-empty bottle of bourbon on the other. He lifts his glass towards me and points to *Die Hard* playing on the screen. I peruse his titles and am shocked to discover that Charles Bronson movies are still available for rent in this part of the world.

'Having a bit of a love-in?' I say.

Eldon pats the chair beside him. 'You fuck that girl again?' he asks. 'I noticed her shoes. Any good?'

'Megumi's shoes are fine.'

'In the sack, wise apple. I'm tired of you and the big guy always making jokes behind my back. Is she a good *lay*?'

'Geezus, Eldon, don't beat around the bush.'

The way his eyes are flitting, I'd say he's at that stage of drunkenness when he's both here and not at the same time. I'm talking to bourbon through the voice of Eldon. He must own a dozen sleeveless white undershirts, because they're all he ever wears around the house.

'She do anything weird to you?' he says. 'You think she'd dress up like a schoolgirl if you asked her?'

'I'm sure she's been asked before. Are you alright, Eldon?'

He sits up and beams, pouring himself another drink. 'I'm great.' He realises his poor hospitality and stumbles off his chair to the kitchen to find another glass and the bottle of cola. I sit down at the end of the table and he shifts in his rigid chair to face me, but his body is not quite aligned, so he's on an uncomfortable-looking angle.

'I was on the train today,' he tells me, 'and there was this business guy reading this comic book about girls being mutilated. This one girl had her eye where her nipple should have been.'

'That's disgusting.'

'It was sick as anything. But this guy was just sitting there, not embarrassed or anything. That doesn't show much respect. In the South we treat ladies the right way.'

He tells me about his wife – how they met, what he calls their 'courtship', their wedding, and early days of marriage. By the time he starts into their descent, I'm staring at the TV remote control, attempting to telepathically activate the play button. I recognise this zone we've entered: confessional regret. I know he needs this moment, but I don't want to have this conversation. We haven't reached the point of interpersonal intimacy where I can bear his greatest sorrows and accept his point of view. But I can't get up and leave with a polite excuse, because his edginess is making me nervous.

'At some point you stop having sex every day, which is

fine,' Eldon says. 'You think, this is not how most people live their lives, and besides, you can get really sore. Don't get me wrong, I can deal with the relationship shifting into a less physical sort, because I wanted to see my friends a couple of nights a week. Our problems started when she didn't want sex for *months*, for no reason. I'd beg and sometimes she'd give in, but I just gotta tell you, I didn't feel good. When you know you're not revving her engine anymore, you start getting bitter and wonder what she's doing when you're not around. When the sex goes, the rest follows. Even the church understands. They say the purpose of marriage is procreation – well, that's sex now, isn't it?'

He gets off his chair. I have no idea how we got from action movies and bourbon to church doctrine on Eldon's forced celibacy. I should have walked in, nodded and headed straight for the futon. Eldon goes to the bathroom and takes far too long to come back. I knock on the toilet door to make sure he hasn't fallen asleep and he tells me he's fine.

I can hear him sobbing.

18

When I emerge the next morning, Marcus is waving the school rankings.

'Well, good morning, Jamie. Looks like you had a bit too

much headache juice last night. And it looks like your school isn't keeping its end up. Where's your BIGSUN corporate spirit?'

'I can honestly say my school, Shin-Yokohama, is not a socialist outfit. We spell "team": T-I-I-I-M.'

Sunlight is streaming through our kitchen window, the solid beam acting like a barrier of pain between my coffee and me. I fumble a cigarette out of my pack and light it on the gas ring of the stove, risking singed eyebrows. Marcus is about to protest, but I crack open the sliding vent and blow a lung-full of toxins to the outside world.

'Climbing Mount Fuji was on my to-do list coming here,' he says, 'so I'm happy to have the company do the organising. You fancy training together?'

'I'm not joining any all-Japanese martial arts club, if that's what you're thinking.'

I notice a note taped to the refrigerator.

Guys, rinse out all recyclables and take your garbage to the bin area outside every night. The flies are bad and the smell keeps me up at night.
Eldon

'Have you seen this?' I ask.

Marcus looks at the paper and lets out a slow sigh. 'Yeah, mate. I'm doing my best to ignore him. He did get the little room, so maybe it's resentment.'

Eldon must have a hypersensitive nasal passage if he can ply himself with liquor and still smell a minuscule amount of trash. As for flies, I've seen a couple of gnats around the cola bottles, but no infestation.

'We'll go running,' Marcus says, returning to the subject of fitness training. 'That will be the best way to train for a hike up the proverbial mountain. The hills around here are excellent for cross-country conditioning, and I can take a wander around today and draw up a good course.'

I imagine my body as a Greek nude, chiselled and solid as marble. I used to run in high school and university, and could probably stem any pending age-based physical decline with some old-fashioned training. The first few treks might be tough, but I'm sure I'll get back into it quickly. If Shin-Yokohama is going to win the Summer Challenge, we're going to need as much help as I can muster.

The next morning, at eight, we're on the balcony. Marcus is holding on to the railing and doing a series of stretches. He rotates one foot, then the other, and then presses his palms against the wall to stretch out his back and hamstrings. I touch my toes a few times and rotate my shoulders.

'Is that all you're doing?' he says.

'I'm naturally limber.'

'You'll be naturally in traction if you're not careful.'

'Don't worry. I come from a family of adventurers. You have to be able to get up a hill quickly in winter in Canada because of the polar bear attacks.'

He's doing some odd twisty thing with his spine, bending like a yogi. I miss the days when jumping jacks were the sign of a serious fitness warm-up. I touch my toes a few more times, then trail off into a coughing fit.

'Jamie, if you want to be a successful runner, the first thing you have to do is give up the fags.'

'I only smoke when I drink.'

'That's complete bollocks. But even if it were true, I've seen how often you drink. I'm not sure which I'd be more worried about, your lungs or your liver.'

'Lungs, definitely. I've got a happy liver, industrious, a valued member of the team. You won't hear my liver wheezing going uphill. See, I've got this theory that the key to healthy drinking is attitude. I drink in a spirit of celebration, thus relieving stress and rejuvenating my body. On the other hand, a person like Eldon, who has issues and obviously bottles up all his negative emotion, is slowly killing himself.'

'And you honestly think a liver can differentiate between the two?'

'Yes, it does. The most dangerous human state is unhappiness. Drinking makes me happy, which releases endorphins, which makes me a more productive person with many positive side effects.'

'Drunken shags, you mean.'

'There's nothing wrong with that.'

He purses his lips in thought. 'Yeah, good point. How's that Japanese girl of yours?'

'In what way?'

'I don't know . . . *holistically*. Give me an overall feeling for the bird.'

'She's fine,' I say.

I don't tell him that our never over-stimulating conversations are really getting to me. There's only so much a person can stand of pointing to common household objects and saying their name in English and Japanese. My vocabulary is improving, but this is no fair substitute for meaningful communication. I like Megumi, she's a sweet girl, but I wish we weren't moving so quickly into a relationship. Besides, part of me thinks I'm new in this city and there are girls with wild, feral hair to get to know. I've caught glimpses of Cassandra coming and going at the school, but she's always preoccupied with the staff or an evaluation.

'I've been thinking I should take advantage of my western exoticism,' Marcus says. 'But I'm a shy guy. I like my mates, football, and reading the paper on a Sunday afternoon – that sort of thing.'

'Yes, how *is* your retirement going?'

He does another series of stretches I've never contemplated before. Surely he's not going to use all these muscles on a short jaunt up the hill and around the neighbourhood. I do some windmills to kill time.

'How do you approach these girls?' Marcus asks.

'Are you serious?'

'I am. I've thought about asking before, seeing as you've had a fair amount of success, but blokes aren't supposed to bring up these questions. Then I figured you're a North

American and you're all a bit soft, so I don't expect to get the piss taken out of me.'

'You want to know how to approach women?' I say.

'Tell me everything.'

'Well, to start, I sneak up from behind with a rag doused in chloroform.'

'Eldon always said you were a cunt.'

'But if you don't want to take the sociopath approach, I'd say a positive outlook is the key, just like with your liver. People like positive energy. Be yourself and start with light small talk, a few jokes, and the odd compliment. And by odd, I don't mean "I like your left eyebrow."'

'You're a very aggravating man, lad. What if the woman doesn't speak a lick of English?'

'Then move on and talk to someone else. Remember, you're trying to make a connection with another human being. Think of dating in terms of baseball. If you're hitting .300, you're doing well.'

'I have no idea what you're on about.'

'If you get a hit in thirty per cent of your at-bats you're considered a great player. Leave it to a Brit to miss a perfect analogy.'

Marcus stops his manic stretching. 'You mean, I can fail seventy per cent of the time in baseball and still be doing well? That's pathetic. That's not a serious sport.'

'Careful, you're treading on sacred ground. My point is you have to be persistent and optimistic, and expect a disturbingly high rate of rejection. Don't let the constant and occasionally overwhelming dissing get you down.

Females can smell confidence. My advice is look in the mirror every morning, tell yourself you're beautiful, no matter what they say, and vow to flirt with at least two females before lunch.'

'Did you get this from a self-help book? You're beginning to sound like the love child of Timothy Leary and Hugh Hefner.'

'Timothy Leary? Please, I can't abide psychedelics. What's fun about waking up and seeing a florescent monkey eating cornflakes at the end of your bed?'

We trot down the winding back stairs. All's well so far – there's spring in my step and a surge of adrenaline. Marcus nods his head and we turn left up a back alley that winds slowly up the hill.

'Shouldn't we start slow, on a flat surface?' I say.

'Running on level concrete won't get you in shape very quick and it's hell on your legs. Shin splints and all that.'

He pounds ahead and I can't help but be impressed by his leg muscles. His calves bulge, like they've been filled with Styrofoam and zipped up. Obviously he's been running for years, because that sort of density doesn't come from a few casual jogs or six months of turning a new leaf. I think of lifestyle choices and how at some point I fell in love with drinks and late nights and conversation. I wonder if our leisure paths are a result of nature or nurture, whether some of us are built with an instinctive need to remain physically strong despite a world of convenience and comfort.

We hit the first hard slope and my muscles are already annoyed. They want to slow down. They like walking and seem well aware that if we don't reduce this pace, glucose is going to start to burn. I'm shocked that my body and I have become such strangers. In my mind, I was sure that when I said jump, I'd still be able to dig deep and keep up with Marcus, who is loose, happy and isn't even breathing heavily. We turn onto a stretch of road that ascends on a forty-five-degree angle, and I stop.

'There's no way I can do that,' I say. 'My spleen will burst. My hamstrings will snap like piano wire and my lungs will end up shimmying up my oesophagus. I'm all for a nice run, but –'

'Don't worry, we're not going straight up.'

Marcus disappears down a dirt path that arches at maybe a thirty-degree angle, which is clearly better, but still a major drag. His circuit moves around the hill, winding through cherry tree orchards that drop into houses with small enclosed gardens – million-dollar shoeboxes that most people can only dream of affording. The air is filled with the smells of fish and miso soup.

By the time we reach the summit, Marcus is running on the spot, waiting and eyeing me cautiously as I stumble towards him. I push hard to force each foot in front of the other until I reach the first flat stretch of the circuit. I feel like I've eaten a roll of copper wire.

'That wasn't so bad now, was it?' Marcus says. 'Might be time to pick up the pace. You warmed up?'

I'd answer, but the imminent collapse of my lungs prevents even a heartfelt plea of mercy. I weave off the road and collapse in the weeds next to a chain-link fence.

'I can't,' I wheeze.

'What happened to all your positive energy?'

We've been running for exactly eight minutes. Factoring for incline (and the oxygen-starved air at this altitude), this has to be the equivalent of fifteen or sixteen minutes on a straight stretch. Small children are watching us as nicotine and ash rise up from the back of my throat. My calves are filled with burning pain and my shoes feel tight, like my feet might be rubbed raw or simply as swollen as water balloons from impact. My chest is on the verge of implosion and crying is not out of the question. I spit several times, then simply let the acid saliva drain from my mouth like a spigot. After a few minutes, the sensation that someone has lit barbecue coals in my chest begins to subside and I can speak. Marcus is still jogging on the spot.

'I thought you played sports,' he says.

'In Toronto I golfed every Friday night, though usually with a margarita in my hand. And it was in my backyard. I *used to* play sports.'

'The kind in which a seventy-per-cent failure rate was acceptable?'

'I did lots of things. You know how most countries have a mandatory two-year service requirement for the army? In Canada, we've waived the draft, but every kid is still required to play hockey.'

'Ice hockey?'

'Is there any other kind?'

'Field hockey.'

'Sacrilege . . .'

Marcus stands over me, blocking the sun. He makes a move to grab my arm and help me up, but I scuttle away like a crab, my back pinned against the giving chain link.

'Come on, you big girl's blouse,' he says. 'The rest of the route is downhill.'

I point towards the road. 'That looks flat to me.'

'Complete decline. Like what your body is in at the moment.'

He lingers, but gradually gets the picture that day one of my training regimen is over. I promise to walk my already stiff muscles double-time back to the apartment and he disappears.

When I get home, I look in the mirror, checking for grey hairs and crowfeet. There's no way I can tolerate Marcus's looks of disappointment, so I decide that in a month I'll run his circuit and do it in less time than him. This is an enormous and some might say arrogant vow, but no one has ever excelled while aiming for mediocrity. And besides, there's no reason why I can't beat him. I used to be in great shape. I used to play five sets of tennis in mid-afternoon summer heat and go to the gym. I used to buy hydration sports drinks because I really did need to top up my electrolytes.

When you stop paddling, you sink. I don't want to accept time and change while there's still a spark of youth in my gut. If Japan is affording me the opportunity to reinvent myself, I might as well do it right, full on with no excuses.

I go through my cupboards and throw out everything that contains processed white flour or excessive sugar, or is deep-fried. I drink a litre of water and fill up the deep Japanese-style bathtub, hoping that I'll have enough physical strength left in my muscles to pull myself out if I slip under the water's surface.

The heat of the water shocks me, the sensation of pain and pleasure so convoluted that I almost want to cry. I fish my cigarettes from my jeans with one wet hand, light up and take a long drag, watching the ember at the tip burn like incense; then I put the cigarette and the entire pack under water, the ash screaming a hiss of demise. I throw the soggy mess into the corner and close my eyes.

I wake up to find Eldon in the corner using a chopstick to push my saturated cigarette pack into a plastic bag. He grunts loudly, looks at me, but doesn't say anything. I should probably apologise, but I would have cleaned up the mess.

Instead I watch silently, like the doorframe is a television screen and he's a program on animal behaviour: *When Ferrets Clean*. He disappears with the bag, comes back with a spray cleanser and a large sponge, and gets down on his knees and scrubs.

I pull my heavy body from the now-cool water and drain the tub, slipping by him in my towel.

'Missed a spot,' I say.

19

My first morning class next day is with Hiroki, a twenty-nine-year-old guy with a deep infectious laugh, and Yoko, one of the three women from my macabre observation lesson with Cassandra. Turns out she's mostly harmless on her own, a sixty-year-old tennis fanatic and ardent student. She and Hiroki both teach 'cram school', the vernacular for after-hours preparatory classes for high school students studying for university admissions exams. Japanese elementary school is lax, high school is like the army, and university is somewhere in between – there's work, but students are expected to have some fun before they graduate and dedicate their lives to a company.

'I have present for you,' Yoko says. 'I bring you giant grape.'

I imagine a genetically modified fruit the size of my head, but instead she produces a large bunch of grapes. I've never had a job where anyone has brought me a present. Hiroki, meanwhile, has brought in several DVDs.

'I want to learn slang for watching films,' he says. 'If you do not teach me, I will pop cap in your ass.'

'What does this mean?' Yoko asks.

'I will shoot him,' Hiroki says proudly.

'I'm not sure Yoko wants to learn movie slang,' I say.

'It is okay,' she says, sitting up enthusiastically.

'Come on,' Hiroki continues. 'Be a bad motherfucker.'

Before I arrived, I had a mental image of Japan as a country of propriety, rice fields, Samurai codes and cheap electronics. The fact that *Pulp Fiction* and hillbillies are creeping into my lessons – and are more relevant than the textbook – is bizarre, depressing and fantastic all at once.

The three of us go to a language lab and watch various scenes from *Deliverance*. Hiroki understands the part about the pig and finds it quite amusing, and asks several very probing questions about the slang.

'It is different to *Pulp Fiction*,' he says.

'Very astute observation.'

'Is this like America?' he asks.

'God, I don't know. I've never been to the Deep South. My room-mate is from Kentucky and, as weird as he is, he's never brought farm animals into the apartment.'

'Well,' Hiroki says, looking at his notes, 'I be damned.'

I decide our teaching point will be persuasion, as in 'Please don't abuse me, mister.' We do a few tame scenarios: someone is in your seat at the theatre and you have to *persuade* them they're in the wrong spot; you want to get on the next space shuttle and have to *convince* NASA you're worthy. I figure BIGSUN can't fire me if I apply the linguistic dynamics of redneck rape to real life situations.

'Get out of my seat, poor white trash,' Hiroki says.

'That might be construed as undiplomatic,' I say.

He looks at my blankly.

'You have to be nice,' I say.

'*Please* get out of my seat, poor white trash.'

I shake my head, no.

'When do we say "poor white trash"?' he asks.

'Very rarely. It's an insult.'

'Ah,' Yoko says. 'Maybe this is like our saying for old men who retire. We call them *sode gome*, which means "dead leaves to be thrown away", because they are useless to the world.'

'That's a bit harsh.'

'I do not believe this, but many of people do. Japan is very concerned with work.'

'I hate this,' Hiroki says. 'Because I am lazy and only want to go to the new countries and drink beer.'

'You have the right priorities to become a BIGSUN teacher,' I say. 'I thought your society respected old people.'

He looks at his notes. 'Maybe this is *complete shit*.'

'Or Chinese,' Yoko says.

Hiroki tells us about his trips to Morocco, Egypt and the notorious heroin-trafficking Golden Triangle of Thailand. He's been offered drugs and women, been taken to floating markets and been robbed twice. He isn't interested in the typical Japanese package tours and wants to learn English primarily so that he can escape his current life. I feel like I've found a soul mate, though one clearly more adventurous.

'I maybe go to Russia next time,' he says.

'Shouldn't you be studying Russian?'

'English is best language. Everyone know a little English.'

I decide we should get back to the classroom before one of the staff gets frantic about my video-playing breach of teaching etiquette. We've got fifteen minutes left, so I set up a role-play.

'Okay,' I say. 'Let's pretend that Yoko's a visitor from outer space and you're a hillbilly, Hiroki. She shows up at your log cabin in the hills of West Virginia late one night.'

Yoko knocks on the table.

'Go away!' Hiroki bellows. 'I am busy drinking the moonshine and having sex with my sister!'

'Maybe a little more quietly . . .' I suggest.

'I hear you are bad mofo,' Yoko says. 'I am police from outer space to arrest you for the jail.'

'Take a hike, pig,' Hiroki says. 'You do not have anything in me.'

'*On* me,' I correct.

'I am innocent man. Why don't you eat a doughnut?'

'That is it,' Yoko says. 'I am taking you to the downtown to be book.'

At this point Yoko gets out of her chair and pulls out her pretend handcuffs. Somehow, I don't see Quentin Tarantino or Guy Ritchie lining up to buy this improvised script. I notice Cora and Cassandra wandering along the hall, looking in on lessons. Cassandra is looking better than ever, namely because she's wearing a shapely black dress.

'Let's do a new role-play,' I say.

'No way!' Hiroki says, getting out of his chair and grabbing me by the collar. '*Squeal*. I'm going to ride you!'

He makes a cocking sound and points his pretend shotgun my way. Cora and Cassandra are directly outside the door, watching with great interest. Hiroki is happy to have an audience and kicks his performance up to Oscar intensity. He boots over the chair next to me and makes to push me to the ground.

'Time for a kicking,' he says.

Cassandra opens the door and sticks her head in. 'How's it going in here?'

Hiroki smiles. 'Everything is groovy, man. I teach hillbilly a lesson he not ever forget.'

At lunch, Cassandra is sitting in the teachers' room going through a textbook. She flips pages jerkily. I sit down across the table with a mystery bun procured from the local bakery. It could be filled with tuna, chicken, or fish eggs — no one ever knows.

'What's up?' I say.

'I've got an evaluation next class, hillbilly.'

'Who are you evaluating?'

She clenches her small teeth together. 'I'm the one getting watched today. Cora is doing an evaluation for my next contract. BIGSUN believes that everyone in the company should keep up his or her teaching skills, because this helps us all *understand and nourish each other* . . . or some bullshit like that. According to my contract, I'm required to teach eight hours a month and get two yearly evaluations, just like you plebs.'

She fidgets through the book, trying to find a lesson her students haven't done. She finds one, looks at it and grunts. It's the 'Map of the World' lesson. I'm sure she's done going-through-customs and getting-on-the-plane exercises far too many times.

'Do you want the chicken or the fish?' I say.

'I used to do a great adaptation of this lesson. I gave all the students food poisoning on the flight. Explaining medical symptoms is far more important than stressing that you want a window seat.'

She takes a deep breath and scribbles down a series of drills. I thought I'd cop shit for Hiroki's performance, but Cora didn't even say a word. The longer I work here the more I understand that BIGSUN really is about entertainment, not achievement – which is great, because it means I can have a laugh with half my students and grind through text exercises with the more mundane ones. Cassandra scratches out the paragraph she's just written and flips to a new page. Her cheeks are flushed and rosy, and I imagine her skin at this moment is icy cold.

'Are you nervous?' I say. 'You've been doing this for years.'

'Nobody likes evaluations. They're never normal classes. They're always glucky.'

'Glucky?'

'Yeah, you know: unfun.'

'That's not a word. My god, you're supposed to be a language instructor.'

'Sue me.'

Her thin eyebrows arch faintly upwards, the blue in her eyes mottled with flecks of grey and black. I like the way she holds her pen, left-handed at a crooked angle, and sits with her tangled hair falling forward over her eyes.

'Are you coming to my farewell tonight?' she asks.

'I didn't know you were going anywhere.'

'BIGSUN has moved me into another district. They've started so many new schools around Yokohama that the regions have had to be split. I'm having a party at the Murusaki Izakaya at nine.'

'I'm off at five-thirty.'

'So go home, get changed and come back. If you don't make it, you might never see me again.'

She winks. I'm not sure if she's being persistent or casually polite.

'I might,' I say.

'No one ever died wishing they'd slept more.'

'Except maybe Japanese people who work eighty-hour weeks.'

We say it at the exact same time: 'My hobby is sleeping!'

I go home that evening and run, this time alone, so that I don't have to use up my desperately needed oxygen on anything as mundane as talk. I pace myself, going ultra slow along the winding path. When I get to the top, I rest for a few minutes, resisting the urge to fall once more into a heap by the chain-link fence, and then push along the straight. I run by the baseball field through a residential neighbourhood and along a schoolyard. The road goes into steep decline and I'm surprised at the amount of energy I use bracing against the slope.

After a shower, I collapse on my futon, my body as useful as a wet sandbag. My limbs want to nap and rebuild, conserve precious energy for the next time we have to run for no apparent reason, but my mind is firmly fixed on Cassandra.

An hour later I'm standing outside Shin-Yokohama station moving anxiously from one foot to the other, doing what I hate most in life: killing time by myself. The kiosk has sold out of English-language newspapers and I'm not in the mood to people-watch. Being foreign can be such an effort sometimes, the ability to communicate a constant struggle. I pretend I'm not in Japan. I'm nowhere. Finally, familiar faces come through the doors, including Eugene lighting up a cigarette.

'Wow,' he says, appraising me. 'If you weren't the only white guy out here, I wouldn't have recognised you. Clothes really do make the man.'

I look down at my jeans and T-shirt and realise that Eugene has never seen me without a tie and dress pants. It does feel strange lingering outside the BIGSUN building like a civilian, especially when the students notice me. They poke each other, point and giggle as they wave, my authority and status dented by denim and short sleeves.

Cassandra must be excessively popular, because our long wooden table at the *izakaya* is jammed with bodies. She's the centre of attention, hovering above the crowd, holding court, laughing and sucking back drinks like a ficus taking in water. Her voice has risen several decibels above her restrained, professional BIGSUN tone.

'Did you bring a gift?' she asks.

'Just my company,' I say.

'Bloody cheapskate.'

'You didn't give me much notice.'

'I posted a sign last week on the teachers' wall, next to Cora's list of ten awesome warm-up games for housewives . . . Which explains why no one saw it. Glad you're here, anyway. We'll talk.'

She says this last bit as a tall guy with blond hair and long, reddish sideburns pulls at her sleeve. He's holding up a banana on a skewer. Small heaters and bowls are being placed on the table by hurried staff.

'Chocolate fondue, Tokyo-style,' Paul says. 'Have you heard the term "Japanisation"? It's the belief that Japan takes the best of the world and *allegedly* makes it better. You know, VCRs, automobiles and genetically modified square watermelons.'

Plates of food appear non-stop – skewers of chicken, small pizzas, sushi, noodles and rice. We're each given a hot white towel sheathed in plastic. Paul takes off his glasses, pulls out the towel and places it against his face.

'You can wipe your hands, face and the front of your neck,' he tells me. 'But if you wipe any other part of your body, especially the back of your neck, you're considered an animal. As foreigners, we've got to be conscious of etiquette.'

When he's finished, he throws the towel at Sally across the table. This sets off a chain-reaction fight that I'm sure the locals find sensitive. Eugene, the elder statesman, breaks up the game.

'I'm all for fun, people, but some of us have to live here for the rest of our natural lives. Let's not piss off the locals too badly. Besides, I'm trying to eat and don't want Paul's sweaty towel on my *takoyaki*.'

'Spare us your sexual euphemisms,' Paul says. 'They're embarrassing, you thinking about my sweaty love towel.'

'I want to be culturally *in*sensitive for a change,' Sally says. 'This country is killing me. I was eating a sandwich on my way to work today and this old, hunched woman grabbed my arm and told me not to eat on the street. She said, "No do in Japan!"'

'Yeah, that's considered impolite,' Eugene says.

'Fine,' Sally continues. 'Eating on the street is bad, but a salaryman pissing against the subway station wall is fine. I get it. That makes sense. Wearing shoes inside a house is heinous, but spitting wads of phlegm on the sidewalk is acceptable.'

Eugene cuts a piece of potato croquet with a deft jab of his chopstick. 'Hey, I didn't say it was right or wrong, but it's not our country. One of the things that makes Japan so fascinating is its ability to tolerate inherent contradictions; it's all part of maintaining societal harmony. Take for instance a serious salaryman who tells his boss he's a total asswipe. If he's drunk at the *izakaya*, nothing will be said the next day. If he's sober, he'll be asked to quit.'

'I don't understand.'

'That's because you haven't let go of your western preconceptions of normal and acceptable. You're trying to apply your idea of right and wrong to a completely different culture. My advice is enjoy but don't try to analyse the strangeness of Japan.'

'Bah,' Paul says. 'Don't listen to the professor. My advice is next time anyone goes off on you, lash out and ask if they have *Barakumin* blood in their family — that's the lowest caste of the Edo Dynasty. It's like saying your family was bred with rats or hasn't evolved beyond orangutan.'

As I listen to the mild carping, I think of *kaiten sushi*, a type of restaurant where you sit and pick plates of food off a conveyor belt that weaves its way around a circular counter. Half the time I don't know what I'm putting in my mouth. Sometimes I discover sensational new tastes, like sweet tofu or raw tuna with green onion, and other times I realise why we don't eat raw clam and sea urchin in North America. I decide that Japan itself is a *kaiten sushi* restaurant, where the good and bad experiences come in equal measure. Clearly, Sally is having a raw clam day and needs to blow off stress by complaining. But tomorrow she could very easily have a sweet tofu day and never want to leave the country. The intensity of being in a minority in such a foreign place is bewildering and invigorating at the same time.

A drinking game breaks out to my left. Jumbo bottles of beer fill small water glasses. I like the communal feel of eating at a large chaotic table, pouring drinks for one another, sharing each small portion. Eugene talks about his naval days, more specifically about getting reprimanded as an MP for arresting a colonel who was driving while drunk.

'He was clearly in the wrong,' Eugene says. 'But the military has its own rules. Looking back, I can see how fed up I was with my life.'

'Tell me about it,' Sally says.

'Someone feeling homesick?' Paul says.

'I'm fine. Most days I'm perfectly happy to be here, but sometimes I wish we had halodecks, like on *Star Trek*, so I could pretend to be back in Australia for a while.'

Paul makes a long mocking *waaah* sound and chews riotously, his shoulders hunched up in laughter. 'You are a geek! You've been doing so well hiding it all this time, but now you're broken.'

'Fuck you, Paul.'

'You should be so lucky. I once made a girl come so hard she threatened to nail me to a cross and call me the Messiah.'

'They do that when you pay them . . .'

'*Oooh*, whimsy from Sally. You definitely need a good lay, what with all that pent-up tension. Unfortunately, *gaijin* girls don't have sex in this country.'

At this moment, Cassandra leans back, stretches behind Sally and yanks Paul's hair. He yelps and rubs the side of his head, the chopsticks in his fingers coming dangerously close to taking out my eye.

'I could sue for that,' he says.

'Leave her alone,' Cassandra says.

Paul's got a point regarding the lot of a *gaijin* girl, though. Japanese men don't pursue foreign females with the same tenacity as Japanese women do foreign men. Women are expected to be rail-thin, demure and feminine – an updated version of the geisha principle – and so western females are often too big, loud and assertive to be considered attractive. The topic turns to body issues, which in Japan are tragic.

Students routinely come to school with wounds on the back of their hands from bulimic purges, and there's more . . .

'Women buy tapeworms and stick them up their asses,' Eugene informs us.

'You're joking . . .'

'Unfortunately not,' Cassandra says. 'A friend of mine called me on his mobile a couple of weeks ago, bored out of his mind in Shinjuki. He was supposed to be seeing a movie with his girlfriend, but she was locked in her bathroom. Her tapeworm had come out, so she had to reinsert it, which takes a while, because the worm has to crawl back inside.'

'Where does a person buy a tapeworm?' I ask.

'Chinatown. And they're not cheap. They cost hundreds of dollars.'

Sally props her elbows on the table. 'God, I miss Brisbane.'

I don't realise how drunk I am until I get up from the table, put on my plastic slippers and stumble towards the toilets. When we came in, everyone was given a pair of flimsy flip-flops and a key to a locker in which to store his or her shoes. I try to calculate how much I've consumed, but with people constantly topping up my glass, it's impossible to know – not that it matters. I've got no car, no responsibilities and no place to be until tomorrow afternoon.

Paul is speaking passionately when I get back to the table.

'There's no way I'm climbing a mountain. I'd rather have sex with Yori the humpback in level two.'

'You'll be there,' Eugene says.

'See, I won't. I'll get a doctor's certificate, bad case of twenty-four-hour polio. I didn't take this job to risk my life for company PR.'

'What about the school ranking?' Sally asks. 'And the bonus?'

'I hear what you're saying, but this is the thing: I don't care about the money. I don't even care about you people. I know you think I do, but really, I don't. Occasionally, I pretend to enjoy your company, but that's because I get bored on my own. I can't help it. I'm a weak, weak man. And who else am I going to hang out with, the students?'

Paul fishes around in a crumpled pack for a cigarette. I don't like Marlboros – way too strong – but just the sight of that beautiful white cylinder gives me a jolt of intense joy. My body leans forward on impulse and I stare at the pack. Paul looks down and offers me one, sliding the package across the cluttered table. He flips open his silver lighter aggressively, holds the smoke in his lungs, and blasts it towards the corner of the ceiling. Eugene pours beer into my glass.

'The race is mandatory,' Sally says. 'And I could use the money. What do you think, Eugene?'

'Well, I'd like nothing more than to take an extra month's salary from BIGSUN and then give in my notice. Besides, I was raised in the military and am not programmed to go against the team. There's some sort of microchip in my skull. All I remember is the injection in my arm and waking up on the galley floor.'

The pack is still open on the table, filters pointed my way for easy access. I drum my fingers on the bench, faintly aware that my drunken glaze of jocularity has been punctured. Sweet, nicotine-laced smoke tickles my nostrils and I take several long slow breaths, deciding that second-hand smoke doesn't count. I look at the cold skewers of chicken and potato patties on the table – everyone has had their fill. I should buy gum. I should run more. I should invest in some meditation tapes.

I should have one last cigarette.

'Jamie, how do you feel about climbing Fuji?' Sally asks.

'I'm with Eugene,' I say. 'I'm not sure why, but this feels like something I want to do. We don't have a stellar-looking team, but if we start training now –'

Paul bellows and blows smoke in my face.

20

In Japan, the bill is divided equally, no matter what time people arrived or how much booze and food they consumed. As a rule, you want to get to the *izakaya* early and stock up on cocktails. Eventually, of course, the system works out for everyone, because of the changing shifts. On an early shift you win; on a late one, you pay for your co-workers.

We all throw in our share, retrieve our shoes and head back into the neon glitz of the night. I haven't gotten up the nerve to talk to Cassandra one on one, and wonder if attempting to flirt with my boss is a good idea. A poster by the ticket machine at the station states simply: 'I believe myself!' I wonder if this is a sign, the universal exclamation mark prodding me towards action, or just another example of advertising in need of an English proofreader.

I decide I'm reading too much into this fate business, but when I get off the train at Azamino, Cassandra follows. We both appear surprised and strangely embarrassed to discover that we're neighbours. She lives a block away from my apartment, down a side street.

'No use going home early,' I say.

We go to a bar across from the station and order gin-and-tonics from a funky young cat with 'Choose Life' written across his T-shirt in florescent pink. We make small talk, like this is the first time we've ever met, which in a way it is because we're not caught in our roles of teacher and boss. She's been in Japan for a couple of years – BIGSUN promote people quickly, as the average teacher only stays seven months – and is vague about her life in Australia.

'Why did you come to Japan?' I ask.

'I don't know. There was an ad in the paper, it sounded interesting and I needed a change. How about you?'

'I had my head slammed into a cop car.'

'Excellent! I like the sound of this.'

I tell her everything – Triple C, Maggie, George Harrison, and the creeping rigidity of life. I tell her that jobs start out as a way to make some money, a bit of a laugh, but after a while you discover that's you. I had hot flashes that I'd be working the panel at a crappy radio station at midnight until death. In a couple more years I'd give in to corporate coffeehouses, start buying a fudge brownie on the way up the elevator, a muffin at break; I'd get lazy, sleep later, and wake up one day with a solid ball where my waist used to be. This version of me would read industry magazines and go to trade shows. My social circle would shrink. I'd masturbate more, go out less, and begin to desperately rely on television. And then, at a merciful point in the future, wasted on Twinkies and all-meat pizza, I'd have a heart attack, alone in my bachelor apartment while attempting to clean hardened cream soup out of my chest hairs. And no one would find me for weeks.

'You've given this some thought,' Cassandra says.

'I'm very introverted for an extrovert.'

'Well, the longer you stay and get to know the foreigners here, the more you realise that most people are running away from something. Usually it's a relationship break-up or a bad job.'

'Which one is it for you?'

The corner of her mouth curls up tentatively and she looks over my shoulder. 'Like I said, you have to stay a while before people divulge their secrets . . . So your radio job was pretty bad?'

'No. *I* was the problem. I've been thinking about my situation a lot since I've been here, and I've come to the conclusion that I see life differently from most people. It's a great big empty space that needs to be filled. I think I've always had an acute sense of life being short, but that goes back to my mom passing away when I was in university. I want to accomplish something to prove I've been here, which is why I'm thinking of taking a film course. It's modern, spiritual graffiti – like hieroglyphics or cave painting.'

She sits facing me with her chin on her hand, her eyes staying on my face, making me know I've got her full and undivided attention. There's no one else in the world but us at this moment. We're cut off from the bar, the clatter of glasses, the rev of cars, the neon, humidity, memories and needs of life.

'What kind of movies would you make?' Cassandra asks.

'One of my ideas is to make a true war picture. It would start like *Braveheart*, with a pacifist trying to stay out of a conflict growing all around him – politicians are acting ruthlessly and injustice is rife. Clearly there's a moral imperative for him to act, but he doesn't want to risk reprisals on his family. A short time later, as always happens, his wife and kids get killed by marauders, either the government forces or rebels, whatever, and so he's drawn into a cycle of vengeance.'

'And he defeats an entire army with a bag of grenades and cunning?'

'That's the traditional Hollywood plot line,' I say, 'but remember, my film will be *different*. Picture this: we're fifteen minutes into the movie, the kids are decapitated and our reluctant hero has set out with his three grenades; he finds the enemy encampment, then, just when we're set to see him spring into action and unleash martial arts skills previously unsuspected –'

'Because he's a dead-handsome pig farmer.'

'Just as he's about to attack, one of the enemy steps out of the trees and blows half his head off with an AK-47.'

'And?'

'And nothing. For the next two hours the camera doesn't move from his corpse. The enemy soldiers rifle through his pockets for money and steal his boots. He gets cold and begins to decompose.'

She's expecting more – a miracle, maybe the hero's not really dead, perhaps he's wearing a bulletproof vest, or in this case, a bulletproof skull. She motions to the bartender for two more drinks. My vision is getting blurry, but she's showing no signs of slowing down.

'And you expect people to stay and watch this movie?' she says.

'Absolutely not. To get the full effect, we'd have to lock the doors of the cinema and force the audience to stay, which is probably against a few laws and civil liberties. But I think my movie would be the most accurate depiction of war ever made: no heroics, no speeches, just a complete and utter waste of human life.'

'It's insane.'

'War or the movie?'

'Both.'

'Exactly.'

Emptiness is beginning to creep over the room, bringing us into film noir, all black, white and shades of grey. The only exceptions are her red lips, flushed cheeks, and fingernails painted like port wine. Colours are moods. I wonder what blind people associate with anger, danger and love if they can't see red and don't know that hearts and stop signs look the same when you're too far away.

'Do you like *sake*?' Cassandra asks.

'I've never tried it.'

'What's your blood type?'

'Why? Will I become so paralysed that a trip to the hospital is likely?'

'No, for *maximum contentmanship* you should order the appropriate *sake* for your body. The Japanese believe that blood type helps to determine a person's characteristics.'

She passes me the menu.

A: serious, industrious.
B: creative, ideas.
O: easygoing, relaxed.
AB: strange mix.

She orders us some AB, and it arrives in a ceramic flask with two shot-glass-sized cups. She pours for me, then vice versa, and we toast. The liquid is warm and sweet, with a pure octane kick at the end. I have to chase it down with mouthfuls of cold beer.

'My god, that's awful.'

'You get used to it,' she says.

'That's what people say about everything in this country. It should be the national motto.'

There's a buzzing sensation in my brain. Clearly the *sake* is attacking key areas of my cerebral cortex, knocking out brain cells like Muhammad Ali. After this point, everything is bent. We end up in a karaoke bar. Two guys with afros are at reception, one of whom is wearing a light blue T-shirt that has 'Girls Just Want to Have Fan' written across the front.

'*Nomi hodai?*' Cassandra asks.

This turns out to be the all-you-can-drink special. We're ushered to a booth the size of a large bathtub, inside of which is a leather sofa, coffee table and large TV screen. Cassandra flips through a book of songs, makes a couple of selections using the control pad and begins to sing A-ha's 'Take On Me', like some bad dream of the 1980s. The words flash across the screen accompanied by a video of a Japanese couple meeting at the beach.

Gin-and-tonics arrive with frightening frequency and we work our way though the English selections. Two things surprise me: how familiar Elton John songs are; and how amazingly cathartic sitting in a closet slurring lyrics loudly can be. At dawn, we stumble down the streets of Azamino arm in arm, still belting out 'Sweet Caroline'.

Cassandra stops.

'Isn't this your apartment?' she says.

'I'll walk you home.'

'It's not far. I'll make it.'

'But what kind of gentleman would I be? I want to make sure you get home alright.'

'This is a *safety* country. It's only one block away.'

'But I need to know where you live, for the next time I

have an urge to sing "Piano Man". We don't work together anymore, so I might never be able to find you if I don't go now.'

'I'll be in touch.'

She's trying to unglue my arm from hers, but I don't want to let go. We've got a night's worth of momentum happening and there's no rational reason to stop here on the cold street, not when there's a perfectly good futon to be messed up. If my skull wasn't so numb, I'd explain this to her. Instead, I kiss her, and she lets me, but only for a brief few seconds.

'I had a nice night, Jamie.'

I can't do a thing as she waves and turns away. I watch her go, not moving until she disappears around the corner. I try very hard to navigate the stairs. They seem to move as I lift my feet, sliding away like slippery eels. My key doesn't fit into the lock very well, but eventually the barrier gives and I stumble into an apartment thick with *tatami*, old ozone and stale air.

21

There's no law that says two people should fall into bed after a spectacular night, but certainly there should be. This is what I'm thinking the next morning as I soak under a hot shower, denying that a *sake*-fuelled hangover is crushing my skull.

I run.

I begin to run every day. I stop calling Megumi and refuse to answer her messages. I might be a shit, but I can't bring myself to explain in pidgin English that things just don't *feel* right between us. She must understand that this relationship can't go anywhere. And besides, I'm pretty sure she has other *gaijin* boys on the side, having seen the messages on her phone.

I don't care. I've never cared. And that's the problem.

I throw myself into self-improvement and try not to think about women until I get clear in my mind exactly what I want. I run for myself, wondering about movies, desire and my ultimate purpose on the planet. My very existence – sleeping, teaching, eating and running – becomes meditative. When I'm following my ever-expanding circuit up the hills and along the cherry orchards, my mind falls into sync with the pace of my feet and I'm able to find momentary peace.

My lungs fill.

I get stronger.

The very idea of a cigarette becomes repulsive.

(Most of the time.)

The days slip past like a deck of cards being shuffled into one another and I become very accustomed to my new job, and these co-workers who comprise my social circle. Today, Paul is chewing his pen and lingering thoughtfully over a file. This indicates that the student is young, flirtatious and open to the power of suggestion. He'll write something cute and manipulative for the lesson and capitalise the next time she requests a look at her file.

'I've come to a conclusion,' Eugene says. 'The effectiveness of my day is directly related to the comfort of my underwear. I accidentally bought extra large, which you'd think would be great legroom-wise, but they keep wedging in the back. Whenever I wear the damn things, I have terrible classes.'

'Mate, you're a man in desperate need of a hobby,' Paul says.

'Mock if you will. My advice is to make a friend of your underwear. I don't want to see you kids make the same mistakes as me.'

'You've been a great help,' I tell him.

'Hey, that's why I'm here. Of course, soon I'll be here a whole lot less. If you notice the schedule, I've cut my hours back. I'm doing two and a half days a week, and I'm going to quit at New Year or as soon as we win the Summer Challenge. I need to make enough cash for the kids' Christmas then it's *hasta la vista*.'

'Isn't that Spanish for "Which way to the brothel?"' Paul says.

Eugene has been secretly running his own small school forty minutes down the train line for the past year, doing night lessons to help supplement the family income. Obviously, business is picking up, as his attempts to poach students have become more visible and he's been handing out business cards in the lobby during smoke breaks.

I can't decide what to write in my last student's file.

'Do you guys have any suggestions for Yuka?' I say. 'She's been coming to BIGSUN for five years and can't seem to get past level six.'

'Don't stress out about her,' Eugene says. 'She's completely hopeless.'

'There must be *something* I can do to help.'

'Nope, her brain's full. I've been working with her for a solid year, but she doesn't have the ability. Don't worry about the book. Kill the lesson with small talk.'

'Seems like a waste,' I say.

'Ah, new teachers . . . I know she's frustrated, but she doesn't listen well and obviously never studies at home. I've got more motivated students to concentrate on. In time, you'll learn to use the armed forces method of teaching: *save who you can.*'

'He's right, mate,' Paul says. 'Don't try so hard. In time you'll develop a healthy loathing for a large number of students, namely the ones who are insane, boring or don't put in any effort. In my opinion, students who can't get to the next level in a year should be encouraged to stop learning English immediately. We should let them cash in their lesson tickets for merchandise – cigarettes, chocolate bars, *Hello Kitty* toilet slippers – things they can really use.'

I can see his point, but the fact that Yuka even shows up tells me that she's not a total lost cause. Some people have more trouble with language then others. I'm still stuck on the weather.

The next morning, I finish my run and go inside to find Eldon in the kitchen, furiously scrubbing a mug. He's bought some steel wool and is sweating profusely despite the air conditioning.

I say hello. He looks at me and says nothing.

I go through more stretching exercises. When I started running, I could barely touch my shins, much less my toes. Now I can hold the back of my ankles with my knees straight. Marcus comes out of his room, wrung out with sleep. He stumbles to the bathroom, urinates extremely loudly with the door wide open, and then comes back into the lounge room.

'Nice work, mate,' he says. 'I'm in admiration of your spine. I haven't been able to stretch like that since I hurt my back playing football. What are you up to now?'

'Forty-five minutes.'

'Still a novice then. I can practically hear those Summer Challenge yen hitting my bank account.'

He goes towards the kitchen, but is stopped dead by Eldon's death glare. Eldon rinses out the mug and drops its still-stained remains onto the dish rack. Marcus slides by, puts on the kettle and watches, clearly fabulously amused.

'I told you to leave it, you daft little fairy,' Marcus says. 'We each got a mug, so I don't understand your problem.'

'The *apartment* got three mugs,' Eldon says. 'We share everything – it's in *the contract*. These are my mugs as much as yours.'

'Use one of the other two. You're far too stressed for your own good. And there's nothing unclean about those dishes.

The British Empire was built on tea-stained cups.'

'Uh-huh, and where is it now?'

'Across the Channel from Calais, right where it's always been.'

There must be something liberating about being absolutely huge. There's no chance that Eldon will take a swing. In fact, he'd either have to get on a chair or take a great leap on his scrawny pigeon legs to get near Marcus's chin.

With a grunt, Eldon puts down the steel wool and walks to his room, slamming the door violently behind him. Marcus sighs, takes one of the non-stained cups out of the cupboard and dangles a tea bag over the top. I stop stretching. Marcus pauses and follows my eyes to the cup and back.

'Well, I'm not going to use the one contaminated with steel wool. I'll puncture my oesophagus.'

Clearly, I'm on his side. Yesterday after Eldon made his breakfast, washed his dishes and left for work, I found two unwashed spoons in the sink and a note: 'I will not wash everyone's stuff, Eldon.'

Marcus bobs his tea bag up and down. He's very particular about his tea, insisting that the water has to be at a full boil when it touches the bag. If it has stopped rolling, he'll dump out the perfectly good drink and put the kettle on again.

He appears to be vibrating.

He yanks out the tea bag, slams down his spoon and storms toward Eldon's room.

'And stop arranging the bloody shoes in the cupboard.

I like them messed up. Also, rubbish only goes out twice a week, so I'm not trotting down to the corner every night, no matter what you think.'

I pat him on the back and decide to finish my warm-down on the terrace. I've been watching the street more than usual lately. I'd like to say that this is part of my meditative state, but perhaps it isn't.

Today I get lucky.

Cassandra emerges on the far side of my apartment building, marching towards the station. She must have come out of Lawson convenience store when I was bent over stretching my calves. I shout out her name, but she's wearing headphones, so I'm forced to take off down the circular stairs, my bare feet pounding on the steel. By the time I hit concrete, she's well down the road, but I take off at full sprint, all this training worthwhile. I'm shouting her name, feeling foolish, but the music must be cranked up high because she doesn't even flinch, at least not until I catch the strap of her bag and collide quite soundly with a telephone pole. When I look up, she's in instinctive defence mode, her legs splayed and fists up, her eyes wild.

'Sorry . . . about that,' I pant, untwisting my fingers from the bag strap. 'I've been . . . calling you, but . . .'

She pops a headphone out of her ear and shuts off the disc. There are dark circles under her eyes and her hair is pinned up haphazardly with flower pins. Obviously I've caught her at a bad moment.

'What are you listening to?' I ask.

'Suede.'

'Good CD?'

'I'm enjoying it.'

'Where are you going?'

'Gym then work. But you didn't chase me down the street to play twenty questions, did you?'

She's looking at me with a bit too much fear to make this a relaxing and casual encounter. I get up, wiping the gravel and dust off my hands.

'I don't have your phone number,' I say.

'Oh, right.'

She digs through her bag and finds a pen and paper. Without saying a word, she jots down her number and hands it to me. I look at the curves of her handwriting and think even penmanship can be cute and endearing.

'Is this your real number?' I ask. 'Or have I come off looking like a potential stalker?'

'You'll have to ring to find out.'

'I should let you go.'

'How have you been?'

'Good.'

'Classes going well?'

'Yeah, everything's great. Don't let me keep you.' I hold up the paper. 'I'll call you sometime. We'll have a drink, or thirty, while singing ABBA's "Voulez-Vous".'

She gives a slight wave, puts her earphones back on, and leaves, looking back once with a faintly amused smirk. I've never run after anyone in my life. I'm not sure whether to be proud of this or mortally embarrassed, but as she disappears it doesn't really seem to matter. I've got her number.

22

Eldon is brandishing a frying pan.

'Hey,' he says. 'Got any idea why my eggs taste like curry?'

'Indian chickens?' Marcus says.

'You've got to thoroughly wash the frypan. If you don't, bacteria's gonna build up and then we'll all have to go to one of those Japanese doctors. My students have been telling me some horror stories.'

I grab Marcus, hand him his electric hair clippers and nod towards the bathroom. I wasn't planning to do this procedure this morning, but feel the need to keep my room-mates separated. I wonder why they can't at least coexist in tense silence like a disgruntled married couple, for my sake.

'My fin is driving me crazy,' I say. 'It never stays up because the humidity completely kills my gel. I'm in no mood to pay eighty dollars for a cut, so we're going to get creative.'

I stand facing the mirror wondering how this mess can be fixed.

'Maybe you can take an inch off the top,' I suggest.

Marcus jockeys for position, his elbows up and his eyes looking for the right place to begin. The razor begins its electric hum. He takes a swath of hair between his large fingers and jabs with the clippers. They grab and pull.

'Aaargh! Gently...'

'Guess what?' he says. 'I've got a date with a girl who works in the Korean barbecue place in Tama Plaza. I've being going there to eat a couple of nights a week. She doesn't speak a lick of English, aside from the obvious "What's your name?", "Hello", "That's cute" and naming her favourite vegetables.'

'That's the basis of all inter-cultural flirtatiousness,' I say.

'She's very attractive. We're going to a movie in the next couple of weeks. At least, I think we are – the details got a bit dodgy near the end. But I should get to see what all the fuss is about.'

'They don't have movies in Britain?'

'How many inches did you want off?'

'Come on, don't lose your sense of humour. Maybe you can try to cut more smoothly. You're on a strange angle.'

He stands back and looks at his work from various perspectives. He makes a humming sound, cuts a patch from the left, then one from the right. He grimaces and looks up to see if I've caught the expression in the mirror.

'How'd you ask her?' I say.

'I said, "You like American movies?" She said yes. I said, "We go movie together maybe" with questioning intonation, and added "*desu ka*" on the end so she'd know I was asking.'

'Very skilful. BIGSUN would be proud to know you're disseminating broken English.'

'I thought so.'

The teeth dig in and grind. I wince and Marcus apologises, taking more shallow passes and working the follicles down more gradually. But it's no use. What was a lopsided fin has now become a frayed broom end. We stand silently staring at my dishevelled head.

'You know what we have to do, don't you?' Marcus says.

'Tag question,' I murmur.

'You know what we have to do, *weren't we?*'

I look at his gleaming skull.

'You'll be much cooler,' he says.

'Temperature-wise maybe.'

I nod reluctantly and he begins to hum happily, the clippers coming to life. As the blades descend to my scalp, I have the feeling this was his plan all along.

Eugene is wavering from foot to foot above me, anxiously waiting for the chimes to start. His philosophy is the sooner we get into the classroom, the sooner we'll be done and on the way home. Sally comes in for the afternoon shift with only five minutes to spare.

'What happened to your head?' she says.

'I choose not to answer.'

Unfortunately, I can't completely avoid commentary on my new look. In my classroom, Yumiko, Mrs Yamaguchi and Yoko have reunited and are laughing in amusement as I enter.

'You cut very much,' Mrs Yamaguchi says.

I mumble an affirmative and sit down. Graciously, she explains that only criminals have shaved heads in Japan. 'It is way to shame them.'

'Maybe prison is why you are a little fat,' Yumiko says. 'Too much food and no exercise.'

'Yes, you must eat very much,' Mrs Yamaguchi concurs.

'Maybe spent half salary on food,' Yoko says.

I want to point out the difference between density and fat – the North American physique versus the Japanese – but instead I retain my professional demeanour and silently imagine dropping all three of them into a hungry brood of freshwater crocodiles. I suddenly realise what Sally has been saying for so long about verbal abuse. The Japanese have a reputation for being understated, for placing great importance on etiquette and saving face, but what people don't understand is that there's a strange paradox in what someone can be blunt about and what they cannot. For instance, it's rude to directly decline an invitation, but telling a person they have horrible acne is perfectly acceptable. And students will do a lesson they've done a dozen times without complaint out of respect for the *sensei* (teacher), but have no reservations about saying a person is too fat, loud, obtuse, lazy or smells odd.

Some people take this paradigm even further. A smirking Mrs Yamaguchi tells me that most Koreans are criminals and that after the 1923 Tokyo earthquake, the last major quake in this region, the locals blamed the Korean nationals working in Japan.

'They make a big crowd,' she says jovially, 'and chase all the Koreans and kill them. These many people are afraid and are thinking Koreans are *causing* the disaster.'

'They are very silly long ago,' Yoko says.

'But I still do not like the Koreans. They are so lazy and not smart.'

'Ah so, this is true,' Yumiko agrees. She looks my way, throws up her hands and shrugs, as if to say, *What can you do, these things happen.* I sigh pointedly and open my textbook.

'But they make excellent tasty *kimchee*,' Yoko says suddenly, as if in apology. 'I am very fond. Jamie-*sensei*, can you eat *kimchee*?'

'It's pickled cabbage. Of course I can eat it.'

'But it is very spicy,' Yumiko says, startled. 'Can you eat sushi?'

All three seem overawed that my digestive tract can handle root vegetables, raw fish and a bit of rice. After twenty minutes of probing my diet and offering helpful advice on which foods are best for my colon (a much appreciated new vocabulary term), we get back to the topic of my bald skull. After much debate, Yoko decides she likes it, because I now look like Andre Agassi, her favourite tennis player.

I tell Paul about the level of anti-Korean xenophobia at lunch.

'Well, mate,' he says. 'A couple of years ago, the mayor of Tokyo came out with a statement saying that if a major earthquake occurred, police would be authorised to use force if necessary to keep the *gaijins* from revolting.'

'Yeah, yeah,' Eugene says. 'But every country has its crackpots. Remember it wasn't that long ago that we were calling the Japanese "yellow monkeys" and refusing to recognise them as real people.'

'It wasn't *two years* ago,' Paul says.

Cora has posted a map of Fuji on the wall and assigned us sections for the Summer Challenge. I'm happy to see that the relay race only encompasses the upper half of the mountain, from 'station five' onwards. Because of his constant carping, Paul has been pencilled in to take the first leg, which means he'll only have thirty minutes of climbing.

On the train home, I thumb my mobile and punch in Cassandra's number several times, hanging up before all the digits run through. I haven't been afraid to call a girl in years, not since high school, and the sensation is unsettling. Outside Lawson's I dial again and resist the impulse to cut and run.

From the tinkle of glass, I can tell she's in an *izakaya*. Cassandra sounds genuinely glad to hear from me – although that could be inebriation. I offer to meet up with her, but she's in Tokyo and isn't sure where she'll be by the time I take the forty-five-minute ride into the city. Instead she tells me to come over to her apartment tomorrow night, after work.

23

For the first time in my life, I iron a T-shirt. The fabric is warm and soft against my skin and feels great with the air conditioning cranked to high. I'm hoping Cassandra will wear lipstick red enough to look like blood in the moonlight. Marcus comes sauntering out of his room and leans against the doorframe.

'Useless household chores,' he says. 'You're either terminally bored, mental or off on a big date.'

'I'm popping around to a friend's place.'

'Female, Japanese, fond of making miso soup?'

'No, I'm going to a teacher's place for a few drinks.'

Marcus perks up. 'Oh, mind if I come? I don't have anything on tonight and am bored rotten. I've watched all of Eldon's movies and can't face the gym. I think I've pulled a hamstring. It's been tight for a couple of days now.'

He makes those sudden movements of someone organising a plan in his head, calculating how much money is in his wallet and deciding which pants to wear. I debate the best way to crush his spirits.

'I *want* it to be a date,' I say.

Marcus raises his eyebrows and stops fidgeting. 'I see. You don't want your best flatmate Marcus messing up your operation. That's your game. Ah well, I should really get to bed early tonight anyway. I'll just entertain myself by watching *The Happy Kitten Loving Jokester Hour*.'

'That's a great plan.'

'I'm being pathetic so you'll let me come.'

'I know, but this is the girl I accidentally assaulted on the street the other day.'

'Ah . . . say no more.'

Cassandra's lips are pomegranate red. She's making sangria in a large pitcher already filled with sliced limes, lemons and oranges. Marcus might as well have come along, because Cass's room-mate Tawnie is staying in for the night, probably as a buffer. When I arrive, she's on the balcony beating the crap out of her futon with a long wooden mallet, not as a show of force, but because bedding has to be hung in the sun and beaten every week to kill small red mites. I watch, sprawled on a *gomi* leather recliner retrieved from the street.

Gomi is Japanese garbage, which often includes perfectly good stereos, TVs and furniture. There are no used-goods shops in this country – it's bad form. There are also very few garages or extra rooms for storage, so when the latest technology or fad appears, old but functional goods get taken to the curb to be scrounged over by *gaijin*. Unlike my monastic hovel, Cassandra's apartment is full of consumer items and character. There are pictures on the wall, including a blown-up aerial shot of the crowd at last year's Fuji Rock Festival, an outdoor event à la Glastonbury or Woodstock.

Cassandra hands me an ancient phrasebook entitled *Practical Japanese*, given to her by a student.

Mado kara mitara yuka no ue ni sitai ga arimashita.
(When I looked in through the window, there was a corpse lying on the floor.)

Haka o makura ni tsukaimashita.
(He used the box for a pillow.)

'Isn't that the greatest thing in the world?' she says. 'It reads like something written by a deranged sadomasochist. It was published in 1954, so all I can figure is that Japan was still traumatised by the war.'

'What does that have to do with using a box for a pillow?'

'Hardship, Jamie. Their manufacturing industry was so badly damaged that feathers were a luxury . . . What have you been up to?'

I tell her about running, life at Shin-Yokohama and Sally's continued homesickness. We talk about how nostalgia for home can slowly ruin the good elements of life in Japan. Tawnie joins us and we begin a slow journey towards losing all feeling in our extremities. I hold up my glass.

'What did you do to this sangria?'

'I added tequila,' Cassandra says. 'Is that wrong?'

'It's a-typical and bordering on lethal.'

'We can't rightly call this "sangria",' Tawnie says.

'Well, we'll name it after me, a Cassandra.'

'I know your name,' I say. 'You're my boss. We were introduced.'

She kicks me with her bare foot, and then rests it next to

my leg on my chair. Her toenails are bright red, too, the colour of sex, danger, and moist strawberries on naked ice cream. She catches me.

'Don't look at my feet,' she says. 'They're ugly.'

'Everyone thinks his or her feet are ugly. They're the feature that most reminds us that we're descended from chimpanzees.'

'What are you saying?'

'I have no idea. The Cassandra is making me light-headed.'

And that is the truth. Her feet are beautiful, not in any specific sense, except that they are attached to the rest of her body and there's no need to break up the package. Even as I'm watching her speak I'm thinking of carrying her to the bedroom only a few feet away. I'm thinking about kissing away all her lipstick and undoing the buttons on her blouse one by one, maybe even with my teeth if I can manage, all of which distracts me terribly from the conversation.

'Life is all about adapting to change,' Cassandra says. 'You can't hold onto the past. Take old friends, for instance. They're like clothes, if you don't wear them for a year, throw them away, because your style has obviously changed.'

'But styles come back,' I say.

'That's true . . . Okay, throw most of your friends away, except the ones that have a classical elegance.'

'How do you tell the difference?'

'I don't know.'

'So you're admitting your philosophy is flawed.'

'I'm not admitting anything. The Cassandra is a strong drink and produces its own logic. Quite honestly, you can do whatever the fuck you want with your wardrobe. But I propose a toast: to new friends and to the future, the only place worth going to.'

We listen to a lounge music CD imported from France that Cassandra has become obsessed with. She sings along to Donovan and dances around the apartment with her arms swaying above her head. Tawnie tells me about travelling through South-East Asia and never finding a shower. She says her hair became so matted together and congested with ticks and lice that she had to have it completely shaved off, just like mine. She tells me about bone-breaking disease in India, how she was so sick in Calcutta in a cheap hostel sleeping on a foam mattress that every time she moved, even just to roll over, or scratch her head, it felt like her bones were being shattered with a sledge-hammer.

'You should become a Contiki spokesperson,' I say.

'It was the worst pain ever. I kept hitting my head against the wall to try to knock myself out. Luckily, I was travelling with a friend who kept me hydrated and didn't let the rats near my bed.'

I wonder why we do these things, why we run away from our homes in spite of danger and disease and loneliness so intense that you become heartsick.

Tawnie runs across the street to get more wine, returning a few minutes later with two bottles. As she's yanking out the cork, her small body hunched over the bottle between her feet, Cassandra's mobile phone goes off. Cass cups her hand over the mouthpiece and goes into her room, the conversation drowned out as she passes the stereo speaker. Tawnie tips wine into my glass.

'Tetsuya,' she says.

'Isn't that a breaded pork patty?'

'You wish. He works at Super Rag, the clothing store by the station. They've been on and off for a while. He's a nice guy, but I'm not convinced he's good for her.'

Cassandra is back at the table within seconds. I shouldn't have expected anything – I'm the one who chased her down the road; I pressured her into getting together; I've been attempting to flirt outrageously while slowly going cross-eyed on a tequila-spiked Spanish specialty. The girls wander to the kitchen area and talk quietly under the guise of getting cork out of the bottle. I get up unsteadily and motion towards the door.

'I should go,' I say. 'I'm on middle shift tomorrow and need to sleep. I've had a great time.'

A funky-looking guy in a blue and red T-shirt passes me on the corner and I'm sure he's Tetsuya. He looks like Cassandra's type, with messed-up spiky hair, a perfectly trendy wardrobe, and a cool sauntering walk. He's carrying a bottle of vodka, so I'm assuming the party will continue without me.

Thankfully, the apartment is empty. I hope Marcus has gone to Tama Plaza to flirt with his waitress friend. I raid Eldon's

Maker's Mark and sit at the kitchen table switching through the channels until I get to *London Boots*.

According to an English-language newspaper, the show involves two comedians known for their 'insanely comical dyed hair' (red and blond) who tease an array of young and beautiful women. In part one of tonight's episode, they go into women's homes to read their diaries. In part two, they set up girls to see if they will cheat on their boyfriends. Most Japanese programs are reality-based – strange mutations of '70s North American variety shows that feature cruel stunts, humiliation and a lot of high-pitched squealing, mostly from the men. In fact, the Japanese invented the whole reality TV phenomenon, being the first to decide that locking a person naked in a room for an entire year surrounded by cameras was an entertaining idea. The world is *such* a better place for it. I can't understand the dialogue of *London Boots*, but the gist is clear.

The doorbell rings, rattling through the midnight air, reinforcing the apartment's emptiness. Cassandra is standing outside with her lips pursed and her cheeks flushed.

'That was rude,' she says. 'You have to come back.'

'Don't worry. I'm good.'

'I was taken by surprise. Tetsuya said he'd be over in five minutes, and I didn't know what to say. I don't know if you noticed, but I've been drinking a lot tonight and my judgment is probably a bit impaired.'

She ends this with a slur, as if to convince me. Her lipstick isn't blood red in the moonlight. In fact, most of it has come off, though through no act of mine. I decide her lips don't need ornamentation. They're thin and delicate and perfectly fine on their own.

'I'm really okay,' I say.

She shakes her head. 'No, you chased me down the street. I hadn't showered, had no make-up on, and you still called me. That shows enterprise. I like being desired.'

She stops as Eldon's door flies open. He steps into the hall in his sleeveless undershirt, a green, liquid-gel eye mask on his forehead. I can't remember if they're for reducing stress or diminishing wrinkles. He squints at us.

'Y'all mind taking the conversation somewhere else? You've got your booze volumes up. I'm not mad, but I am trying to sleep.'

Cassandra stumbles out the door and down the steps, where she commences to kill herself with uncontrollable laughter. I follow, hoping Eldon can't hear our cackles through his window.

'That's your room-mate?' she says.

'Yeah, he's one half of a double homicide waiting to happen.'

'Are you coming back?' she asks.

'I don't think so. Not tonight.'

She considers this with what I'd like to think is tragic disappointment. But I have no desire to know my enemy. I can't cope with his flashy jeans and spiky hair at this point.

'Thursday's your day off, right?' she says. 'I'd like to take you to a part of Tokyo westerners never see.'

She won't say what the significance of this mystery place

is, but tells me the experience will be fantastic. The only catch is that I have to be up and ready to go by five.

Come six-thirty Thursday morning, I'm staring into a gelatinous fish eye. We're in Tsukiji at the world's largest fish market. I hadn't been sure what to expect, but several acres of dead and dying aquatic life certainly wasn't it.

'Where's the fun in this?' I say.

'Life experiences aren't always meant to be enjoyable,' Cassandra says. 'I didn't promise fun. I said the day would be *fantastic*, and if you look that word up in the dictionary you'll find it's closer to extraordinary than joyous.'

'Your tone suggested a good time.'

'This is rewarding. You'll thank me.'

The market is huge, the size of several aircraft hangars, and smells surprisingly tolerable considering the thousands of tons of sea life contained in its halls. Apparently the place supplies pretty much every *izakaya* and sushi shop in central Japan. I've never thought hard about where my food comes from and am surprised at the scale of this operation. Food production doesn't equate easily with manufacturing, but that's precisely its nature. The tertiary product is brought here, secondary refinement takes place in a kitchen, and the waiter provides the final service. There's a sudden honk as a pug-nosed diesel cart barrels by, barely missing my elbow, leaving me wondering how my obituary might read had I stepped left at that precise moment. *Jamie Schmidt killed by a Samurai golf cart filled to the gills with polystyrene boxes.*

We meander through rows of simple stalls, composed of plain wood and unadorned with anything besides plastic sheeting. Cassandra steams in front of me, getting out of the way of a man with a bag of live eels, her blonde hair bouncing in time with her steps. There's no air movement in here, and humidity, as usual, is high. She's got a nice back, long and shapely, that clings to her T-shirt. I've never been attracted to a back before. I wonder what happened the other night at her apartment – no doubt, Tetsuya stayed and they probably had wild and creative sex in all manner of strange and exotic positions. For the most part, this strikes me as fair, because there's nothing between Cass and me; but I want the sweat on her skin to be mine, not that of some trendy salesman from Super Rag.

'Everybody seems to be in a pretty big hurry,' I say.

'And this is the slow time of the morning,' she says. 'The real bidding happens at the wholesale auction before five, which is so completely nuts that visitors aren't allowed access.'

'That's a shame. We could have gotten up at three tomorrow and trekked in. Is this what you do for fun?'

'What would you rather be doing?'

'Sleeping, like normal people. Speaking of which, how late did your get-together go the other night?'

'I'm not sure. A couple more hours. Tawnie's a character, isn't she?'

Two men in overalls and rubber boots run a six-foot-long frozen tuna through a bandsaw to our left – it looks like a perverse high school shop-class stunt – the grinding drowning out our conversation. I can think of several things I'd rather be doing, and they all involve my futon. We move past restless trays of crab, large crayfish and lobsters that crowd us on both sides. Two-inch baby crabs crawl over top of one another in a small bucket.

'Hey, cute,' I say.

Cassandra looks over my shoulder. 'Those will be battered, deep-fried, and served with mayonnaise. I'm not sure if people eat the shell, but I wouldn't be surprised. This isn't a pet store.'

I imagine keeping one of these crabs in the bathtub, making sure to top up the water with bath salts, and letting my crustacean feast on an unsuspecting Eldon's genitalia as he wanders in for his morning shower.

'I don't think I'll ever get used to seeing baby animals being eaten,' Cassandra says.

'Maybe you were a mother crab in a past life.'

'First you compare me to a chimpanzee, and now a crab.'

'Can I blame the Cassandra?'

'No, the statute of limitations on stupid drunken remarks only extends to a hangover, and even that's pushing it. Please have the courtesy to compare me to something cute.'

'Okay, you look like a kangaroo, especially around the eyes.'

She doesn't stoop to comment. We wander by crates of squid and purple octopi, sea snakes and creatures that challenge years of evolution, bizarre half-shelled mutants that look like they've stepped out of a sci-fi movie. The place is astonishing in a Discovery Channel sort of way, but disturbing for its sheer scale. Human beings consume so many living creatures. My foot slips into a pothole of slimy water in the cement and I curse loudly.

'If I'd known we were coming to a fish market, I could have worn running shoes.'

'It's just water. Buck up and be a man.'

'Like Tetsuya?'

'He sells women's jeans. I don't think that qualifies as a testosterone-fuelled occupation.'

Ignoring my cue for discussion on the topic, Cassandra walks on. Most of the people working here are men, but there are a few thick-boned, ruddy females scattered around. A group stands contemplating us, pointing and discussing our presence at length. The fish intestines splattered on their aprons only increases the allure. I smile and wave.

'How's that for a *Vogue* cover shot?' I say.

'Don't be cruel.'

'We could get photos of them in slinky, off-the-shoulder overalls and the latest rubber boots. Or we could have them naked, lined up covering their naughty bits with large shellfish. Some say the scent of tuna can be an aphrodisiac.'

'Please stop waving.'

'Why? I'm sure they don't mind the attention. They're probably excited that we're interested in their lives. People like to think that what they do is unique and special. We're validating their sense of worth and building self-esteem. And besides, they were staring at us first.'

An old man speaks to Cassandra in Japanese and lifts the

lid of a large pot. Inside is an assortment of odd shelled creatures, their beige insides bulging out like swollen bladders. The flesh looks fake, almost like plastic, and is the colour of butterscotch pudding. The man pokes the aquatic anomaly and laughs. Cassandra chuckles politely, takes my arm and leads me away.

'What were those?' I ask.

'I have no idea. He said something about sea hearts. This has been very enlightening, but I've got to get out.'

'Had enough rewarding life experience for the day?'

'You could say that.'

'Was it fantastic?'

'Most definitely.'

We emerge into the morning sun, which is blinding after the dark confines of the market. From the heat evaporating the salt water on the asphalt, I can see this is going to be a scorcher of a day. We stumble across a decrepit wooden bridge, dodging several pug carts, and take the first side street.

'The guidebook suggests we do breakfast now,' Cassandra says. 'In one of the many sushi restaurants in Tsukiji.'

'I'm more inclined to take up vegetarianism. A person can overdose on culture. But you know, I'm from North America, so by spending a day with me, you're expanding your insight into my fine continent.'

We end up in a coffee shop in Ginza, sucking on lattes, eating biscotti and being as western as we possibly can be. Despite my disdain for chain stores, today the predictable oak counter, wooden tables and art deco lamps are strangely comforting.

'I've got fish in my nostrils,' I say.

'Inhale the Guatemalan dark. Breathe deeply.'

She leafs through her pocket guidebook and comes up with several stellar options for the rest of the day, including the Tobacco and Salt Museum in Shibuya and the Kite Museum in Nihombashi. There's a Ramen Museum in Shin-Yokohama, devoted to the history of the noodle, and the Shitamachi History Museum in Ueno, which promises a re-creation of the plebeian downtown quarters of old Tokyo. That could be exciting. We could also go shopping at the Shibuya 109 department store, featuring such stores as Sheep Dip, Pep and Shy, and Chup! Instead, we decide to have another coffee.

'I'm concerned about Eldon,' I say.

'I don't know why, he looked perfectly normal to me.'

'Marcus wants to kill him – and I mean that literally. His behaviour is getting worse, more erratic. I think he needs to get out and socialise. He used to go to Shinjuku and Roppongi, but lately all he does is drink alone and watch action movies. I can't tell you the number of times I've woken up to incoming helicopters and sporadic gunfire.'

'You should suggest he rent comedies.'

'You can afford to be casual about my situation, because you've had the good luck to end up with only one roommate, who aside from a propensity towards contracting rare and truly horrific diseases, seems sane.'

'On occasion, that's debatable, but I get your point.'

'You know, when it comes to accommodation, BIGSUN needs questionnaires. If Eldon had written *I'm an anal compulsive neat freak with suspect social skills and a sleeveless white undershirt that will be worn at all times*, I'm sure we wouldn't have come up as a match.'

'Now you're just flattering yourself. But I can bring up your idea at the next regional meeting so head office can immediately veto it. As for Eldon, he's obviously lonely. That's the great and terrible thing about this country: the *gaijin* need one another to stay sane. Does he know any other teachers in the neighbourhood?'

'I don't think so. He works in Tokyo.'

'There's only about twenty teachers in Azamino. Why don't we organise a roving party, with stops at everyone's house? We'll have themes based on food or drink. One apartment can do Jamaican, with rum, reggae and Bob Marley. Another can do Hawaiian *luau* – god knows there's enough pineapple around.'

'It's the official fruit of summer.'

She's getting very excited and rummages through her bag for a notepad and pen. I like the idea, though I've seen a fair number of weird *gaijin* in the supermarket. I've made a point of trying to speak with them, but several don't want to be stopped or know me. Marcus thinks they've been in the country too long and have either gone native or are sick of putting an effort in with the revolving door of ESL teachers.

Cassandra makes a list of people she knows and their addresses. She suggests we design a flier in the afternoon to be faxed to the local school and posted at the train station. This girl is worth more than ruined sandals.

That night, I take her up my running hill. I show her a Shinto temple I found on my route. It's ancient and spooky, with rows of graves snaking along the edge of a steep cliff. When we come to the baseball field, Cassandra tries the lock on the fence door.

'What a bunch of bastards – the only decent piece of green space in the neighbourhood and they have it locked up. Are they afraid that people are going to steal the turf? These are the things that get to you after a while.'

'Have you never been up here?' I ask.

'No, why would I?'

She has a point. This is residential space with no shops or parks. I want to suggest because of the view, but the horizon stretches away from us as a grey mass of rooftops, electrical wires and railway lines.

We sit on a bench facing the forbidden field and I tell her about my family. I explain how my mother died from lifelong kidney problems stemming from a severe bout of childhood food poisoning. I tell her a bit about my dad. Admittedly, he's been on my mind lately. We email, but I haven't been able to call him, because I know he'll be maudlin and I'll end up depressed about our relationship.

'Wasn't it difficult to leave him?' she asks.

'I love the man, but I can't forfeit my life. Besides, he's got his job, golf, and dental hygienists to date. I'm not sure what the allure is, but he's just started seeing his second one this year.'

'How do you feel about that?'

'At first I was worried, because dentists have the highest

rate of suicide among professionals. When Dad dated the first hygienist, I kept asking if she looked depressed, had random crying jags, or had been talking about "the time after I'm gone". He got really annoyed.'

'Are you always this flippant when asked a serious question?'

I meet her eyes. 'Often.'

'And how does that make you feel?'

I laugh and look out over the swaying cherry trees, fully green and well pruned. Cassandra is picking at her fingernail silently. I'm attempting to let her in beyond this present life, but it is difficult. In some ways I'm more comfortable floating on top of emotion, not in the depths.

'Here's what you need to know about my father,' I say. 'My mom used to organise a barbecue for friends and family every July first, Canada Day. It was huge, and she spared no expense – fillet mignon, lamb chops, salads with those radishes cut up to look like miniature roses . . . After she died, Dad tried to keep the tradition going, but friends were always my mother's department. The first year was fine, because everyone made an effort, but from that year on, the party got smaller and smaller until this year when he bought a disposable hibachi and we roasted hotdogs on the front lawn of his condo while drinking cans of beer.'

'I don't know whether to laugh or cry.'

'Yeah, I know. My point is that we both need to move on. Our traditions have become moribund. With me gone, hopefully next Canada Day he'll make a few telephone calls and go golfing with his buddies.'

'That was a very good, non-flippant answer.'

'Thank you.'

'Being a parent is hard, though. It's a cliché, but you never realise what it's like until you have a child of your own.'

'Yeah, I know. I've heard that too.'

We watch petals vibrate in the wind. During this part of my run the ground levels off and the going gets easy. There are two months left until Fuji, at the end of the climbing season, and I feel more determined than ever.

'You're a nice guy, Jamie.'

'I don't see the point in being anything else.'

'Before I ask the next question, you've got to know that I don't let very many people get close to me. You can't expect a lot from me.'

'You need one of my kidneys, don't you?'

She laughs. 'No – at least not at the moment . . . Do you want to kiss me?'

'I've wanted to kiss you since the baby crabs.'

And we do.

24

I tell Eldon about the moving party and suggest we go with a North American theme, using our numeric advantage to force Marcus to wear a basketball shirt and say things like

'Gosh, ain't that swell' and 'Would you like another hotdog with relish?'

'No way,' Eldon says. 'I don't want people I don't know in my apartment.'

'But they're all BIGSUN teachers. Well, except for one hostess, but she's mostly harmless. She might even let you rip off her stockings at the end of the night if you play your cards right.'

Cassandra has made friends with a Brit who works in a hostess bar and makes a bit of extra money at the end of the night by letting one lucky businessman rip her stockings off. There's no sex involved, just tearing polyester and a smile.

'I don't care,' Eldon says. 'I don't know them.'

'You'll *get to know* them – that's the point. A stranger is just a friend you haven't borrowed money from yet, and it'll be one night without a commando movie, something different, social . . . If anyone tries to steal the TV, I'm sure head office will be able to track down the perpetrator.'

Eldon grunts loudly. There are only three beer cans in front of him, so he should be at a pleasantly lubricated stage. I want to say that he needs this party because human contact will make him feel better. I don't want to be his enemy. He turns to face me.

'I'm not going to be responsible for your people doing damage to this apartment. I'm sorry, that's how I feel.'

'We'll be here the whole time. And the party will keep moving, so our place will be full for an hour, tops. You can even shut the door to your room.'

'That's not the point. I'm responsible for the living room, kitchen and bathroom. I can't afford to buy a new washing machine if things go awry.'

I lose my train of thought trying to process this remark, and Eldon presses play. I've never been to a party where the heavy appliances have been damaged.

'I thought Southerners were big on hospitality,' I say.

'Don't disparage the South.'

The front door rattles, the walls shake and Marcus comes in. He slips off his shoes without noticing me standing in his direct line of vision and stops short only when he's about to run me over.

'How was the date?' I ask.

He makes a low philosophical *mmm* sound. 'It was alright. The movie was good, we smiled at each other a lot, there was a certain amount of listen-and-repeat on the way back to the subway and we didn't go for drinks. All in all, I felt like I was at work.'

'I take it you won't be seeing her again?'

'I don't think so. I have to find a new Korean barbecue restaurant, which is too bad, because their prices were very reasonable and the menu was bilingual. But there's no way I can go through that fiasco again.'

'D'yall mind?' Eldon says.

He points at the TV screen, as if he needs utter silence to listen to machine guns ripping through a jungle. Marcus scratches his hairless head impatiently.

'It was a bad experience,' he continues. 'But I should be used to those.'

Eldon grunts and pauses the movie. We all linger in silence. I nod towards the front door, but Marcus bites his large lower lip and shakes his head gently. Eldon presses play once more.

'Still miss the smokes?' Marcus says.

'Yeah. The cold sweats have stopped though.'

'That's progress.'

Eldon hits stop and throws the remote onto the tabletop, where it slides to the end and slips over to the floor. He pushes back his chair, takes his remaining full beer and looks at us in defiance.

'I think we need to have a discussion about respect.'

'Haven't you seen this movie?' Marcus says. 'I swear you watched it the other night.'

'That was part one. This is the sequel.'

'Oh right. The girl dies in the end of this one on a rubbish tip, because the bloke in the black suit is a double agent.'

Eldon's eyes narrow. 'Old Europe,' he says.

'What does that mean?'

'You heard me.'

Eldon takes a step forward and Marcus shoves him backwards against the wall, which, being made from softwood and paper, gets tattooed with a perfect skull indent. Eldon gets up and takes another run, but Marcus easily wrestles him to the ground.

'I'm not paying for that damage,' Eldon says.

'At least it wasn't the washing machine,' I say.

Marcus turns his head. 'What?'

'It's not important . . . Marcus, get off him. Eldon, watch

your movie. No one said living abroad would be easy, but for fuck's sake, let's try to keep the violence to a minimum.'

Marcus and I end up on the balcony. We lean over the railing and look at the lives going on around us: women are gathering clothes from the lines, a pizza delivery driver is tearing up the hill on his moped, and the usual assortment of teens are hanging around the convenience store. The boys appear to be having a spitting contest.

'He attacked me,' Marcus says.

'I know. Thank god you're studying aikido.'

'Does it strike you as wrong that we're both sharing a balcony while Eldon monopolises the lounge room and kitchen?'

'Yes.'

'Should we kill him?'

'Cassandra thinks he's lonely.'

'We're all lonely! But at least some of us are trying. Think of it from my perspective: I just had one of my worst nights and don't need that stress. You know, I have the feeling she went out with me out of some sense of obligation, like it would be a loss of face to decline.'

'I'm sure that's not true,' I say.

'She barely spoke.'

'She was probably just super nervous. You know how Japanese people are afraid to make mistakes.'

We stand in silence for a few seconds. The boys have ended their spitting competition and are now punching one another soundly on the arms.

'I definitely have to study Japanese,' he says.

'Make sure to learn the phrases "Are you a carpenter?" and "Can you fix a head-sized hole in my wall?"'

He bellows with laughter.

Thanks to Eldon's obstinacy, our party doesn't happen. I can't very well convince complete strangers to open their homes for bacchanalia and then explain that my house is off limits. I feel like I'm back in high school and my father has locked the liquor cabinet. But the lack of one social event pales in light of other developments. I'm proud to say that Tetsuya quickly becomes a non-factor in my life as Cassandra and I move into a routine – namely, I get out of my apartment and crash at her place every night. Inevitably one of us has an early shift in the morning, so I leave by eight, walk two minutes down the road and go through my usual shower and shave. This is the best sleepover arrangement of my life. I don't even have to buy a second toothbrush.

We share one day off a week and end up as cultural voyeurs, travelling around Tokyo and surrounding areas to explore. We go to Odiwara Castle, an authentic recreation of a Shogun palace with a nifty snack bar and gift shop on the top floor, just like in ancient times. We eat in such fine establishments as the Yakitori Club. ('Would you please let's show you our heart full services with various taste of yakitoris and beverages? You could surely enjoy the most dramatic night in "the Yokohama"!')

We shop in places like Book Off, the Fabric Shop ('The grain and fabric living pose') and Bang Bang For Clothes.

We suck on Kiss mints 'for skin freshness', before our lips meet. And our drink of choice is Key Coffee – 'The excellent taste produced by the blend technique of KEY COFFEE which has crystallised through the long experience' – procured from one of BIGSUN's thousands of vending machines.

I begin to enjoy and experience Japan in a new way. Because she's been here so long, Cassandra takes away my fear. She leads me into bars and clubs I never would have found, teaches me how to order food, and points out things of strange beauty. On our way home from the station one evening, she stops to watch a salaryman spinning his umbrella merrily above his head, a small act of individuality in a sea of conformity.

'You have to look harder in Japan,' she says. 'In other places, everyone is trying desperately to show that they're special. Here, people hide their personalities and need to be brought out.'

Today Cassandra is waiting for me beside the gates at Sakuragicho train station. She's lingering by a stand-up noodle counter, sending a text message on her mobile phone. I look around and see four other people doing the exact same thing. She's wearing a black skirt and sleeveless T-shirt with a bohemian red cloth bag hooked across her chest. I watch for several minutes, the way she purses her mouth, puts one foot in front of the other, and runs a hand through her tangled blonde hair. Finally, as if sensing, she looks up, directly at me.

'What were you doing?' she asks.

'I didn't see you.'

'I'm the only white person in the crowd. How hard am I to miss? God, I go to all the trouble of making myself look beautiful and end up a wallflower.'

We take the moving sidewalk towards the harbour, like two characters straight out of *The Jetsons*, and enter the gleaming main hall of the shopping plaza. A small man in a tuxedo plays a grand piano and sings what I vaguely recognise to be 'It Had to Be You'. We look in bag shops and bookstores and an astounding number of accessory shops. Cassandra buys a polka-dot hat, bobby pins and hair elastics with large plastic bubbles.

'Don't you already have these things?' I ask.

'Yes, but I don't have the right colours. Who knows when you'll need blue? Accessories make an outfit. A moderately good-looking person can wear a flour sack, but with the right shoes, earrings, clips and jewellery, no one will care.'

Cassandra is firmly in the now, looking around greedily at everything that spins within her orbit, talking ferociously and walking quickly. We have a bite to eat in an 'authentic' British pub, watching people eating fish and chips with chopsticks. I'm not sure that they have wedges coated with dried fish flakes in the UK, but I'll have to ask Marcus to be sure. At the table behind us, a fifty-year-old man is flirting with a girl in her late teens. It could be a date or a father–daughter day out.

'There's a hot new video game at The Deep,' I say. 'The object is to undress a schoolgirl.'

'Surprise, surprise . . . A friend of mine got off the subway last week and there was a man bent over sniffing her seat. I'm not expecting the country to conform to my standards, but a bit of decorum would be nice.'

She licks salt from her lucky fingers, and I realise I'm in awe of this girl. She's vibrant and confident, not given to moments of indecision. My sense of her power goes beyond her position of authority in the BIGSUN hierarchy – it's *her*. We walk along the harbour and make our way towards the amusement park. Cassandra stops, shading her eyes and looking up at the world's tallest ferris wheel.

'You up for it?' she asks.

'For you, I'll take the ride.'

We buy tickets and get in the short line, winding our way around a pretzel of steel barriers. We're ushered into a ten-by-ten metal cage with glass sides, and a bored-looking man in his twenties locks the door behind us. The front edge rises and we slowly lift off from Earth.

'I thought ferris wheels were quicker than this,' I say.

'Yes, but we're not paying to go around seven times and vomit up a sausage. This is to enjoy the big view.'

We hold hands and I think that I can remember the first time I held a girl's hand in every other major relationship in my life, but with Cassandra I can't. It had to be in the last three weeks, probably on one of our day trips, but the act was so *easy* that I can't remember the moment.

The big view is disappointing, the dense humidity and pollution haze restricting the horizon to a few thousand yards, but the ride is smooth. The harbour is lined with cruise ships and commercial vessels groaning under loads of steel containers. Halfway to the top I begin to sense just how large this wheel actually is. We're over a thousand feet above ground, suspended in midair. I imagine being here when the big earthquake hits, see us tumbling off the moorings and rolling slowly into the harbour, locked in this cage.

Cassandra moves from one end of the car to the other, snapping photos. Finally she sits down, puts her arms around my waist and kisses me on the lips.

'Is anyone in the cage below us?' she asks.

'No.'

'Good. The one ahead of us is empty too.'

She smiles and begins to undo my pants.

'You're joking,' I say.

'Why not?'

I've never contemplated midair copulation before – it goes against my species instincts – but the danger factor is intoxicating. By the time we reach the peak, I'm thankful for both smog and skirt season.

When we get to the bottom, we're flushed and giggling stupidly. The minder unlocks our cage and we tumble back into Japan, this temporary displaced world where we've come to meet. We take a walk along the water and listen as waves dash themselves softly against concrete.

'Jamie,' she says, 'you're the most fun I've had in a long time.'

'And you, Cassandra, are definitely the best boss I've ever worked for.'

25

Every action has a reaction. Two days later, a familiar figure is lingering at the bottom of my stairs. She's in a red skirt and black top with the words 'Why Am I Right Too Much?' written across the front in silver. Her face turns into a dramatic cotton-candy pout when she sees me.

'You no call back,' she says.

'Hi, Megumi. I've been busy.'

'Too busy for Meg-meg-*chan*?'

I've known this was coming, half hoping she would take my disinterest as a hint and spend more time with her other *gaijin* boyfriends. But ignoring a person in Tokyo doesn't have the same gravity as in Canada, because Japanese people are always short on time. My complete lack of communication could mean I've been working eighteen hours a day and sleeping in my spare time. Or my boss may have decided that the company needs to go out after work more, bond through karaoke and toxic levels of *sake*.

'I'm sorry,' I begin.

'That okay.' She grabs my arm and moves towards the stairs. 'We go play Bump of Chicken.'

I'm about to tell her I've been playing bump of chicken with someone else when she hands me a CD cover, featuring sneering young men in leather. Apparently, Bump of Chicken is one of Japan's hottest punk bands. Megumi disappears up the stairs before I can say another word and ducks into my unlocked apartment. I have the sense that I'm doing Japan all wrong. I'm so clearly a tourist, fumbling over the language and customs, taking young women for granted, eating sandwiches on the street and not attempting to understand their society. I've been frivolous.

By the time I get inside, the music is blaring and Megumi is dancing around in tiny circles with a dizzy grin. She coos and takes my hands, forcing me to spin with her. The music is surprisingly good and her wiry body feels fine pressing against me. I could run across the street for some drink and spend the evening in. Nothing would have to happen, and we could just hang out, have fun . . . Except I can so clearly imagine Cassandra's expression if she were to turn up. And the girl pressing against me is lovely, warm, and such a dangerous temptation. Suddenly, more than anything in the world, I don't want to hurt Cass.

'I can't do this,' I say.

'You dance okay. Move leg more.'

'No, Meg. I'm seeing someone else.'

'I'm seeing you too!'

She dances around me, a full three-hundred-and-sixty-degree turn with twirls. Like true New York rockers, Bump of Chicken play two-minute three-chord songs with manic energy, so I don't have long to collect my thoughts. At the end of the tune, I turn off the music and the pout returns.

'You're a really nice girl, Megumi,' I say.

This is the point in English where the person takes the hint. 'But I have a new girlfriend.'

There's a flicker of sorrow, but only for a second.

'That okay,' she says. 'We have language exchange, no problem.'

'No sex,' I say.

'Maybe yes a little?'

She slinks, her eyes focus, as if it's a game – Seduce the *Gaijin* – and we've entered a new phase. She turns and walks into my bedroom, shedding her skirt and pulling off her top. She slides my door closed as her bra begins to fall.

I hear Eldon shuffling around in his room as I walk out the front door and head down the street to Cass's place. She won't be home for another hour or more if she goes out with co-workers, but I'm happy to wait on the front steps. I wonder how long Megumi will wait, naked with the air conditioner on high, before she gets dressed and leaves. I feel guilty and gutless, but maybe this short-term sting of hurt pride and ruined friendship is best for us all.

26

A strange reverberation takes hold of me as I climb the long row of stairs towards the daylight of Shin-Yokohama. The morning is as hot as a sauna, as usual, and is perfect for a festival. Three Taiko drummers are set up in the station square, their heavy bass beats pulsing through the air, affecting my cardiorhythms. They stand before steel kettle drums, lean muscles rippling as they attack the instruments in karate stances, jerking and thrusting forward and back, white headbands across their foreheads. The drumbeats are low and rumbling, clearly ominous and contrary to the amused faces of the hundreds of weekend spectators. They should have set up these drums a hundred and fifty years ago on the hills of Shimoida when Admiral Perry brought his black ships and forced the reclusive Japanese to trade with the world. The sailors would have mutinied, broken the masts, and swum back to sea.

Food kiosks are being set up all along the square. There's an *okunamiaki* stand (seafood pancake covered in dehydrated fish flakes), and one specialising in *takoyaki* (octopus balls coated in sweet sauce). Another stand offers 'sour hotdogs', which I hope means they come with sauerkraut, although with this heat one never knows for sure.

Near the entrance to the BIGSUN building, a crowd has gathered around what appears to be a giant inflatable fish. Pretty girls are holding placards and men in suits are yelling through blow horns as television cameras and microphones bob above a cacophony of heads. A girl in a short skirt and blue blazer approaches me and offers a sample of brownred matter in a tiny plastic cup.

'Foundation for the Enjoyment of Whale Meat is happy to offer this wondrous fresh selection,' she says.

I politely decline, wondering why this promotion doesn't violate the no-eating-on-the-street rule. Sally waves from a nearby planter, where she's sitting with a coffee watching the spectacle.

'Feel the love,' she says. 'I've never seen people get so excited by the consumption of an endangered species. Think what they could do with a couple of pandas and a barbecue.'

'It's not the most eco-conscious place in the world.'

'Tell me about it. I did a class on the Great Barrier Reef last week, mainly about how it's eroding because of pollution and drunken oil-tanker captains beaching themselves monthly. I said sightseeing tours should be stopped, but the students reckoned Australia should attract more tourists and get as much money as possible until the reef disappeared.'

'A difference in methodology.'

'Of course, my new boyfriend is different.'

Sally is looking at me with barely contained glee, her perpetual look of fatigue gone. Before I can ask, she gushes forward, tapping me on the leg like she's sending a telegram down the line.

'His name is Reiji and he's a total spunk. He's a friend of a friend and we'd met a few times before, but he'd never speak to me. Saturday night, thanks largely to the warm *sake*, I went after him, realising that I was never going to get a date in this country if I waited for a guy to make the first move. And you know what, he likes me! He really likes me!'

Her index finger is threatening to wear a hole through the thigh of my pants, so I get off the planter and motion towards the school. A man with a blow horn chooses this precise moment to blast a message of encouragement through my fragile eardrum and I decide that today my brain isn't wired to cope with either the sight of hundreds of people eating raw blubber, dense humidity, or amplified fanaticism. Unfortunately, my desires aren't shared by the masses, as the school is filled with students, all combining the festival with an hour or two of study. Eugene is helping the staff at the front counter.

'You didn't try the whale meat, did you?' he asks.

'We resisted,' I say. 'That was a nice tag question, by the way.'

Eugene chuckles. 'What I meant to say was: you didn't try the whale meat, *are you*? You made a wise decision. It contains about two hundred times the maximum level of mercury allowed for human consumption. The whale lobby is encouraging people to slurp up blubber until their brains turn to brie and they can't remember how to work the toaster oven.'

Eugene moves seamlessly between his administration duties and detailing how people in line are killing themselves with the sample cups in their hands. He explains that a couple of years ago, Harvard University and two Japanese toxicology laboratories went around testing samples of whale meat in supermarkets. Ninety-five per cent of what was labelled whale meat was actually dolphin and porpoise, but the toxicity levels were still too high.

'Gives a whole new meaning to a love of Flipper,' I say.

'Yeah, well, after the W-A-R, with all the shortages, whale meat was an inexpensive way of feeding the masses. This being Japan, they had to revere it so that people wouldn't feel like they were eating crap, so it became tradition.'

Amazingly, the thumping bass of the drumbeats courses right through the cement of the building, tampering with my normal breathing and leaving my nerves desperately jangled. Luckily, my first student of the day is Takashi, one of my favourites. He's unusually tall for a Japanese person, at least six foot, and his stature seems to have affected his personality, which could be described as clownish. We're practising dinner party etiquette.

'Okay,' I say. 'You've had too much to drink, but your host is offering another gin-and-tonic. How do you politely decline?'

'I do not drink gin-and-tonic.'

'Yeah, that could work.'

He waves his hands. 'No, really. I do not like the flavour. This is serious. It taste like gasoline.'

I ask him to imagine it's some drink that agrees with his palate, and then I spend five minutes explaining 'palate'. Finally, I offer him a beer.

'No, thank you,' he says. 'I am not a great drinker.'

'Or?'

He thinks hard. 'No, thank you, I am going to vomit.'

'That would definitely work. Okay, now reverse the situation. You're the host, I'm your guest and we've just finished dinner. What might you say now?'

'Please do my dishes.'

'Yeah, but that might take the fun out of your party. Why don't you invite me into the living room to relax?'

'I live in one room.'

Apparently Takashi's mind isn't on entertaining today, so

we close the books and simply talk. He tells me that his father expects him to join the family company, but that he wants to quit the export business to become a travel agent. He fidgets and asks me about my life in Canada and tells me, like so many other students, that some day he'd like to work in North America.

I'm sitting there thinking there's no way that I could survive being Japanese. I spent my twenties bouncing from one vague ambition to another and have never had any real pressure to settle into one job. For all the Gen-X angst in the western world, compared to the east, we're all pretty free to make our own choices. Of course, Japan offers more stability and continuity, and a greater sense of common good over individuality. The Yin and Yang is immense.

'Which country's way do you think is better?' Takashi says.

'I'm not the right person to ask. If everyone in North America were like me, we'd still be living in caves and lighting fires by rubbing sticks together.'

At lunch, I sit at a table and work my way through a bento box. Next to a small piece of cake is a segment of what I assume must be custard. I shovel half into my mouth and discover it's actually mayonnaise. I spit it back into the box, reassured once more of my own ignorance.

Maybe I don't belong anywhere.

After work, I do some research on the Internet about whaling. Because of the world ban, Japan is not supposed to harvest whales, but the government encourages fishermen to kill hundreds of Minke whales as scientific samples. Under international law, the samples aren't to be wasted, so the meat is auctioned as soon as the ships return each spring. The International Whaling Commission can't do a thing about it.

I explain this to Cassandra later in her room.

'Loopholes strangle the world,' she says.

'Doesn't this make you feel like doing something, like organising a protest to educate people?'

She looks at me for a few seconds, the tension around her eyes telling me she's had a long day too. The company has been putting pressure on her to get sales up at satellite BIGSUN schools, but the market is already saturated with ESL schools and the economy is in extended recession. She returns to applying polish to her naked toe-nails.

'We're foreigners, Jamie. There's nothing we can do. Don't be such an American.'

'What does that mean?'

'This country has its own ways. If they want to change, that's going to have to come from inside. There are lots of things wrong with Japan, but a bunch of preachy English teachers aren't going to make a difference. And besides, there are a lot of things the country does better than the west: the cities are clean, there's barely any crime and people will always stop to help you. So maybe they know what they're doing. I used to get really frustrated like you, but I've learned to accept the place. There's no use.'

'You sound annoyed, almost like you *don't* accept it. If I didn't know you better, I'd say you –'

'Don't finish that sentence. If you do, you might be sleeping alone tonight.'

'Touchy touchy. All I'm saying is people do change the world, Cassandra. Where would we be if Martin Luther King accepted the status quo, or Gandhi waited for the English to spontaneously leave India?'

'I'd be right here, in this room, talking to you about whales.'

She lifts a foot to her mouth and blows on the polish. I don't say much and wonder if a night in the home hammock might be in order. Cassandra sighs, puts her foot down and screws the top back onto her bottle.

'I always knew some day something about this country would fail to surprise me, and then it would be time to leave.'

'What's failed to surprise you?' I say.

'My attitude. I know how you're feeling, Jamie, but I've been here too long and I'm exhausted. I'm tired of new teachers coming and marvelling over the trains or the food or the fact that bananas are wrapped individually. I'm sick of businessmen looking at my breasts and housewives asking why I'm not married. I'm tired of whale meat and squid snacks and buying beer from a vending machine. I look around and don't know who I am anymore. I feel a real need to go home and talk to people who know me, get my head back on straight.'

She stops there. She shuts off the stereo and extinguishes the incense by jamming the stick upside down in a potted plant. I expect her to shut off the light, plonk her head onto the pillow and be snoring softly in a matter of minutes, and am surprised when her terse anxiety turns to warm affection. Kisses fill the space where talk should be.

'Can we forget about the outside world for the rest of the night?' she asks.

Her warm lips nibble my earlobe.

'What world?' I say.

'Until tomorrow, this room is all that exists.'

Welcome to Planet Us.

27

A couple of days later, I walk into the staff room and am surprised to see UK Roger, my teacher during the training phase, sitting on a foldout chair eating noodles and reading the newspaper.

'Hey, remember me?' I say.

'The guy who bought me drinks. How can I forget? How are things, Jamie?'

'Good enough. Not thrilled by this inter-school run up Fuji, but everything else is interesting. Are you competing?'

'No, trainers are exempt. It's one of the perks. That and the fact that we barely teach.'

'I thought you said you loved it.'

He doesn't reply, just raises his eyebrows sceptically. 'Seen anything besides Yokohama yet?'

'Not really.'

'Yeah, why bother. Seen one temple, seen them all, and behind the temple will be a 7-Eleven and an *izakaya*. You have to love modern Japan. Of course, officially I didn't say any of that, because I love this company ... How's your race training going?'

'Good. I've been running every other day, mostly at night because of the heat. I'm up to seventy-five minutes and burn extra energy by jumping away from cockroaches on the road while screaming like a little girl.'

'Asian cockroaches are a treat.'

That's an understatement – they're the size of my thumb and they fly. Better yet, they've got a nasty habit of playing dead, lying on their backs in stairwells and on hot pavement. When you get close they make a high-pitched whirling sound, like an air-raid siren, begin to spin around, and then shoot up into the air. I've had several ricochet off my body like rubber bullets.

'Why are you slumming at Shin-Yokohama?' I ask.

'I'm interviewing Cora for the job of assistant district manager.'

'Cassandra's job?'

'Yeah, you know Cassandra?'

I smile, thinking I've got the inside track on good news. If Cass's job is up for competition that can only mean one thing: *promotion*. The way she works, a rapid rise up the ladder isn't surprising. I wonder if she knows yet.

'Cass will be excited,' I say.

'Yeah, she seems keen to go home.'

'What?'

'She put in her resignation last week. It was sudden, but you get used to these complications in this country. Everyone has to go home eventually.'

I go to the toilet and lock myself in a stall. I can't breathe. There must be an explanation. She's mentioned leaving at various times, but every *gaijin* does that – it's a coping mechanism, the safety valve of knowing you can always escape the urban crush and your own overwhelming foreignness. There has to be some mistake, a mix-up in communications. Maybe she's been offered a job with another company and has made an excuse, or maybe there are two Cassandras.

At lunch, I'm in the Prince Pepe Hotel looking at my cigarette options: Lark, SomeTime Fresh, Peace and Hope. I'm assuming the last one implies 'Smoke these and hope you don't get cancer.' My mouth runs dry and my skin feels like it's being run over by a cheese grater as I put in my coins. So much for self-improvement, so much for running and betterment, love and working towards a fucking goal. I go for a walk to keep my mind moving, not stalling, not thinking about the fact that Cassandra has decided to leave Japan and hasn't even bothered to let me know. My forehead feels like white-hot metal. As I light up, I remember a story a student told me about a smoking contest between two construction workers in Hong Kong. A crowd gathered and the betting apparently got pretty intense, at least until one of the workers finished number one hundred and twenty-seven, and dropped dead of nicotine poisoning.

This is good. Tales of death and self-destruction are what I need right now. Forget life renewal and being able to walk up stairs without nearly passing out. Who needs lung capacity? I walk around the back of the station and stand on a bridge admiring the view of the waste containers, trucks unloading steel, concrete and wire. I light up my first cigarette in months and take a long drag.

'Fuck, fuck, fuck!!'

I toss the smoking tobacco off the bridge as well as the rest of the pack. If I weren't wearing expensive leather shoes I would kick the crap out of the nearby post. Instead, I slowly walk back to my job, not in any way in the mood to make conversation.

My next class is a one-on-one with my cram-school-teacher friend Yoko, she of giant grape fame, tennis fanaticism and *Pulp Fiction* slang. I ask her about love and she humours me, the teacher, telling me about how she fights with her husband. She says that though she loves him now, she didn't when they first married, not that she had much choice. She was nearly twenty-two, in danger of becoming 'Christmas cake' – unwanted and uneaten dessert going stale on the shelf – and he was her best option. I almost wish my dilemma were so easy.

'Men and women do not understand the other,' she says.

'I'm forced to agree.'

'And Japanese men do not have skill to talk to women. In high school, they go to school eight o'clock to three o'clock, and after do mandatory sports club, cram school and homework. They have no social time, so they are uninteresting. Later, they work alone at computer and get strange thoughts. But women have no choice but to marry for money.'

'Who is in control of the relationship?' I ask.

'The man thinks he, but I am most powerful behind the closed door.'

Yoko tells me she decided to learn English because she and her husband have been hosting exchange students. Her husband took a liking to a girl from New Zealand and would sit at the table laughing with her and refusing to translate the conversation. The day the girl left for home, Yoko beaned him with a tennis racquet and signed up with BIGSUN.

'I can't condone spousal violence,' I say, 'but I admire your spirit.'

We spend the next few minutes learning 'condone' and 'spousal violence'. She particularly likes the latter phrase and vows to use it in conversation with her husband tonight.

I debate calling Cassandra to cancel our night's plans, wanting to get my thoughts straight before confronting her, but in the end I head for Yokohama. We stick to our kitsch plan and check into a love hotel. Because rents are so high, there are a lot of households full of extended family, so to be alone, couples go to hotels specialising in rooms for a night or a few hours. There is no stigma. Of course, that doesn't mean I don't feel awkward and perverted as a very pleasant fifty-year-old woman at reception checks us in and asks if we'd like to buy lubricant.

An hour later Cassandra and I are lying in bed watching a man on the TV as he twists and pinches a woman's nipple, kneading her breast like unleavened dough and making some terrible facial expressions. She's squirming away, screaming, '*Itai, itai!*'.

'I think that means "It hurts",' Cassandra says.

'This is the worst pornography I've ever seen.'

'I'd agree, but I've never watched porn before. We can switch it off. We've had the love hotel experience.'

'Do you have a checklist of things you have to do in this country?'

'Yes.'

'Well, you'd better hurry.'

This was supposed to be our weird Japanese love night, but I can barely contain the urge to shout and beat the bedcover, which happens to be covered in a really repulsive plastic sheet, like those used for chronic bed wetters. Cassandra seems oblivious to my mood and I can only rationalise that she's distracted by the misery of her betrayal. Or maybe she's trying to work up the courage to beg me to come to Australia.

I look around at the warped velvet wallpaper and the old furniture. This is the least modern place I've encountered in

Japan — it's like a 1950s roadside motel. The air conditioning is faulty and the street noise rises up like static. The smell of the room suddenly comes to me: cheap cleaning products and body fluids. Cassandra tries the radio on the floor.

'Can we leave and come back?' I say.

'I don't know. I'm pretty sure we lose the room if we leave. It's a let-by-the-act not let-by-the-night sort of place. Anything bothering you?'

'I'm fine.'

'You seem tense.'

'Should I be?'

Strange hotel rooms reinforce the feeling that all is temporary. I'm lying naked with a woman I barely know, who will disappear in a matter of weeks. No one in this country knows me, and I don't know them. We're all friendly shadows, parodies of ourselves, pretending to be what we aspire to, making great gestures and ruminating about our future grand plans. Japan is our make-believe world, where everything back home is better and all our current problems are connected to the limitations of this country.

'When were you going to tell me?' I ask.

'Later.'

'You're aware that I know you're leaving?'

'I'm not stupid. Roger was going to Shin-Yokohama today. I thought it would be easier if you heard it second hand, in a business setting, because the decision is purely job-related. My contract expires soon and I've decided not to renew.'

'That's it?'

'I don't want to commit to another year.'

'But we're having fun.'

'Yes, but that's not always the basis of worth. I could stay another year, hate my job, get tired of what I love here and end up with an unrewarding segment of life experience. I don't want to waste my time.'

'Thanks.'

'You know what I mean – you know exactly what I mean. It's like how you felt in Toronto: I've jumped the shark. Besides, there are other considerations . . .'

I'm confused and can't find any rational arguments to counter my own stupid phrase, except that I've fallen in love with her. She has become Japan to me in a very short time. She tucks her head into my shoulder and we fold together like an Annie Lebowitz snapshot. We go to sleep and I wrestle fitfully against the heat and unknown sheets, the smells of other people's love and loss, and the presence beside me. After a time, the air conditioner cuts out again and we touch with only fingers, as it's too hot to hold one another tightly.

28

In confusion, I do the only logical thing and get completely intoxicated with the king of indifference, Paul. We go to an American bar, replete with road signs, country music and a coin-operated mechanical bull in the corner. The waitress is from Newcastle in the UK, but because most Japanese people can't distinguish accents, she was deemed American enough to lend authenticity to the place. She's on a working holiday visa and is leaving for Korea in a couple of weeks. Naturally, Paul tries to flirt, and is instantly rejected.

'Nicely done,' I say.

'Why don't you have a go, mate?'

'I've got a girlfriend.'

'You don't honestly think it's going to work out with Cassandra, do you?' he says. 'She's already given you your marching orders, even if she does want to keep you around until she leaves. You're old enough to know a bloke has to be clinical about relationships. Be a free man, enjoy it. Don't be one of those weepy, miserable, blurry-eyed dreamers.'

'I'll find a way to make her stay.'

'Trust me, I've been here for a few years, you've got to accept that people leave. Don't get attached. Stay aloof. God knows you'll shag a lot more women that way. Did I tell you about how a mate and me met these two girls the other night and ended up getting head in a karaoke box? Show me another country where that can happen.'

I'm not sure if I invited Paul out tonight as the voice of reason, sleaze or as inspiration to stay committed to pursuing Cassandra. As usual, he turns the conversation to more pertinent matters and asks which student I'd want to be trapped with when the big earthquake hit.

'I'm not playing this game tonight,' I say.

'I'd take Sumi, the pregnant one, just for kicks. She's got so much anger, it's sexy.'

We have a couple more drinks before a Japanese country and western band takes the stage. The men are in stars-and-stripes shirts, blue jeans, cowboy boots and ten-gallon hats. They start with 'Achy Breaky Heart' and boot-scoot around the small stage. I never thought anyone could do injustice to a Billy Ray Cyrus song, but apparently 'blakie halt' is a real tongue twister in this country.

'Come on, mate,' Paul says. 'You're getting me down and this noise is doing my head in. Why don't we go to the massage district and get a couple of hand jobs? You pay, but I'll pick out the girls – we'll get fat ones, because they're always so much more attentive.'

I swish the final dregs of beer around my glass. Paul bobs his head in mocking agitation.

'Would you forget about the girl,' he says. 'Besides, you're looking too needy. She won't respect you if you sulk. My philosophy is if you want something to love you, ignore it. If it doesn't come back, fuck it. Or better yet, fuck something else . . . God, I'm horny tonight.'

We hit the humid streets and double-back to the school to meet up with Sally, who is on late shift. Before she appears, the students flood through the doors, including Hiroki, who comes over and proudly hands me a demo CD of his band, Blandlands.

'You know,' he says, 'like Terrence Malick film.'

He describes them as a cross between Pink Floyd and Eric Clapton, which is reason enough to hurl the disc against the nearest brick wall; but I'm touched by the gift. They're playing their first live gig on Friday and he desperately wants me to come. I ask if it's normal that a band makes a CD before actually playing in front of an audience, and he says he thinks so, because technology in Japan is so advanced and venues to play music are so limited.

'We practise in Yoyogi Park,' Hiroki says. 'Every Sunday. So this is not number one gig, but only first in real club. It is cool, man.'

Paul watches a girl in six-inch platform heels and a fluorescent green dress stroll by. She's talking on a mobile phone, her handbag hooked over her arm, and is moving so slowly and awkwardly that a hairline crack in the pavement could bring her down. Every year in Japan there are at least ten platform-shoe-related deaths. Girls tumble down subway stairs, or trip and fall in front of oncoming traffic – that sort of thing. Death by fashion.

We head to a nearby park with Hiroki and Sally's trophy boy Reiji in tow, stopping to buy drinks and fireworks (*hanabe*). Japan doesn't have the same safety restrictions as other nations on fireworks and we're soon equipped with powerful weaponry: bottle rockets, roman candles, screamers and Chinese crackers. We requisition a picnic table under the high voltage wires, the only green space in the area, and start lighting up the moody sky. There are dark clouds roiling around, thunder in the distance and the odd faint spark of lightning.

Reiji is shy, but friendly, smiling and apparently terrified to speak English to anyone but Sally. A couple of men in dirty jackets are sorting through the garbage nearby, picking out cans.

'You don't see many homeless people here, do you?' I say.

'There are more compared to years before,' Hiroki says. 'If you go to Ueno Park, you see Tent City pushed in the corners. It is filled with salarymen who left their families after the bubble burst.'

'The financial crisis?'

He nods. 'No job, no money, too great of pride to face wife and children as a failure.'

'I've been to Ueno,' Sally says. 'I had a man come and ask what I thought of interracial marriages – turns out he used to be a high-level BIGSUN student. I talked to him for a while, but he was a bit psychotic.'

'Did you shag him?' Paul asks.

'The way you compensate is sad.'

'You did!' Paul says. 'Sally shagged a homeless man!'

To everyone's surprise, Hiroki produces a pouch of magic mushrooms. Apparently they're legal in Japan and available from a shop in Shinjuku. We all chew a few rubbery heads and stalks. Paul puts a firework in an empty beer can. He lights the fuse and retreats. After a few seconds there's a deep hiss, a gunshot crack and a blast of orange resin in the air thirty feet above our heads.

He tries the trick again with two screamers, tying the fuses together, but as he ducks away the can falls sideways and the projectiles explode in the direction of a Japanese couple sitting peacefully on a bench by the water. The fuse crackles as the bomb beelines to target, my lungs vacating oxygen, my mind thinking only of forced deportation, arrest, or fleeing across the highway and down the river. Time slows to an agonising slow motion as the couple turns towards the hurling ball of explosive coming their way. Only seconds from impact the firecrackers snap into a brilliant red.

The two lovers don't yell, and the boyfriend doesn't come over to beat us senseless; instead, they get up and walk away slowly. Thank god for the pacifism in this country.

'The *gaijin* are revolting,' Paul says, uncharacteristically embarrassed. 'Take that whichever way you want.'

If we're being culturally insulting, neither Hiroki nor Reiji seem offended. In fact, Hiroki is doubled over crying with laughter. He can't speak for several minutes, during which I become faintly aware of my own tingling fingers and the welling of euphoria in my chest cavity. The mushrooms have arrived.

We work our way through the fireworks. Hiroki and I decide to get more drinks and spend thirty minutes staring at the beautiful rows of silver cans in the convenience store until a clerk comes up cautiously.

'Okay?' he asks.

I give him a thumbs-up and he goes back to the counter. In any other country I'd be soundly abused, if not thrashed and arrested, but in Japan my individual right to be insane isn't questioned; at least not as long as my failings don't affect the masses. This is the liberation in the system, one of many safety valves designed to allow individuals to blow off stress and carry on with their obligations. We are all free to drink, play violent video games, thrash a guitar in the park and routinely spend entire nights in a small rented box singing off-key to Carpenters hits. I turn to Hiroki, who is snoozing peacefully against the cooler door.

'I love this place,' I say. 'I understand now.'

Despite protests, I trek off to catch the last train at one in the morning, but when we pull up to Centre Kita, several stops short of home, the engines cut and the carriages drain their human cargo. I stumble along the platform to the main gates, where I find a railway worker.

'*Azamino je nai?*' I ask.

'*Hai.*'

There are no more trains for the night. He directs me to the taxi stand, but I find there's nothing left in my wallet, because I've spent my last yen on booze. I discover another great thing about this nation: most bank machines close on Sundays and holidays, and after 5 pm on all other days. I sit on the station steps and attempt to clear my head as a light rain begins to fall. I try to convince two taxi drivers that my room-mate will pay them, but they wave me away with their white gloves and press the button that automatically closes the passenger doors.

I'm vaguely insulted that they wouldn't trust an incoherent sweaty *gaijin* with no cash, dilated pupils and beer stains on his T-shirt. Wisely, I decide to walk home, following the tracks, which I know will eventually run to Azamino station. There are only three or four stops, so I figure a solid sixty to ninety minutes and I'll be tucked away on my futon sleeping like a heavyweight KO'd in the fifth. I hike by convenience stores and students on mopeds hanging out like Hell's Angels. I try to keep the electrical overhang in view, but this is difficult, especially when I come to the outskirts of the town, where urban congestion gives way to small cottages and rice fields. The road goes up a series of hills and within twenty minutes, the railway line disappears into a tunnel that runs through a rather large mountain.

'Shit,' I say. 'Forgot about that.'

In my hazy mind, the notion of climbing the fence and taking my chances inside the pitch-black gaping mouth of the tunnel is a good one. The trains have stopped running for the night, so the only thing I'd have to be careful of are repair crews coming down the line. I stumble up the rocky incline only to find a security fence topped with barbed wire.

A few minutes later I'm back on the road, cresting yet another hill, trying to figure out where the tunnel might exit. Unfortunately, the road is winding and the rain begins to fall hard enough to obliterate my view and extinguish what's left of my spirit. I come to a stony temple and sit on a rock bench as the rain berates me for my ignorance. Shintos believe that demons take the form of foxes in the night and move across the landscape looking for victims. I glance around nervously. I'm in no way superstitious, but sitting in the middle of nowhere in complete darkness, I'm poised to run at the first weird noise or bony hand pushing up through the topsoil.

In the heart of the building, a small statue of Buddha stands surrounded by traditional offerings of oranges and rice for relatives in the afterlife. Beside these are modern supplements – canned coffees and Kit Kat bars – as if the dead need to be kept up to date on new trends and products.

I think of religion and ritual, of fortunes hanging in neat rows above a well, and I realise I could die and no one would know why I was alone and wet in a temple beside a rice paddy far from home. I think of my mother and wonder if she'd be proud of the man I've become, high on edible fungus but taking on the world as best I can. If I allowed myself to believe in an afterlife, I'd imagine her looking down and laughing her ass off at my current predicament. Maybe she has arranged all this to teach me about urgency, love and the wonder of folly.

As I leave, my feet give way on a slick of mud and I find myself sprawled out in long grass with clouds moving swiftly above. Despite the cold and damp, I put my jacket over my head and fall asleep in the softness. When I wake, the rain is driving harder and my watch reads 2.30 am. I decide to hike back to Centre Kita and wait under shelter for the first morning train.

I'm slumped across from the station on a bench with my eyes closed, thinking of Cassandra. I don't want to think of her, but I don't seem to have any control over my brain at the moment. Images and impulses are tumbling around like socks in a drier. I can't wander through this city without her. I can't imagine one day soon waking into the light of day, stark reality and solitude.

I don't want the people I love to always leave me.

Someone taps an umbrella against my leg. I expect this is station security coming to run me off, back to the rice field, so I mumble a polite 'Fuck off', not looking up. I'm not in the mood for confrontation, and hope my foreignness will be enough to make this person give up in general apathy. But no, the umbrella taps my thigh again. I open my eyes to see a man my age hovering above me, ensconced in the requisite briefcase and blue suit ensemble. He looks at me like I'm a jigsaw puzzle with no edges. I hope he's not one of our students.

'Okay?' he says.

'Been better. But yeah, I'm okay.'

'*Aparto?*'

'Azamino.'

I point stupidly down the track. He looks around, his lips puckered, and waves his hands towards the station. 'Trains no.'

'I caught on to that one, too. Thank you.'

He moves away and motions for me to follow. I'm acutely aware of my vulnerability. Despite all reassurances that Japan is a safety country, this is a bit too close to the classic abduct-drug-and-sodomise-the-stranded-runaway scenario. But I'm probably being paranoid due to excessive hillbilly classes with Hiroki. Besides, I'm sure I could overpower this guy if need be, stomp on his little head and crush his glasses under my shoe.

He stops at a large Kawasaki motorcycle, opens a container unit on the back of the seat, takes out a helmet and puts in his briefcase. He undoes his tie and throws it inside, then closes the unit and swings his leg awkwardly over the beast. He's small for the bike, but handles it roughly, like it's a steer needing to be broken. I think back to the mechanical bull in the American bar and can barely suppress jittery laughter, my eyes swimming in tired tears.

He kicks the bike to life and motions for me to hold him around the waist. There's no extra helmet, so I expect he'll go slowly . . . which of course, is the exact opposite of what he does. Maybe he's trying to impress the foreigner, make up for some perceived ego difference due to physical size, but he bolts off the curb like Han Solo jumping into hyperspace. The fluorescent lights of the noodle shops and electronics stores seem to bend and refract as we hit the first straight.

Even more worrying, my new friend is barely hanging on, his arms straining to keep hold of the handlebars, the machine wobbling and shaking beneath us. I think we'll be dumped at any minute, imagine the bike hitting a patch of slippery salaryman vomit on the asphalt and sliding into Fanny, the beauty salon at the end of the street.

My driver turns at the intersection and we lean together, like we're a close second in the super challenge and have one last shot at glory. The bike is slow to come back to an upright position, but Jacques Villeneuve doesn't seem to mind, or notice, as he opens the throttle and sends us bullet-like onto the highway, where Porsches and Jaguars are doing their own mock time trials. The dead of night is speed time in Japan, when people pursue their driving hobbies.

I can hear my new friend speaking, his head turned incrementally to share some speed-blurred observation with me. But the translation is lost in the wind stinging my face and the thought of my head ending up Humpty Dumpty–like next to the sign that reads 'Clean is the Love of Japan'.

Despite the terror and raw ache in my cold inflamed hands, I'm keenly aware that we're not going to Azamino, at least not along any route I know. And this is confirmed when the bike comes to a standing stop – the back wheel rising as our G-force motion abates – in front of a white apartment complex. I get off and stagger around, my hair tangled dense like steel wool. My driver takes off his helmet, smiling wildly, and motions towards the building.

'*Aparto,*' he says.

'Great. Thanks for the lift. Now I can enjoy being stranded and disoriented in a different part of town. Where are we? *Doko wa desu ka?*'

'*Me aparto.*'

'Oh for . . .'

I'm sure this is his idea of extreme kindness, but I was perfectly fine on the cold damp bench with the knowledge I'd be bucketing towards home around dawn. He starts walking, again motioning for me to follow. I'm in no mood for a sleepover and complimentary language exchange, but there isn't much I can do. And he's too damn cheerful to insult.

He slides a magnetic card through a scanner and the front door pops open. '*Seido*' is written on the wall, the only thing in English. It's an experience, I tell myself. Cassandra would be proud. It must be in the top twenty on her list, right after Crush Heart of Trusting Canadian.

'Me company,' he says. 'I Yoshiki.'

'You're great company, Yoshiki. Don't let anyone tell you different. My name is Jamie.'

'Ja-mui-*san*.'

'Close enough.'

He bows and sticks out a business card, holding it in the tips of both hands. He's in product marketing. I make it clear that I'm short on cards at the moment. He laughs and waves me away, like I'm the one being ridiculous. Of course I don't have cards.

'Teacher?' he says.

'Yeah. With BIGSUN.'

'Ah, good school. I no study now.'

'Thank god.'

'America?'

'Canada.'

He thinks hard for a few seconds. 'Rocky Mountain.'

'There are several, but yeah, that's right. Thank you for not saying "Celine Dion" like everyone else.'

'She-N Towwa?'

'CN Tower, right. That's in Toronto, my home. I'd make a phallic joke here, but let's face it, all the good ones have been done already.'

'Ni-a-gu-ra Farus!'

'Yes, Niagara Falls is around there too. But we could spend hours in the cold discussing landmarks . . .'

He nods, as if he understands completely, and we go inside and down a well-lit hallway, the sheer burden of colour and clarity threatening to burst open my cranium. He puts a key in one of the doors. We slide off our shoes and step into slippers. The apartment is a room, a self-contained bachelor pad with a small kitchen area in the corner, a TV on a nightstand and two futons, one occupied by a sleeping man.

Yoshiki speaks, kicking the covered body with his socked foot. A mole-eyed face emerges from under the pillow, looks up at me and no doubt tells his room-mate to get fucked. At least, that's what I'd do. I make all the apologetic motions a person can with his hands and facial expressions, bowing stupidly and stepping backwards.

'You are okay,' the mole says, sitting up. He runs a hand over his hair and takes a few moments for his head to clear. He grabs a pack of cigarettes from the side table and shakes one out, offering them to me. My willpower staying amazingly strong, I decline.

'My name is Tomo,' he says. 'You want drink?'

This appears to be a done deal, because Yoshiki has already brought over three glasses, Santori scotch and a bottle of cola from the fridge. He pours and we toast, as if we've been assigned to the same table at a bar mitzvah. The walls on Tomo's side of the room are bare except for a single Yomiuri Giants pennant, but Yoshiki's side is covered in movie posters and pictures of western celebrities ripped directly from magazines.

'You miss your train?' Tomo asks.

'Yeah.'

'You can get first one at six o'clock. Not far.'

My mind registers a pattern in Yoshiki's pictures.

'Geezus, it's a shrine,' I murmur.

'Not a shrine,' Tomo says. 'Yoshiki only a little crazy. You like Tom Selleck?'

'Tom Selleck!' Yoshiki says. '*Kompai!*'

We toast our favourite hirsute '80s icon and peruse the pictures together. There are copious shots of the *Magnum P.I.* years – the garish Hawaiian shirts, red sports car, Robin, and the Dobermans. Below these are posters for *Three Men and A Baby*, *High Road to China*, *Mr Baseball* and *Lassiter*; and various Japanese ads featuring a beaming Tom holding instant coffee, electric sandwich makers and ramen noodles hanging from chopsticks a few inches from that huge bushy moustache.

Yoshiki then pulls out a scrapbook filled with photos, postcards, clippings and a letter from the man himself, the letterhead from the 'Tom Selleck Fan Club, Los Angeles'. This obsession must be a few years old, because there's a photo of a younger Yoshiki standing on the *Magnum P.I.* estate in Hawaii. He's got a very weedy moustache and is wearing a white suit jacket over a turquoise mesh shirt, giving the peace sign and beaming wildly.

'You sure are wetting yourself in that one,' I say.

He nods enthusiastically. He's got T-shirts and stickers and far too many items for a grown man to be hoarding. But I smile, because the room is warm and dry, and Tomo is laying out an extra pillow and blanket on a spare futon. Yoshiki is trying very hard to get a point across in English. The third time he repeats the word, I understand he's talking about the TV show *Friends*.

'Oh yeah,' I say. 'Tom Selleck played Monica's boyfriend.'

Tomo says little, but he seems unwilling to go back to sleep, saying 'It's okay' every time I tell him I won't be offended. We admire Mr Baseball for about twenty minutes more and then my mind and body short-circuit completely. I make several polite but inarticulate sounds, say '*Domo arigato gozaimasu*' until Yoshiki stops bowing, and then pass out within seconds of hitting the floor.

At quarter to six, Tomo wakes me up. I'm given a postcard of Tom, Steve Guttenberg and Ted Danson to remember the night by, and with great thanks, re-emerge into the early dawn air.

29

'It happens all the time,' Sally says. 'I went on vacation to Nagoya and couldn't find a hotel. A family made me stay with them for the entire weekend, and even drove me to the station on Sunday to catch my train home. They barely spoke a word of English, but they were really friendly and fun.'

I thought my adventure story would cause more than a ripple, but apparently everyone has experienced this sort of random kindness. My lack of sleep turns out to be a surprisingly effective teaching tool as I ride a frenetic day-long wave of pure adrenaline. Half the time I can't gauge how loudly I'm speaking, and at one point I nearly fall off my chair. Everything is hideously funny, even the student who tells me his hobby is eating *yakisoba* noodles. Okay, that was still incredibly dull.

My final lesson before lunch is with a dentist, who tells me how she and her husband went to the Greek island of Mikonos for their honeymoon and accidentally ended up at a gay nude beach.

'I am only woman,' she says. 'But we keep on clothes. But many men and many *chin-chin*.'

'People were making celebratory toasts?'

'They not cooking.'

She explains '*chin-chin*' and I'm very surprised it has taken me this long to learn the Japanese word for 'penis'. The sexual terms and innuendos are usually the first words to be learned in a foreign language. From all indications, the experience was a touch emasculating for her husband.

During a free lesson, I make some additions to the staff calendar. The fifth is now officially Be Kind To Jamie Day, the eighth is Stress Out Cora Day, and the twenty-first is Dress As Your Favourite *Harry Potter* Character Day.

'Good to see you're using your time to prepare afternoon lessons,' Cora says. 'That's the kind of work ethic we like to see at BIGSUN.'

'I'm on a roll. Preparation will only slow me down.'

She looks into my eyes, grimaces, but she doesn't seem to really care that I'm a body in motion that will collapse if allowed to relax for more than five seconds.

At lunch, I read an article about a twenty-four-year-old man who worked for an ad agency and committed suicide because of stress, fatigue and depression. His parents sued the company successfully. The article goes on to detail a report that outlined corporate Japan's dependence on unpaid overtime, stating that if all unpaid OT were eliminated, nine hundred thousand jobs would be created.

I think if I lived here, if leaving wasn't an option, if I had been born into this grind, I'd probably have an unhealthy obsession with schoolgirl porn or an '80s television icon as well.

When I get to the apartment, UK Roger from head office is sitting at the kitchen table drinking tea and watching the news. He slurps up the dregs in his cup and hustles to the kitchen to wash it out.

'I didn't think you'd mind if I made a cup,' he says.

'Is there a problem?'

'I've just come to inspect your former flatmate's room.'

'Sorry?'

'We got a call yesterday that Eldon had moved out. You must have noticed he hasn't been around.'

'I've been sleeping away lately, at my girlfriend's place, in rice fields and corporate dorms . . . You know how it goes.'

'Apparently Eldon's living in a *gaijin* house in Tokyo. He's paid up here for the rest of the month, so technically we're not supposed to move anyone in until the first, but we have a high demand for accommodation at the moment. Don't be surprised if you get a new tenant sooner than later.'

'Did Eldon give a reason for leaving?'

'He said he had to get out because of a personality conflict. It happens more frequently than you'd imagine. The pressure of living with two strangers at close quarters is difficult. Say, you might want to soak these cups to get the stains out.'

'Don't you start.'

Poor dumb Eldon. If razor shavings in the sink freaked him out, sharing a communal bathroom with a hundred other people in a *gaijin* house will shatter his mental health completely. I try not to smile, but my burnt euphoria has left me with little control over my facial muscles. I wonder what information Eldon has passed on to head office.

Roger disappears with his clipboard into the now-vacant room, as if there are enough items to require a list of contents. I close Marcus's door. The *tatami* is starting to smell badly, filling the place with a wheat/barn stench, and I don't want him to get reprimanded.

'I'll have someone come by to replace the bedding and futon,' Roger says.

He hands me the pen and asks me to sign off on the inspection.

Marcus knocks, slides back my door, and pokes his newly shaved head inside. It looks like a freshly baked bun suspended in midair. When he sees I'm completely shattered and in a mild coma, he opens the door further and comes in for a chat.

'Hey, mate,' he says. 'Any idea why there's a futon jammed behind the washing machine?'

'That's Eldon's reparation payment to me. I figure having a second futon might compel Cassandra to sleep over more often. She can add some excitement and class to your otherwise bland life.'

'Oh good. You get a new bed and nightly shags, and I get to share the place with more people. Maybe we can rent out the lounge room to gipsies . . .'

'Do you know how uncomfortable it is sleeping two people on a single futon?'

'No, but I'd like to find out. By the way, why is Eldon getting new bedding?'

'You haven't heard?'

I'm sure we'll hear complaints from our neighbours about the excess noise as Marcus shouts for joy.

30

Cassandra and I spend our next day off in the Tokyo suburb of Kichijogi. We're doing what we always do – poking around shops, looking at the local temple, and grabbing a bite to eat. We pretend to be normal, a couple moving towards the future, as we wind our way through a series of indoor markets and end up in a store entirely devoted to the innocuous pink cartoon cat Hello Kitty. The doorway is pink and white, with cat's ears and a pink ribbon at the top.

Overkill is not a concept recognised by the Japanese. There are *Hello Kitty* toilet seat covers, dust mops, cameras, CD players, spaghetti strainers, spatulas, kimonos, clocks, watches, potato chips, and a ten-thousand-dollar kids' miniature car. Every corner, aisle, shelf and tile is pink and white, and nauseatingly cute. The shop girls wear pink uniforms with ribbons in their hair and shout happy slogans with every purchase.

'This is appalling,' I say. 'Does the world really need *Hello Kitty* mayonnaise?'

'It might be fantastic. You haven't tried it.'

'This is how I imagine the world feels on Prozac. All soft hues and easy on the eye, but essentially plastic and poorly made.'

'Don't suppose you're overreacting?'

'No. This very well could be the portal to Hades, or one of them, though obviously not the one Dante stumbled upon. I've always imagined that Hell was a children's television program filled with overly happy men and women in pastel colours singing frothy, gleeful songs with bad lyrics and inconsistent meter. "Come on, you know the words," they'd say over and over and over again. We'd be singing "A Hundred Bottles of Beer on the Wall", except we'd start somewhere in the millions. And then, when we finally got down to the single digits, Satan himself would show up dressed in a giant foam-rubber rabbit suit and we'd all be forced to do something humiliating with a skipping rope.'

'I take it you don't want kids,' Cassandra says.

'I haven't decided. You?'

'Err . . . No comment.'

She hands me a *Hello Kitty* breast pump, which I drop onto the floor in horror. A very nice, perky young girl scurries over to help me pick up the box. She smiles widely as she hands it back, not at all surprised that I'd be looking for a milking aid.

We wander beside the stream through Kichijogi Park. The day is hot, even more blinding hot that usual, with air as thick as condensed milk. I can't say I've become used to the heat, but I have learned to cope with the discomfort. Like everything else in my life – hangovers, death, emotional attachment, and girlfriends leaving – I turn to denial for strength.

Baby turtles linger along the edge of the water, disappearing if we step too close. In the middle of the lake, paddleboats shaped like giant white swans move across the placid surface. If countries were drugs, Japan would be acid; Canada, a mild sedative (according to Marcus); the US, crack; and Britain, booze. I'm not sure what Australia would be, never having been there, but looking at Cassandra leaning over the turtles, her reflection staring back at me off the water's surface, I'm inclined to say ecstasy, a pure endorphin rush pumping through the synapses.

I want to see pictures of her as a kid, as a teenager, from last week, from all stages of her life. I want to see the boys who broke her heart. I'm greedy for insight; I want every moment of her life, not just now. We sit on the grass, stretched out without urgency, her head on my lap. A group of passing teenage boys makes no secret of trying to look up Cassandra's skirt, so she drapes her bag over her knees.

'Do you carry pictures in your wallet?' I ask.

She sits up and pulls out a day planner. One section is a mini picture album containing half a dozen photos. She looks like her mother. I can see the chin, the lips, and the shape of her face. There are photos of a baby and a girl of about three. Cassandra clears her throat and flips the plastic.

'My niece,' she says. 'And this is Simon's twenty-first.'

People in varying states of intoxication smile rubber-faced and appear soundly flushed. It's summer, with boys in button-down shirts and girls in light dresses. The drinks are wine, beer and multicoloured cocktails.

'Birthday?' I say.

'Yeah. Twenty-one is big in Australia, and England, I think. Everyone dresses to the nines and we have a big bash.'

'Which one is Simon?'

She points to a drainpipe in the garden, near an open patio door. There's a happy face painted on steel at eye level. On the ground is a semicircle of gifts.

'Simon's a drainpipe?' I say.

'Yeah. We even printed up invitations. Everyone brought a present and at all times someone had to be talking to Simon or sharing a joint with him, something social. After all, it was his night.'

I look up to see the corners of her mouth pushed out wide into a cheeky smile. She looks like a squirrel storing nuts.

'Sometimes you need an excuse to have a formal party,' she says.

We soak in the sun until the thick dry grass begins to sting our legs, and then wander back along the stream toward the restaurants. There are a lot of bikes. Hundreds of shiny steel handlebars face us in columns, like loyal veterans in the May Day Parade in Red Square.

She wants to push me away, because we're from opposite sides of the planet, meeting in the middle, as *gaijin* in a country outside our natural spheres. But anyone with the will to come here has to have hope and curiosity and a need for romance – the belief in the gut, those shades of grey, coupled with danger and love, both red, both affirming most distinctly the tenacity of life.

'Are you sure you want to leave Japan?' I say.

'Why, because I might not get perved at so much back home?'

'Maybe you just need a break, like a month away.'

'If I go, I won't be back. I know that on a cellular level. You're big on intuition, so you must understand. Let's not ruin the day by talking about this.'

People on bicycles filter past, languidly peddling and moving as slowly as the faint gasps of breeze that push through the cherry trees all around us.

'Maybe I could book my two-week vacation right before the Christmas break,' I say. 'That would give me a month in Australia. We could see how we feel.'

'Jamie . . .'

'It's no pressure. I'm not expecting marriage, or even a commitment, but we do enjoy each other's company. We could keep this going. That's all a part of using time and living life. You feel this is the right time to go, and I feel like following is right for me.'

'You're not being realistic. I don't know where I'll be staying. Anything could happen – I could get to Australia and decide I want to go to Paraguay. I'm not reliable. You should forget about me.'

'Impossible. And as for South America, I'll take my chances. I've got nothing to lose, except of course *you*.'

She brushes stray bits of dry grass from her dress. 'Try to understand. I'm going back to the real world. I've got people in Australia, and I'm going to have a life completely different from this place.'

'Maybe I could fit into that world.'

'No. I'm telling you to save your feelings. We need each other here, because otherwise we'd end up like Eldon. But when I'm gone, you'll find someone else. I'm sorry, leading you on wasn't part of my plan.'

'None of this was part of any plan. I thought I was going to date a very nice Japanese girl, learn the names of every vegetable, and listen to way too much Celine Dion, but apparently human beings aren't as predictable as they think.'

'What are you talking about?'

'Maybe nothing is real. Maybe nothing is as solid and reliable as we pretend.'

'Did you do something weird with a Japanese girl and a vegetable?'

'You're missing my point.'

She smiles, wraps her arms around me and hovers inches from my lips. She touches my lips with a finger and forces my face into a false grin.

'Jamie,' she says, 'you have to know that I'll miss you so much and that you've been the greatest surprise in my life for a long time. But that's why we should leave this relationship with happy memories, not stupid fights. There are things you don't know about me.'

She puts her finger across my lips to stop me from speaking and shakes her head, no.

31

Cassandra takes an extra job on her days off and most evenings to raise cash before jetting home, so my once erotic mornings are now spent staring at the fire-retardant rubber coating on the ceiling. I feel as if I've assumed someone else's existence, slipped into his body and his less compelling life. I want to escape, find relief, but that's negated by the fact that I've already run away from home. There's nothing to do but eat repulsive giant white toast and get on with life – his life, my life, whatever. I slide, my concept of time corrupted into waking and teaching and ending up in my room at night without remembering how I got there.

I walk through Shin-Yokohama station, dragging myself through the crowds, people weaving in front of me, fabric scratching my arms, shuffling and warm. I feel my patience about to implode. What used to be a source of fascination is now frustrating. Faces march by and I wonder how long I will last in this place, isolated by an inaccessible language. I think of speech, how even my best students lack precision when speaking about emotion and feelings. Even though Cassandra and I speak the same language, I have no idea what she's about or how exactly she feels about us.

Mid morning, Paul and I are sitting in the teachers' room. He's sending flirtatious text messages on his phone and I'm reading the newspaper.

'Anything interesting happening in the world?' he says.

'I don't think so.'

'You're here early, *isn't it?*'

'I didn't feel like hanging around my apartment.'

'Right. It is much more fun hanging around BIGSUN, waiting to teach deprived housewives. Keep this up and you'll be working at head office. You do know you're looking like shit, right?'

I don't bother answering.

'I'm a bit bagged myself,' he says. 'I went to Sakuragicho for Sea Day yesterday, watched two hours of fireworks and then marched back to the station with thousands of sweaty Japanese people. It was like the Baatan Death March, but the clothes were more colourful.'

'Sounds like a good time.'

'It was horrid. I usually avoid going out on national holidays, because I don't like getting cattle-prodded onto trains, but my girl wanted to go. I've started dating one of the Japanese staff from Tama Plaza.'

'How long will this one last?'

'I don't know. She's an advanced speaker, gets my jokes and has no qualms about stimulating my prostate to help me come. It could be love. We'll have to wait until we get through the hormones. You can't take a relationship seriously until at least seventy shags. It's scientific. I've run the trials.'

The bell goes and a slow progression of co-workers shuffles in. After five straight months of hyper humidity and heat, summer is beginning to catch up with us all. Everyone looks drawn and worn down, moving slowly and staying close to the air conditioning vents.

I'm looking out the window as the bullet train pulls away from the station. Below me on the street is wave upon wave of navy blue, all men drowning in the same jacket. My first student, however, is obviously not caught in this ocean. He's wearing an all-white suit with polished white leather shoes. He tells me that people often confuse him with Jackie Chan, which is natural considering he's twenty, weedy and has a mouth full of steel braces. He says his mother has been breaking into his room to rearrange the fifty cologne bottles in his cupboard so that all the labels won't face outwards. He's tried locking the cabinet, but she still gets in.

The following student is wearing a USS *Arizona* hat. I wonder if he realises the significance and decide I have to break one of BIGSUN's primary rules: I ask him about the Second World War. He tells me it ended in 1949 and that Japan won.

Eugene is in the teachers' room at lunch and I tell him about my suspect day.

'My dad's uncle was in a Burmese prison camp building a railroad,' he says. 'They used to shove bamboo under people's fingernails if they weren't working hard enough. Every family has a story, I suppose.'

Eugene tells me that there are three main reactions to the war: remorse, anger and denial. Even though the subject is never taught in schools, a lot of people know that Japan treated its enemies inhumanely, committed atrocities in China, and was the aggressor. They carry some sense of national shame. Some blame the west for Hiroshima and Nagasaki, and for its long-standing treatment of Asia and Asians as second-class, inferiors to be colonised or dictated to. They feel Japan had no option but to assert its influence by force. Others simply look to the future and seem content to know that these conflicts are years and generations removed from modern life. In a strange way, I can understand the feelings behind all three viewpoints.

In the afternoon we have two earthquakes, or perhaps one earthquake and an aftershock. Either way, the vibrations are intense enough that my students pause and wait to see if this is the Big One. We linger, wondering if this shaking will be our demise, if this will be the moment when the architecture can't withhold the strain and the building accordions down upon itself with its human cargo inside.

'Yesterday was my day off,' a student says. 'I went in a coffee shop and read a comic book about Mesopotamia. Do you know this place?'

'Egypt.'

She nods enthusiastically. She gets very excited, shifts back and forth on her chair and looks at notes she has made for today's class. She tells me about Cleopatra and King Tut and the astral alignment of the Great Pyramids.

'No one knows how the stones are in the order,' she says. 'No one knows why. Some people believe there is a great plan by aliens and we are all slaves.'

We are all slaves – to history, conformity, fate and our natures. I think of Cassandra and how she has changed me fundamentally in such a short time. Compared with evenings spent with her, grand aspirations like making films seem trivial. Ambition is only graffiti, an urge to make the world know that you exist and yearn for recognition. Suddenly, Cassandra has filled that need. She's enough.

On the way home, I stop at a travel agent. The walls are filled with offers promoting hotels, traditional *ryokans* and hot spring resorts in Hakone and Atami. I end up at Cassandra's door.

'I haven't seen you for a while,' she says. 'How have you been?'

'Good . . . I didn't think you'd be here.'

'But you came anyway?'

She hasn't invited me in. She looks exhausted, her eyes weighed down with black circles. We're standing in the doorway. Behind her, Tawnie is stretched out on a futon in front of the TV. Cassandra runs a toe across the stoop, a chipped red nail sliding against grey concrete. We're both watching it.

'Did you feel the earthquake today?' I say.

'No. Was there one?'

'I felt definite movement. It's been a while. I want to go away for a weekend. Something we can remember each other by or tell our kids about years from now.'

She laughs and looks like she might just have missed me. She motions for me to come in and we go to her room. She tells Tawnie to finish the movie without her and we close her sliding door.

'I've booked my ticket,' she says.

'That's great.'

'You don't have to pretend to be happy for my sake.'

She tells me about her new part-time job, a private school run by a man with no office, just a mobile phone. He books rooms around the city and she has to find them. All of her students are old women, who, remarkably enough, are even less interested in learning than the BIGSUN crowd.

'Honestly,' she says. 'Most of the time they refuse to say anything in English. They giggle and speak Japanese. We end up talking about clothes and men. They can't believe I'm in my late twenties and not married. I'm learning loads more Japanese than they are English.'

'Seems like a good enough reason to stay.'

'Stop it.'

She looks out the balcony window over the tiled rooftops. The slogan on her wastepaper basket reads: 'Waybe: there is something attractive about this goods. And these are daily life necessities. Dust Bin 905.' In the distance the garbage truck is approaching, blaring a happy jingle and an indecipherable refrain.

Around Mount Fuji there's a forest where men and women have long gone to commit suicide and where magnetic instruments no longer work. Compasses spin out of sync, people get lost, and unexplained phenomena occur. In the 1950s a British plane lost its instrument panel and crashed into the mountain, killing a hundred and twenty-three people. At temples, people hand-make a thousand origami swans together as a physical prayer for recovery.

We are all slaves.

'You know that photo of my niece in my wallet?' she says finally.

'Yeah.'
'That's my daughter.'

32

That night I'm hooked by strange raving dreams and visions of being lost in the pockmarked concrete skin of urban back alleys. The doorways become snarled mouths drawing me in, then suddenly I'm on a plane full of people who aren't even touching their cellophane-wrapped Danishes. We're flying towards Mount Fuji when the instrument panel goes haywire.

I wake up with a start. I change into my running gear, stretch on the balcony and hit the dead streets. At first, my body and mind both resist this unorthodox move. I'm jumpy, skittering away from shadows that my mind interprets as rats and vines that turn into snakes. I feel the wind running up my spine, fuelling irrationality. But then, as my breathing takes on its rhythm I begin to calm down, the constant drop of shoe on pavement like a heartbeat.

Cassandra has a four-year-old daughter whom she hasn't seen in two years. Emily lives with her grandparents and sees her father on weekends. Cassandra is here because she couldn't cope as a single mother and because she's not qualified to do any job that would support two people. She sends a portion of what she saves back to Australia every month via money order.

What this all means to my future is anyone's guess.

I push harder, running against circumstance and choices, the crazed pain of my calves and the copper taste coming from the back of my throat. I pump my arms hard as I come up another hill, not breaking stride, unwilling to lose even a fraction of my pace to gravity and incline and the casually indifferent forces of nature. As I come to the stairs, I feel my resolve give and stumble to the railing, holding on, kicking at bushes and gripping my hair in my hands.

I cry for Cassandra, and for myself. A wall breaks and in this one moment I feel every heartache I've ever known: my mother's death, my father's loneliness, and my lack of certainty in every aspect of my life. So much of life is a magnetic forest throwing us off course.

I walk slowly to the twenty-four-hour Hot Spar and buy an international calling card, go to a phone booth across the street and call Maggie at the flower shop. Oddly enough, she's not the least bit surprised to hear from me. I tell her everything.

'I'd hate to think I'm growing up,' I say. 'I feel lied to and cheated, but I still think I love her. I have no desire to be a parent, and yet the idea of being with Cassandra is still more appealing than staying here or coming home.'

'There is more to life than boozy nights and casual sex.'

'Yeah, unfortunately. I don't want to think about how many other things I've been wrong about. My life seemed pretty good in Toronto and now it seems completely screwed up. Maybe coming to Japan was a mistake. Do you think I strived too hard to compensate for the shark?'

'No. You're a victim of your nature, and that's nothing to be ashamed of. God knows, you're never dull. Besides, I like the fact that you're half crazy and often dangerously spontaneous, because you make me feel like anything is possible, even if it's not.'

'So you're not surprised by any of this?'

'I'm more surprised that you quit smoking. I can't imagine you without nicotine. It's just not you.'

'Apparently it is.'

Personal history strikes me as unreliable. Maybe we're never what we think, always morphed and distorted by lenses and refractions, forever in a state of becoming.

'What are you going to do?' Maggie asks.

'I don't know. Cassandra leaves in ten days and I've got a mountain to climb. She doesn't want me to follow her and has a child. I'm still under contract for half a year and don't have nearly enough money saved to go back to school.'

'Jamie?'

'Yes?'

'Call me when you get into Sydney.'

33

The band Blanky Jet City are playing an afternoon concert at Shin-Yokohama Stadium down the road, and by lunch, the station square is swarming with teenagers, university students and grubby-looking ticket scalpers in ill-fitting tracksuits. Girls in thick pink make-up with their hair in pigtails waddle around on platform shoes, huddling into giggling groups. The men are young and pensive, with ducktail hair and loads of black leather clothing. The temperature is thirty degrees, so maintaining that stoic cool must be agonising.

A scalper in an all-white tracksuit comes towards me, rocking back and forth in an exaggerated swagger, his chest pushed out like a pigeon. His bottom lip dips, revealing messed-up teeth jammed together like puzzle pieces in the wrong slots. As he gets closer, I notice his hair is tightly permed.

'No tickets thanks,' I say.

'You my sister.'

I keep walking, but he steps in front of me with his hand out. He tilts his head to look at me more closely, then pokes his index finger into my chest. The only people taking notice of the scene are other ticket sellers, a few of whom are drifting our way.

'You my sister,' he says again.

'I don't think so.'

'You no like sister?'

'I'm not really into Japanese music. Excuse me.'

The smell of cheap terry cloth, old smoke and *natto* (fermented soybeans) is thick in my nostrils. He pokes me again and steps closer. The only thing my mind can compute is that a pimp appears to be threatening me for not wanting to sleep with his sister. I look around, but there aren't any other BIGSUN teachers in the square. There aren't even any *gaijin*, just a couple of thousand Japanese people who clearly do not want to get involved.

'I don't want any trouble,' I say.

'My sister nice.'

'I'm sure she is, but I don't want to fuck her.'

From the way his eyes bug out, I can tell this is the wrong thing to say. I'm taken from behind by the shoulder and am about to go into full scratching, clawing and eye-gouging mode until I realise that Eugene has pushed me out of the way and is walking the scalper backwards, speaking in aggressive Japanese. I expect the other scalpers to swarm, but they're looking away, going back to the business of trying to unload tickets. Obviously Eugene speaks better Japanese than he lets on.

The scalper barks and yells, but from the way he's moving away, I can tell there's not going to be a fight. The permed head turns to me and says something in a tone that can best be described as a whine. Eugene comes back, puts his arm around me and we walk towards the school.

'I told him if he wanted trouble, I could get a dozen

Marines from the base in Yokohama and we'd have a fair fight. These guys are such pussies when you mention the military.'

'Is it a good idea to threaten the Yakuza?'

Eugene snorts. 'These guys aren't Yakuza. They're scalpers and wannabes. Think of them as Mafia fans, or the Mickey Mouse club. This is as close to petty criminals as you get in this country.'

'What did he want?'

'He said you and your friend ruined his family's honour by using his sister. He's obviously got the wrong guy or it's a new scam. I guess the economy isn't what it used to be and the lower classes have to find new and more creative extortion schemes to make a living.'

Eugene's reward for saving me from a potentially bad terry cloth burn is a six-thousand-yen fine from BIG-SUN, because he's gone over time on his break and the staff have been forced to reschedule his next lesson. I insist on paying the charge, but he waves me away, saying he'll take the incident to head office and get the mess sorted out.

'If anything,' he says, 'I should get a bonus for being the muscle around here. I'm the tough guy, the hammer, the Shin-Yokohama goon.'

When I straggle home that night, I discover that our new room-mate has arrived. He's short, pale and looks like he's slept the night on a garbage tip. He's wearing a grey shirt that I'm sure isn't supposed to be that colour and a pair of bizarre, lace-less, fake leather loafers. If I were to guess, I'd say he's combed his hair with a side of bacon. He juts a hand towards me.

'David Haliburton-Smidges,' he says.

We're obviously being punished for having run Eldon out – head office hates us – or else this is the act of a higher power, testing the limits of my human endurance. Marcus comes in at this moment and stops in the doorway, his nose twitching.

'That rubbish really needs to be taken out,' he says.

He sees us standing in the middle of the lounge room and smiles.

'Right, mate, you the new blood? Hope you don't mind shavings in the basin and a bit of oil left on the counter top, because if you do, I might have to set your futon on fire while you're sleeping in it. I'm Marcus, nice to meet you. Last room-mate was a bit of an odd job, but he was American, just like this one here, so what can you expect, right? The memo from BIGSUN accommodation department said you're from my dreary rain-drenched shores.'

He says all this in one long breath. David stares at him, meets his hand with a limp shake, then drops his arm back down to his side. The corners of his lips arch downwards and he leans back ever so slightly to take in Marcus. I've become quite used to the imposing bulk, shaved head and rambunctious energy.

'Wait until you see the nipple rings,' I murmur.

'You new to Japan?' Marcus asks.

'No,' David says. 'I was living in Kawasaki, but there was a rooster down the road that would wake me at five o'clock every morning, and the others refused to swap rooms.'

'Oh right. Roosters in the city.'

'We were in a very suburban area. If you'll excuse me, I must unpack my valise.'

Marcus glances at me, his eyebrow arched, as if looking to be let in on the joke. But no, this man standing in front of us with his greasy skin and beady eyes isn't kidding. He is not a work of imagination or comic character come to life. God help us, he's real and in the flesh.

34

Cass is out with co-workers for a final farewell. I've been invited, but can't face the inevitable three cheers that will surround her departure. We haven't mentioned her daughter since the night she told me – I haven't asked and she hasn't offered – but Emily has been with us, sitting on the edge of the futon, looking over the neck of the wine bottle, coughing during those unusual lulls in conversation. I haven't mentioned chasing after her, going to Australia, or seeing those endless blue skies and miles of white, pristine beaches. We've simply been together, trying to wring out every last second of togetherness, discovering as always how badly relationships work without a future to anticipate. She says at one point that maybe we can meet up in Asia for a vacation, but that's after several bottles of wine and neither of us take it very seriously.

At least Marcus seems glad to have me around. We're bored and are amusing ourselves by playing Decipher the Cultural Significance, a game we've just invented. It's been fascinating to discovering how little the world knows about my country, apart from *Degrassi Junior High*.

'Tragically Hip,' I say.

'Clothing store?' Marcus says.

'No.'

'A new piece for the space shuttle, like that *Canad-arm*.'

'No, they're a rock band.'

Marcus snaps his finger. 'That was my next guess.'

'Timbit,' I say.

'Ice hockey player.'

'No, but disturbingly close. You're half right.'

'Midget ice hockey player?'

'It's a deep-fried doughnut ball. You know how your standard doughnut is round with no centre . . . ?'

He winks and shakes his finger at me. 'Ah, right. That's brilliant. But what does it have to do with ice hockey?'

I tell him the story of Tim Horton, the humble hockey player who started the nation's most successful doughnut chain and died in a car crash – a myth central to our very being. Sure, we could have some great military hero as our soul guide, but Canadians are secure enough not to need violent drama as the cornerstone to our psyche. Besides, doughnuts are much more appealing than battles, death and dismemberment.

'Toque,' I say.

'That's not a word.'

A key fumbling in the door interrupts us and we freeze, knowing it's too late to bolt to our rooms and close the doors. Marcus scrambles for the remote control and switches on the movie we'd been watching before boredom and a beer/diet cola run sidetracked us. I look at my watch. With all the fun and frivolity I've lost track of time and will now suffer at the hands of –

'Oh. Hello,' David says.

We mumble greetings and make every effort to look engrossed in the action on screen. The atmosphere in the room changes, both emotionally and scent-wise. The air is hung with discomfort and weight, like we've submerged to an aquatic level that will surely induce the bends. I can *feel* David watching the movie. I can also detect his rampant body odour.

'Is this a Rodgers and Hammerstein musical?' he asks.

'No,' Marcus says. 'It's *The Matrix*.'

'I must admit I don't watch much television . . . Oh, I like his costume. He looks very French. They have such a way with wearing leather, don't they?'

David continues to stand in the middle of the room looking at the screen. For a second, I think he's going to feel the awkward silence and trundle off to his lair, but instead he sits down and pulls his tie askew.

'What a day I've had. We were out at an *izakaya*, and

well, you know how a man will start boasting when he's drinking . . . My manager was saying he could sing falsetto, and I bet him he couldn't, because I've sung in choirs for most of my life and we all know the difficulty of the range.'

'Amen,' I say.

'But he had quite a good falsetto. I lost one thousand yen. I can be very reckless when challenged. Of course, I felt the odds were in my favour and don't apologise for the wager. I suppose I'm as much a victim to the male ego as any of us.'

I used to think I was very good with people, able to find common ground with even the dullest individual, but my time in Japan has shaken the foundation of this egalitarianism. I've been interred with not one, but two socially deranged misfits.

'A Japanese female by the name of Megumi came by the apartment this morning,' David says.

'Tell her I moved,' I say.

'Oh, she wasn't looking for you. She was looking for the previous tenant.'

'Eldon?'

'Yes. She appeared very upset. Apparently she's having trouble locating him. If you know his new address, pray leave it on the table in case she returns.'

'I think you've made a mistake,' I say. 'She's my ex-girlfriend and she definitely wasn't looking for Eldon. But if you want to tell her I moved, pray do. It would be much appreciated.'

David shrugs testily. 'I'm not lying.'

Marcus lets out a deep sigh. David leans over in front of him, blocking the TV. For a second I think he's going to plant a kiss on his lips.

'Do you want me to stop talking?' David shouts. 'Am I bothering you?'

Marcus picks up his can of diet cola and swishes the shallow remains, taking one last swallow, apparently unable to articulate a response. David stomps off to his room.

'You know,' I say, 'I think he loves you.'

'I don't understand what we've done to deserve this,' Marcus replies. 'Obviously, people come to this country for only one of two reasons: to gain a unique cultural experience, or because they cannot possibly make it in normal society anywhere else on the planet. Have you noticed that David doesn't own soap or shampoo?'

'It's difficult to miss.'

'I thought at first that he was using mine, so I placed my soap at a strategic angle and marked the level of my shampoo, but every day, they're exactly as I left them. As far as I can tell, he coats himself in spray deodorant every morning and heads to work.'

'I woke up when he came home last night, not because he was noisy, but because his smell permeated my room. It came right through the door.'

David comes back out to the lounge room dragging his loose mauve socks across the floorboards, the ends flipping back and forth messily. He fills up a water bottle from the tap. With the door open, I have a clear line of sight into his room. Everything he owns – clothes, book, CDs – all appear to be piled in the corner under the window.

'Right,' Marcus says. 'I'm off to bed. That Rodgers and Hammerstein musical has me buggered. Night, David. Try not to wake us up when you take your shower tomorrow morning.'

I can't face isolation in my small paper cell, so I go out walking. I phone Cassandra and surprisingly she's on her way home, so I meet her at the station.

'I thought you'd be out all night,' I say.

'I wasn't into it. A couple of the guys brought their Japanese girlfriends and they were totally bored, which is understandable considering they could barely speak English. Also, I didn't want to stay long enough for anyone to get emotional.'

'Because emotions are bad.'

Her shoulders sag as we wander down the narrow sidewalk, past Super Rag and the glowing fluorescent eye of the whale hovering above The Deep.

'To be honest,' she says, 'I wanted to be with you, so don't be a prick. I missed you . . . Did you go running tonight?'

'No, Marcus and I watched half a movie and then scattered when smelly room-mate came home. I figure I'm ready for the climb, so I'm letting my muscles rest for Sunday.'

'Do you think Paul will show up?'

'Yeah. We've got an arrangement worked out. If he

thinks he can bail after my months of clean living and exercise, he's sorely mistaken. I'd have to batter him to death with a textbook.'

'Killed by "Do You Have Any?"'

'Lesson 72.'

'I wonder if those lessons will be tattooed onto my brain forever,' she says. 'I'll be eighty and still able to recite the entire dialogue from "Joining the Marines".'

'Lesson 207.'

'*Have you ever handled a gun before? No, sir, but I like action movies.*'

'*Do you like the ocean?*'

'*Do your feet get sore when you wear boots? Because you'll have to march a lot.*'

We look at one another and laugh crazily.

'*Do you want to kill civilians?*' I say.

'That's not in the text. Don't be disrespectful to the BIGSUN lesson dialogue . . . Are you sleeping over tonight? It's one of your last chances to hear me snore.'

'Not if you cash in your ticket.'

She doesn't answer and I don't expect her to. I am loading every phrase, nagging her with my casual remarks and subtle cues. But I'd hate myself if I stood by and accepted her departure with soppy piety, like some pathetic Petrarchan suitor. Give me a slap in the face over a mournful look any day. Failure will always be more gorgeous than regret.

'There's a danger in staying somewhere too long,' Cassandra says. 'You start doing everything badly, not just your job.'

'I love you.'

Even I'm surprised by my stone cold sober confession. We stop walking and Cassandra looks at me, her mouth half open and her eyebrows arched. Japan is full of surprises, so I suppose one last meaningful shock in front of the Hot Spar won't make a difference. This could be highly romantic if it wasn't for the drunken men stumbling out the door with their bags full of *nori* rolls and alcohol.

'I like you,' Cassandra says. 'A lot.'

'If you call me, I'll come. That's all I'm going to say.'

She puts her arms around me, moves her lips towards mine and doesn't unlock them until we're dizzy from car fumes and chemicals. The oceans must feel this way when the moon's gravity draws their tides, this eternal motion, ageless and insuppressible.

I wonder if the saga of Cassandra and me will turn out to be a Hollywood lie, a love story that ends in closure and happy ever after. I've never been keen on tidy endings, because resolution isn't a common element of life. Hope is the only constant, a blissful fabrication based on little more than desire and wishful thinking. I've never understood why people watch movies when they know the guy will get the girl in the end. I don't know why resolution is a need, our emotional imperative. Just for once don't you want to be surprised, don't you want the girl to get on a plane and disappear forever?

35

I look at my watch as we get into Cora's company car and think Cassandra is probably arriving at the airport right now. She'll be lugging her heavy suitcases alone, checking her pockets for her passport and worrying that she might not get a window seat. I see her pixie nose scrunching up as she speaks Japanese to the airline check-in clerk.

Paul's apartment is next to a large fruit and vegetable market. The traffic is brutal and Cora has to stay in the car while we all go inside. Marcus squeezes out, ducking his head to get through the Honda's minuscule doorway. My tower of a flatmate is only here as the hired muscle, reward for which will be a lift to Mount Fuji, where he'll join his own school in the Summer Challenge.

Eugene leads the way and puts his ear to Paul's door. There's music playing (Enya, if I'm not mistaken), and the sound of dishes clattering. Eugene rings the bell and we wait as Paul pretends not to be home.

'This bonus is important to a lot of people,' Eugene shouts at the door. 'So don't be a prick or you'll end up in Yokohama Harbour, rolled in a *tatami* mat weighed down with bricks. We've given you the easiest stretch of the mountain. You'll be done in forty minutes, tops.'

After a few more seconds of what I now recognise more precisely as the Cocteau Twins, I pull out a key and open the door. As usual, BIGSUN has few qualms about teacher safety, privacy or basic civil rights. Marcus and Eugene burst past and swarm first into the lounge room, then into a bedroom off to the right. There's a loud commotion of feminine shouting and a couple of loud thuds. When I get to the doorway, Marcus is sitting on Paul's prone body as Eugene runs his belt around the Scotsman's legs.

'Who the hell is on top of me?'

'Paul, Marcus. Marcus, Paul,' I say, as a means of introduction. 'Marcus's hobbies include sleeping, travelling, tormenting people from the Deep South, and aikido. Hey, this is a really nice place. Why isn't our apartment this good?'

'Accommodation has a vendetta,' Marcus mutters.

'He's got a DVD player . . .'

'I bought that myself,' Paul says.

Eugene points a finger. 'You shut up. As for apartments, BIGSUN was a lot more generous ten years ago, when demand for ESL teachers was higher and the currency hadn't dropped. My first place had a leather sofa and minibar.'

'Story of my life,' I say. 'Born a generation too late.'

Eugene takes a roll of duct tape from his pocket and wraps Paul's wrists together. By this point, however, Paul has begun to laugh, no doubt impressed by our determination and resourcefulness. He is a natural admirer of treachery.

'Fine, you have me,' he says. 'I'm not going to run away, so you can undo my arms. And loosen the belt – I don't want that faux leather to give me a rash. The *kugaru* girls will never come near me again.'

'We'll let you loose when we're at station six on the

mountain,' Eugene says. 'Until then, consider yourself under citizen's arrest. My kids need school uniforms and my wife hasn't had a decent vacation in years.'

'You do know I'm going to crawl, don't you?' Paul says. 'I'll get up the mountain, but by that time Shin-Yokohama will be hours behind. We should forfeit now – gracefully – and go drink *ume sours* around the corner.'

'Marcus, lift him up,' Eugene says.

Paul goes limp. 'You can lead a horse to water, but you can't make him drink!'

'You can if you push his head down far enough.'

Luckily, Paul is as thin as a twig, so Marcus has no problem doing a fireman's carry to the car. Cora pops open the hatch, but there's no way that we can accordion our captive in the small trunk. No wonder the Yakuza imports large Chevys and Cadillacs. Sally, Eugene and I end up crammed into the back seat with Paul lying sideways across our laps, which isn't the best pre-climb set-up, as my leg muscles are stiffening and beginning to cramp even before we're out of central Yokohama.

The drive west takes two hours, the smog keeping Fuji out of view until we're within a dozen miles. Then, the postcard appears, sitting back against the soft sky like a tired Buddha. Fuji doesn't impose or overwhelm; it watches and rests.

'The Japanese have a saying,' Eugene says. 'You're crazy if you don't climb Fuji once in your life, and crazy if you climb it twice.'

'How many times will this be for you?' I ask.

'Seven. It's good exercise. And when you live here long enough, friends and relatives visit, and they all want to do the same damn things. Except for my sister. All she wanted to do was shop, which in my opinion is worse than climbing twelve thousand feet.'

'Twelve thousand what?' Paul says.

'Don't worry, we're only racing up half the mountain. And your section of the relay is only a thousand feet – the grandmother run.'

We pull into a large parking lot, absolutely filled with tour buses, vans and cars. Crowds are teeming across the asphalt, lining up at the noodle cafes, and drinking beers from the dozens of vending machines. There are people of all ages, from young children to elderly men and women who can barely walk across flat pavement, much less get up a mountain. I'm assuming they're here for moral support.

Cora checks us in and we wait as a guy with slicked-back hair hands out bright yellow windbreakers with 'BIGSUN' on the back in bold black. No doubt, astronauts will be able to read the blatant advertising from space. When I put the jacket on, my hand tears through the fabric at the elbow.

'How is this supposed to protect me from the elements on a mountain?' I say.

'Buck up,' Marcus says. 'Back in 1924, Mallary and Irvine went off to summit Everest in tweed blazers and cotton pants. They didn't have Gore-Tex or synthetics. They strapped oxygen canisters onto their backs like firemen and set out to go where no human had ever been. We can't complain.'

'I didn't think of it that way.'

'Of course, they both died in the attempt to summit, but they went exceedingly high. That's the lesson to be taken from the –' His jacket rips too. 'Yes, I see your point. You did pack extra gear, right?'

'I've got a fleece, two comic books and an extra T-shirt in my pack. I left the comics in there by accident, but I figure we can huddle under them if we get pinned down by a typhoon.'

'Good. We're going to move from humid to frigid in six hours, so we need to be prepared.'

'I move from humid to frigid in thirty seconds every time I enter an air-conditioned building in this country. I'd say I'm overly prepared.'

We're gathered around a small stage where several tedious speeches about friendship, team building and inter-cultural understanding are made in English and Japanese by a series of managers. A small contingent of print and TV media record the proceedings, cameras turning towards the mass of teachers at regular intervals.

'You experience more in an hour of climbing than you do in a week,' Marcus says. 'Your senses are fully alive.'

'Have you hiked many mountains?' Eugene asks.

'None. I read that in a book.'

The rules of the competition are explained: five teachers per BIGSUN school have to start from our current position, station five; of those five, one teacher is responsible for carrying the school climbing stick for each section, at which time they can continue the climb or come back down. There are four different approaches to the top and twenty schools – so five teams per route.

Shin-Yokohama is one of the schools assigned the Kawaguchiko approach, which thrills Eugene no end. He's stretching and has become more focused than I've ever seen him, as if he's morphing into professional soldier Eugene before our very eyes. Marcus bids us farewell and goes off with his school to another approach. Always the consummate professional, Paul is smoking a cigarette and making smiley faces at Japanese staff members from other schools.

'I thought you were dating someone,' I say.

'Didn't work out.'

I look at the rocky slope and think about my motivation. A month's bonus would cover a ticket to Australia, a few kangaroo steaks and several Kylie Minogue CDs. I might even be able to afford to see a bit of the country and overcome its debilitating stereotypes.

The starting point for all the teams is at the very top of the treeline. The landscape below is green and lush; everything above is red and black rock. Cora hands Paul the school climbing stick, which will be stamped at every station with a miniature seal (the significance of which eludes me, because I don't see too many barking sea mammals in the vicinity). We walk to the gate and a small Japanese man holds up a starter's pistol. BIGSUN-Machida, one of the schools sharing our route, rushes out at the crack of smoke, but all the other teams fall into line and trudge upwards in pairs. There's no need to sprint in a six-hour race.

The climb isn't difficult. There's a slope, but the pace and incline aren't taxing. I fall in with Eugene and we walk for a time in silence, finding our rhythm. My mind takes on the beat of the steps, clears, and makes me aware of the connection between the mind and body.

Away from the congestion and the urban sprawl, I can feel the spirituality of this place. This is as close as I'll come to ancient Japan, when people believed the Shinto gods lived in this mountain, before the Emperor became regarded as God incarnate and the creation myth was reinvented to start with the imperial family. Most people don't believe or care about religion or the royal family anymore – economics is the god of Japan, and progress negates sentimentality. Even old buildings and architecture aren't valued, as most places are torn down after twenty years. This is both liberating and sad, a natural renewal but without the calming effects of history and the illusion of being part of something lasting longer than a single lifetime. As if echoing my thoughts, Eugene begins to speak.

'You know what I love about Japan?' he says.

'The landscape, the spirit underneath the customs, and the integration of myth and ritual into society?'

'Nope. I love the fact that heated toilet seats are the norm; I love seeing paunchy men with comb-overs on TV hawking kitchen graters, jewellery and rice cookers; and I'm amazed by the sheer excitement I feel when I walk into an import store and see a tin of Campbell's Condensed

Cream of Mushroom Soup on the shelf. It's times like this, removed from life, that I appreciate that shit.'

We walk on for a few more minutes in silence, then he clears his throat. 'Cassandra flying out today?'

'Yeah.'

'That's a tough one. You dealing okay?'

'I'm fine. We weren't together long.'

'True, but this is Japan and I saw the way you two crazy kids looked at one another. Trust me, six months here is like seven years in any other part of the world – fifteen if you're from the Midwest. Besides, you can't measure love in time. I fell for my wife in a matter of weeks and we've never looked back.'

I think about what I know of Cassandra and come up with a list of endearing eccentricities, like her nail polish obsession. She had dozens of bottles in a shoebox at the end of her bed and would change the colour on her toes every night. If she couldn't sleep, she'd occasionally do this at four in the morning. She hums when she reads, and doesn't realise she's doing it. She eats toast more loudly than anyone I've ever encountered, as if her teeth take a running start before hitting the bread. And she murmurs in her sleep, little whimpers when she's cold and the blanket has come off her shoulders.

We reach station six in no time. Paul hands off the walking stick to Cora and lights up another cigarette, sitting down on a large volcanic rock. BIGSUN-Machida, the school that ran off from the gate, is far ahead, but the others are maintaining pace.

'There,' Paul says. 'I've qualified for my equal share of the bonus, and in an hour, I'll be relaxing with a book on my balcony while you fools are sweaty and exhausted.'

'No you won't,' Eugene says. 'I took the house key out of your pocket when you were tied up. You'll get it when Marcus descends, in about seven hours.'

'You're bluffing.'

'Remember that Shin-Yokohama spirit.'

The track continues to meander easily until Cora hands off to Sally at station seven. After this point, however, the path narrows and we're forced into single file in several places. The incline increases like a staircase, the wind becomes a factor, and the ground becomes more slippery, covered in a thin veneer of volcanic dust. The mountain hasn't erupted for centuries and is considered dead, but there's still plenty of evidence of its once awe-inspiring power. The landscape is barren and sharp, all scattered rock and red sand. I'm not sure about our exact altitude, but breathing becomes more difficult, like I'm taking air in but it's low on oxygen.

'I'm dizzy,' I say.

'Lucky you,' Sally says. 'I'm *busting*. If I'd known this part of the trek was going to be slow, I would have gone to the toilet at the last hut.'

'I'd take you people into combat with me any day,' Eugene says.

Our pace slows, though not as much as the other schools. We move into second place and gain considerably on BIGSUN-Machida. By the time Sally passes the stick to me at station eight, we're dying for both the facilities and a rest. We line up at the station hut, a shack made from corrugated tin, and buy green tea and *nori* rolls. I'm definitely light-headed now and my thighs are aching.

Eugene digs out several pairs of gloves from his backpack.

'You're going to need these. From here on up, we'll be using our hands a lot. This section separates the men from the boys.'

'That's sexist,' Sally says.

'Are you coming with us?'

'You must be nuts. Enjoy the rest of the hike.'

The going becomes tedious and Eugene institutes a system where we walk for fifteen minutes, rest for two, and then continue. All talking stops and there's no sound except for feet on ash and the wind whistling through the mausoleum rock. I cease to be one with my surroundings and simply keep going.

Halfway to station nine, we pass BIGSUN-Machida and move into first place for our path to the top. Of course, we have no way of knowing where the other BIGSUN schools are on the three alternative routes.

'We're making good time,' Eugene assures me. 'This is the fastest way in my experience, so I'd say we're in the running to win. *Fuji-san cho*, here we come.'

I'd like to say we surged to the top, were feted by company management and collected our bonuses on the spot. I'd like to say that my months of training, including the blisters and sore muscles, were worthwhile. I'd like to say I double-tied my shoelaces before we set out . . .

As I turn on a narrow edge to gauge our distance from BIGSUN-Machida, my left foot slips and I slide a solid ten feet on lava rock – which, I must say, has excellent exfoliating properties. I don't scream, but I sure do grunt a lot as waves of pain swell in my left calf. Eugene tosses away his pack and scrambles down, helping me get the leg out from under my body.

'Ouch!' he says. 'If we had a hibachi and some buns we could make hamburgers. That's some pretty mangled skin.'

'I'm fine. It's just a flesh wound.'

'Steady on, soldier.'

The lightweight hiking pants I bought specifically for the day are ruined, torn near the knee and stained with blood. I've got flecks of rock and ash in the grated laceration and can only hope that no calcified eons-old microbes from the centre of the Earth have been embedded in the gash. Luckily, Eugene has come fully equipped, like a good boy scout. He washes my wound in disinfectant and dresses it with gauze in a matter of minutes.

'Try not to bleed on my jacket, would you?' he says as he works away.

'I'm trying not to bleed at all, but it isn't exactly mind over matter.'

'Be at one with the cut,' he says, attaching the final dressing. 'That should do it. But you might want to tie that shoelace before you get up and give your leg a test.'

I wobble to my feet, the sharp stabs now a warm ache. My ankle has stiffened, but it's not too immobilised, which is good, because at eleven thousand feet up, my options for descent are rather limited. As I'm limping around in very small circles, our BIGSUN-Machida rivals crest the ridge and wander by, giving little more than anaemic nods.

'I'd say they've climbed before,' Eugene says.

'By their pace and technique?'

'No, by the fact that they don't give a shit about you – if you can stand on a mountain, you're good to go. After all, this isn't the safest hobby in the world. Everyone climbs alone.'

'What are you saying?'

'If this were Mount Everest, I'd be forced to leave you. But seeing as we're only a few hundred feet from station nine, a rest hut and a couple of bags of *wasabi*-covered peas, I'm going to drag your mangled corpse behind me.'

In my mind, the thought of stopping before the summit isn't even an issue. I've come this far and have too much pride to let a missing chunk of leg stop me. I want to be able to tell Cassandra that I succeeded, as if to prove that my life hasn't been affected by her departure. We push onward, not far behind the BIGSUN-Machida pair, and I use the seal-covered walking stick for support. I'm glad to say that my cultural ignorance has shown through once more, as the pole is covered in *signets*, not aquatic animals.

We're met at station nine by a crowd of photographers and news people, who have obviously been taken to the site by helicopter. They ask for shots of us in front of a long line of gleaming vending machines, the sight of which greatly reduces my senses of both endangerment and accomplishment.

'Can we have a couple of photos of you chaps buying products?' the company rep asks.

'We're trying to win a race,' Eugene says.

The slick-haired rep calls over his assistant and speaks in fluent Japanese. The younger man yelps '*Hai!*' and races off to confer with sub-assistants. The whole managerial hierarchy dominoes until a small woman in a skirt and high heels races off toward the BIGSUN-Machida teachers now rising above us.

'I've asked your competitors to pause for a few minutes to keep things fair,' the rep says. 'The faster we snap these photos, the better chance you have of winning the competition.'

We're given hundred-yen coins and quickly go through the pantomime of buying miso soup from a machine. Some things that can be purchased in vending machines in Japan: quail eggs, film, instant noodles, magazines, books, flowers, blue jeans (allegedly), condoms, sexual lubricants, pocket pussies, sandwiches, drinks, deodorant and MINI OXYGEN TANKS!

Places vending machines are commonly found: train stations, street corners, hospitals, shopping complexes and ON TOP OF MOUNT FUJI!

'I've seen it all,' I say.

'But you haven't seen the top of Japan yet,' Eugene says.

There's no way he can win with me gimping along, so

I tell him to go on ahead. He resists far less than anticipated, tossing me his backpack and taking off his sweater. I guess his kids really do need those school uniforms.

'The time has come for shock-troop conditions,' he announces.

'You miss the military, don't you?'

'Tag question.'

'Fuck off and climb the mountain.'

He races away in a full sprint, much to the delight of the media, who run from the corrugated shack, frantic to get this dramatic final pose. I quaff a Pocari Sweat and rest for ten minutes before heading onward. The last section goes more quickly than expected, largely due to oxygen deprivation, fatigue and a wandering mind. Without realising my altitude, I crest a ridge and come to a small temple built into the rock where several BIGSUN teachers are sitting around chatting and admiring the view. We're above the cloud line and the sky above us is deep blue. Eugene wanders over looking mildly despondent.

'I'm assuming we didn't win,' I say.

'We came in second.'

'You couldn't catch BIGSUN-Machida?'

'Oh god, I blew by them within fifteen minutes of leaving you. Unfortunately, there was a blond guy from one of the other routes at the finish line making coffee when I got here. Apparently, BIGSUN-Yokohama teaches French and German as well as English, so they stacked their team with Austrians and Swiss. Fuji is an anthill compared to the Alps.'

Though disappointed, I take a look around at this beauty, think about our unique place in the world, and know that this climb and my training weren't a waste of time. When I arrived in this country, the walk to my new apartment left me winded. I can still feel the taste of raw nicotine and blood in the back of my mouth when I think about that first run with Marcus. Not only has this country changed my body, making it stronger, but I get a very real sense that it has changed me as well. I came to Japan weak, immature and lacking in understanding of the immensity and complexity of life and the world.

'Well,' I say, 'I guess we didn't do this for the money.'

'I did,' Eugene replies. 'I've been up this damn mountain seven times. Do you know how expensive Christmas is when you have three kids?'

'Still, I feel a sense of closure.'

'Just wait until you make the real summit, then you'll have an even greater feeling of accomplishment. There's a weather station on the far side of the crater that is technically the highest point.'

'How long will that take?'

'Forty-five minutes, thirty-five if you double-time it.'

'I'll meet you at the bottom of the hill.'

36

All is calm for the next two weeks. I get email from Cassandra saying she has arrived home safely, misses me and wants to seriously consider a vacation in Asia in the new year. I've been mulling over our situation and think I didn't do enough to reassure her about Emily. I've never thought about having a child, but after a lot of thought, I've decided I could be willing to give up some freedom to be part of a larger union. Maggie was right when she said we all need to change and *compromise*, and I've come to see the word as having something other than a wholly negative meaning.

I only wonder if this conclusion has come too late.

I go to work, trudge home and sleep late most days, becoming instantly lethargic every time I arrive in my neighbourhood. I stand on the balcony at regular intervals watching for Cass's familiar walk among the crowds. The weather has changed, cool relief breaking the wall of humidity, signifying that both climbing season and summer are officially over.

On a good note, the photo of Eugene racing up the mountain made the front page of *The Japan Times* and BIGSUN rewarded him with a half-month's bonus for bringing honour to the company. He collected the money and gave two weeks' notice the next day, as the attention also did wonders to boost enrolment in his small, newly renamed school. The Fast Fuji Runner Language School is a definite hit with ESL learners. He's thinking about having T-shirts made.

Now, on a Wednesday night, with my weekend beaconing and promising a couple of solitary days of rented movies, commotion erupts at the school. As we pack up for the day, two students return from the station and excitedly report that there's a crazy *gaijin* outside.

'He is not clean,' one says. 'He has the bad smell and much hair on his face.'

'He's been around for a few days,' Sally says. 'He came up to me in the station and asked if I worked for BIGSUN. Apparently he used to be a teacher and wanted to know if the company was talking about him. I'm not sure if he's schizophrenic.'

'Did you shag him?' Paul asks.

We go outside and find our mystery white boy sitting on a park bench, staring at the ground. I feel my heart jump. For a man so scrupulously anal about cleanliness, he really has let himself go. His clothes are dirty and look slept in, and his chin is covered in at least a six-day beard. As if sensing me, he looks up and waves.

'Hey, Jamie,' he says. 'How are things going?'

'Umm, Eldon . . . I'm pretty good. Did the dorm not work out?'

'Nah. Too many loud people, and one guy vomited in the sink. I couldn't handle that. Some people are pretty gross.'

I decide this is the wrong time to point out that he smells like sour cheese. He doesn't appear to be drunk, but his eyes are glassy and his focus is completely lost.

'Where are you staying, Eldon?'

'Oh, I was at the Prince Pepe Hotel for about five days, but I lost my credit cards, my passport and all my bags, so they kicked me out. That's fair. I'm crashing in a park near here until I get some money wired and the embassy sorts out a flight home. I have to say I'm looking forward to getting back to the USA, 'cause I really want to play some pool.'

Turns out Eldon shafted Prince Pepe for a week in a honeymoon suite, complete with three meals a day from room service. He'd lost his credit card by that point, but Pepe let him stay out of respect for BIGSUN. I picture Eldon in his white undershirt, eating from fine-bone china and watching cheap action films while sitting at the hotel room table drinking beer. I take him to the teachers' room but the staff freak out – Akiko, the manager of the school, doesn't want students to see him, because it reflects badly on the company.

'No one's going to come in,' I say. 'Classes are over for the day.'

'But he smell.'

'Yeah, I'll give you that. Crank the air exchanger to high and I'll bring in some incense tomorrow morning.'

Eldon is very apologetic and also very hungry. I buy him two sandwiches and an iced coffee from the local Hot Spar, and we all stand around wondering what to do next as he wolfs them down.

'Not enjoying the country?' Paul asks.

'I've seen better,' Eldon says.

'Yeah. Mate, you should check out Tokyo Disney, I hear it's —'

'Paul, can I talk to you outside?' Eugene says.

'What? My students rave about it . . .'

Even though Eldon clearly had problems all along, I'm feeling strangely guilty about this situation, thinking I should have been more understanding. I could have asked more about his wife, their break-up, and the issues that were scratching at his brain. I'm guilty of sins of omission, because, like it or not, we are all our brothers' keepers. At some point in life, we all get broken, like misfit toys, and need mercy and attention. Our apartment nation can be viewed as a microcosm of the world, a miniature parody of war, hate, intolerance and hoarding the television remote control.

'There's this bar down the street from my home in Kentucky,' Eldon tells Sally, 'where beers and shots of bourbon are two bucks on Wednesday night. Don't suppose I'll have time to get down there this week, but I used to go with Sharon, that's my wife, and we'd play pool. She was a real nice girl.'

I get on the phone to head office. Our area rep knows about Eldon, speaks diplomatically, but is overwhelmingly useless and uncompassionate. I understand he's in a difficult position – being the valve between east and west, between company management and our raggle-taggle band of gipsy teachers – but Eldon is a human being in trouble.

'I want to help,' the rep says, 'but it's a matter for the American Embassy. They've been contacted, so they should have a temporary passport ready within the week.'

'What does he do until then?'

'Obviously he can't stay at the Prince Pepe Hotel, but he's also not our responsibility. He bluffed his way through the interview. He didn't say anything about a history of mental illness, because he knew we wouldn't hire him if he did. Technically speaking, he shouldn't be here.'

'Technically speaking, he's in the other room boring one of our teachers with inane details of his life.'

'Since he withheld information, his contract is nullified and he is not a BIGSUN employee –'

'I lived with the guy! It wasn't the most pleasant experience of my life, but I saw him going to work for this company every day. Whether he misled BIGSUN or not, he's here as an *employee*.'

The rep's voice becomes very animated. 'I don't mind if you let him stay with you in your apartment, as long as your flatmates don't object. You're certainly free to provide him with accommodation, but we're not about to pick up the tab for a deluxe hotel room. End of story.'

I phone the US Embassy and speak with the woman dealing with Eldon's case. She says that because he's lost all identification, processing a temporary passport and arranging a flight will take time. No doubt, the fact that he looks like a Taliban militiaman who has crawled from a cave isn't helping speed the process. I give her my contact details and go back into the teachers' room, where Eldon is still talking.

'They got this great bar on, like, the fortieth floor. All the walls are made of glass and you can get some real fantastic views. You can even see Yokohama Bridge, and that's miles away.'

'Yeah, I've been up there,' I say.

'It's really cool. We should go now.'

'We're going to Azamino. You need a shower and some sleep. I'll warn you now, the place isn't as neat as when you left, so don't . . . umm, freak out.'

'I'm fine sleeping in the park, 'cause this is a safety country.'

'You're staying at the apartment. Besides, I think you're still paying rent.'

'Couldn't you have picked up a stray kitten instead?' Marcus says.

'He's not well.'

'He looks the bloody same to me! I swear, this apartment is like the house in *Poltergeist*, except instead of ghosts, it attracts absolute nutters.'

We're huddled on the balcony. Eldon, now showered, shaved and wearing my clothes, is sitting in the living room watching Sly Stallone as Rambo in *First Blood*. It's the first time Eldon's stopped fidgeting and babbling. I explain the situation to Marcus and even he concedes that we may have an obligation. We go back inside and our ex-flatmate looks up with medicated eyes.

'Oh, hey there, Marcus. How are you doing?'

'Fabulous, mate.'

At least Eldon hasn't said a word about the lingering–

decay smell of the apartment. We still haven't seen David shower. He washed his clothes once, hanging them out on the balcony, but even that was suspect because he has no detergent. The mess smelled like a cruel wave of death – dead meat – and was even worse than dehydrated fish flakes. Marcus and I took turns moving the clothes back and forth away from our balcony doors.

'How's your new room-mate?' Eldon asks.

'I'm writing a letter to head office about him,' Marcus says. 'He's very close to getting stabbed with chopsticks.'

'I'd move back,' Eldon says, 'but I don't think I've got a job anymore, and I probably should leave the country. I've made an awful mess of things again.'

Again.

I visualise the progression: Eldon as an overworked lawyer, too much pressure, the job goes, his wife leaves, he's isolated, drinks too much, he rambles around a large house in Kentucky alone until BIGSUN has the bright idea to bring him to Japan.

'I'm sorry things went wrong,' Eldon says.

'That's okay,' I say. 'Life is tough sometimes.'

'I didn't mean to cut your grass, but we should both be thankful she's not pregnant, right? That was a bit of a scare. 'Course, where I'm from, protection is a woman's responsibility, so if she wasn't on the pill, she should have said something before language exchange.'

Eldon stops talking and looks up at me momentarily, before glancing away with an expression of shame. The poltergeist has one icy hand on the back of my neck.

'I know she was your girlfriend,' he continues. 'But you weren't that interested. I could tell, the way you were off with that BIGSUN girl all the time. Megumi was wandering around the apartment looking so upset, and she said it was what you deserved, 'cept of course she said it like, "Jamie bad, me hurt Jamie too." You know the funny way Japanese speak.'

Megumi.

Her brother the scalper.

You my sister.

I reach into my pocket and pull out the *go-en* coin tied to my key chain. Clearly, I've made an awful mess of things, too.

37

Eugene meets me at his local station and shakes my hand like I'm a business associate, not a friend coming over for a few beers. Maybe he wants to make a good impression, so that I'll talk up his school around the students. He leads me down winding alleys and small streets with no traffic. An old man is standing on the yellow lines practising his golf swing with a Ping driver, and kids are playing tag, machine-gun laughter spilling out of their mouths.

'We don't get many tourists in this neighbourhood,' Eugene tells me.

His school is up a flight of stairs. It's an apartment converted into a waiting room and classroom, the shelves full of English books and tapes. He opens a bar fridge, pulls out four tall cans of Asahi and motions to a black and white picture on the wall, from which rows of young lean faces stare forward.

'See that?' he says. 'My first posting, on the USS *Lyndon Johnson*, a floating piece of shit. Say, how'd your room-mate make out?'

'Eldon's back in the States. The embassy fixed him up with a ticket, which he'll have to pay for when and if his finances ever get sorted out. He kept his word and spent every cent he made here, though on what, I'm not sure. Renting movies and drinking beer doesn't cost that much.'

'What about the girl?'

'Megumi won't speak to me and I don't blame her. I should have talked to her about Cassandra instead of leaving her to figure out the situation, but I let myself believe that being evasive was okay because she didn't speak English very well. I'd like to think the whole experience is a lesson learned. At the airport, Eldon was talking about bringing her to America so she could see Celine Dion in Las Vegas.'

'She'd probably be the only Japanese person in Kentucky.'

'I'm betting she stays on native shores.'

Eugene talks about his school, how he's reached maximum enrolment and has even hired a secretary. I tell him about Cassandra, about her daughter, and the use of

Japan as an escape route. Eugene isn't even marginally surprised.

'Happens all the time,' he says. 'Everyone here has something they're running away from. Not that I ran away from the navy, exactly, but I was definitely fed up with the hassle.'

'She doesn't want me to follow her.'

'Do you believe that?'

'What I believe doesn't matter. I'm working in Japan and she's back in her real life in Australia.'

Eugene is waving his hands, swatting away my arguments. 'Blah blah blah. Believe it or not, life in Japan is *real*. I know the seizure-inducing neon and overabundance of pink are misleading, but you do exist as a sentient being in this country. What you do, say and feel matter, and I bet Cassandra got home and discovered that the Australia she created in her mind while away is nothing like what she's got now. You're still a real part of her life.'

'You think?'

'Damn straight. She said she wants to see you again — obviously she said "vacation" because she's too scared to ask for more, knowing a kid is a big matzo ball. You've got a decision to make. I know, because I was in your position many moons ago when I met a real nice woman of my own. Sure, I gave up a few things — career, pension and sense of personal identity — but I don't regret a thing. When you're a soldier you're told to defend God and country, but ultimately you fight for the men and women around you, your comrades and the people you love — the human element. Nothing else matters.'

I finish the warm foam at the bottom of my beer. Eugene is already snapping open a new one for me before I place it on the table. There's a small chalkboard in the corner covered in a child's drawing of dancing carrots, behind which are a series of pictures pinned to a bristle board.

'Those are my kids,' he says.

His children have Japanese and American names. Hiro is Henry. Hideki is Harry. Hiromi is Heidi. His wife believes the letter H is lucky.

'If I were you,' he says, 'I'd get on a plane tomorrow. *Carpe diem* – seize the girl.'

'Are you serious?'

'Hell yes. You can get great last-minute flights in Shinjuku. So you lose two weeks' salary and never, ever get employed by another company in this country again – who cares?'

'I'd have to write a resignation letter and give notice.'

'Screw that. BIGSUN isn't concerned about your welfare; look how they treated Eldon. I say leave spectacularly, with as little professionalism or class as possible.'

He's leaning over the table, his eyes filled with energy. There's nothing holding me here and no reason why I should give up on Cassandra so easily. We kill another couple of cans for courage, and then he leads me through the winding streets back to the station. He walks quickly, as if he's excited about the plan and doesn't want me to lose momentum. He even pays for my train ticket.

'You'll need your money in Australia. Say hi to Cassandra. I always liked her.'

The train is getting ready to leave, so I slide on board. Eugene waves, then runs alongside dramatically as we pull out. He gives me the thumbs-up and stands at the end of the platform, growing smaller until we disappear around a bend.

Marcus knocks on my door. I'm dividing my clothes between items I'll wear again and every piece of formal polyester I bought specifically for this job. Suit jackets will not be a part of my future, no matter how desperate I may become.

'Whatcha doing?' Marcus asks.

'I'm leaving.'

'Ah, yeah. What are you doing right now?'

'Packing.'

'You mean you're *leaving* leaving?'

'Tomorrow morning. I'm sending a letter to BIGSUN. I have to be a good soldier and take care of the human element: Cassandra. Don't you see? This is *real life*.'

'Might I hazard a guess and say you've been drinking?'

'Yes.'

'And now you're going to run away and leave me in this apartment with David the smelly bastard and whatever anal retentive sociopath the accommodation department decides to replace you with?'

'Correct.'

'This is not the sign of true friendship, Jamie. I'll probably get a serial killer this time, one that insists on sharpening all the knives in the house at 3 am.'

I stop jamming rolled shirts into my case and stand up. At this moment, Marcus looks remarkably young, with a pout on his face, like a first grader missing home. I offer my hand to shake, but he pulls me into a hug, his chest like a barrel of oil.

'Take care, Marcus. Stay in touch.'

'I will. And who knows, maybe you'll come back one day to see me or marry Cassandra in one of our tiny classrooms, for nostalgia's sake.'

'I don't think BIGSUN will let me step foot on the property after tomorrow.'

'I'll sneak you in, mate, anytime.'

A sense of unreality overtakes me as I pack away my life once again. I wonder if I'll keep jumping sharks for the rest of my life, and question if this is a dangerous trend beginning.

Goodbye, Diddle Shop.

Bye-bye, cosmetic surgery ads on TV.

Farewell, pink inflatable *Hello Kitty* chairs.

Long shall I miss you, Kinko Sports: 'For all sports and the healthy mind of the sportful people'.

I write a letter to my dad explaining that I've done everything I had set out to accomplish and will contact him with more details from Australia. At the bottom, I write that I think Mom would want both of us to do more with our lives, use our time and never waste love.

I realise that this is what I came to Japan to do – to meet this girl. This was the kick of fate I was feeling, the one that led me into a seedy sports bar and had George Harrison so concerned. And whether or not things work out in the long run, I'm going for the ride, because that's the only way to live, moving towards love and away from loss, but never giving up the fight for experiences. Our fates are a tangled, gauzy web of insanity, our lives resisting even the most basic plans. All we can do is sparkle through the amber of wet nights, clinging humidity, and take strange comfort in the terrifying loss of certainty and hope for the future.